REGGAETÓN CRUISE

Patricio X. Maya

GRADY MILLER BOOKS

Reggaetón Cruise

All names, characters and events in this work are wholly fictional. Any resemblance to real persons or actual places is coincidental.

AUTHOR'S PHOTO by Hunter Pavdolar

COVER DESIGN by fiverr.com/design9creative

ISBN: 978-0-9862734-8-3

Manufactured in the United States of America.

PUBLISHER Graydon Miller

EDITORS Juan David Castilla and Graydon Miller

Please contact the publisher at: gradymillerbooks@gmail.com

1236 1/8 N. Cahuenga Blvd.
Hollywood, CA 90038

A mi abuelo Fabian Solís Cruz, cartógrafo en el Amazonas

Index

THREE

ONE

Supreme Warrior I

Artjom Pärn had woken up late again. Nobody was home except Mitu, the cat. He sat on the edge of the bed. *Ema,* whose name was Marija Pärn, had turned off the heater on her way to the factory. Artjom yawned and went back to bed. An hour or two later, he woke up again, and sat on the edge of the bed again. It was slightly warmer now. He reached for his green hoodie, walked to the bathroom, took a pee, and went down the stairs to the kitchen. There was no breakfast on the counter, though it was closer to lunch time anyhow. He opened the refrigerator and surveyed the contents: yesterday's *mulgipuder*, milk, sausage, and some rye bread from god knows how long ago. There were also eggs, but he wasn't going to make himself eggs. He took out the *mulgipuder* and heated it in the microwave. He ate it with a glass of cold milk and a banana. After eating he walked around the house as if looking for something to do. He turned on the computer that had been Kirill's. Mitu walked up to him and he pet it, waiting for the bite, which usually came when you least expected it. The computer took a while to load up. It was heavy with things past, present, and future. Once it was loaded, Artjom logged into his networks. There were no messages from Kirill. There were messages from his online friends. He responded to those messages. He was starting to share grody memes when Mitu jumped in front of the screen. Artjom grabbed the orange cat by the ribs and that's when it struck. Two little rips, oozing. Artjom sucked out the blood at once. But then he recalled that the day before Mitu had brought a small dead rodent as if bringing a precious prize to the front door. He rushed to the kitchen sink, gargled some nasty Listerine and spit it out. There were dirty dishes on the other side of the sink but he wasn't going to do them. It wasn't his job to do the dishes.

When Kirill was around *ema* always did the dishes. He'd promised her that he wouldn't go to the Hollywood PC room today, but what else could he do? Kirill was in London, and *ema* had gotten a job. He couldn't stay with Mitu, getting bit all day long. He could go play football but most of those kids were assholes, especially Romet, who had it against him for some reason. Artjom didn't like football anyway. The boys always made him goalie because he was chubby and not as fast as the others, but he didn't like being goalie because he wasn't good at being goalie, and he told them, but they made him goalie anyway, and then blamed him if he let the ball through, particularly Romet, who took things seriously and liked to show off his strength just because he'd gotten tall. So Artjom put on his red and gold SF 49ers cap and headed out the door. The neighborhood was gloomy and empty under the white sky. Not too far away you could hear the train, which traversed the eastern edge of Tallinn with scrap iron and wood. He walked to the back of the house, got on his bright lime BMX, which had been Kirill's and put his headphones on. He had just discovered death metal. Riding on his BMX from his house, the long way along the medieval towers, to the Hollywood PC Room in Kalamaja, while listening to death metal or thrash if he felt particularly pumped up had become his second favorite activity. The first one being, of course, gaming, which he'd been good at before, but after Kirill had left, his skills had blown up, as there was nothing else to do, and he was being requested by different gaming groups. He knew some kids in his group (like T-Rex500 out of Kuala Lumpur) had started to get paid to compete. Some others had been brought in to help companies develop games or by military technology contractors to test out different projects. Artjom didn't care much about that anyhow. He was one of the youngest high-ranking gamers in his tier, and most definitely the highest ranking at the Hollywood PC Room in Kalamaja, where he reigned uncontested.

Still he had to pay. The drunken Finn owner would not let him play for free, not even a minute, even though everyone knew Artjom made that shitty PC Room stand out in the competitions. He wasn't getting paid yet. That was a reality. Good thing he still had some of Kirill's remittance from London. He parked his BMX in the back of the mall, took the elevator to the third floor and paid for two hours. He paid for two hours on principle. He knew he'd stay at least three and maybe four hours, though no more, as he had to be home before *ema*. He came in and sat at the best computer with the best headset and the most comfortable seat. At least that the Finn owner knew to give the twelve-year-old rising Planet War Survival III star. Artjom Pärn signed in.

These were the current rankings in his quadrant and tier:

Planet War Survival III

Supreme Warrior Tier I – Alpha Quadrant

Name	Units	Status	Fluctuation*
T-Rex500	78930	Online	1+
xoxo.cutie13	77051	Offline	2+
$doomMetalBo	59088	Online	1-
Alphadomixxx	50047	Online	3-
r-coksF-U666	47901	Offline	5+

* Daily scores calculated at the end of 24-hr cycle

$doomMetalBo put Artjom Pärn's concerns behind. He chose his armor, loaded his machine guns, and jumped into the conflict. xoxo.cutie13 was not online yet. She lived in Melbourne and wouldn't be online for a few hours. This was $doomMetalBo's chance to catch up on the almost 2,000 units she was ahead of him. He couldn't believe that a chick was that much ahead of him. But xoxo.cutie13 was good. She was the only girl in the Supreme Warrior Tier's top five, pretty close to T-Rex500, who'd already been gaming for two hours by the time $doomMetalBo logged in. T-Rex500 was trying to expand his lead, but T-Rex500 wasn't $doomMetalBo's concern now, xoxo.cutie13 was, who, by the way, judging by her brunette avatar, was very cute. $doomMetalBo made it through the Hall of Bombs by clinging onto the roof frost, and right into the Dilapidated Fields where predators started charging at him from all sides. He knew that he couldn't trust T-Rex500. That dude was too fucking double faced and could pretend to have his back only to back stab him out of the blue. The little asshole had done it to CyberF***ingViking, who was a pretty straight-shooting dude, and now CyberF***ingViking wasn't even on the top five.

After slashing the last predators, which took a long time, and finally making it through the Dilapidated Field on his fourth try, which had taken an awful toll on his overall strength measurements, not to mention decreased his ammo, $doomMetalBo sent a message to Alphadomixxx. It was the right thing to do. T-Rex500 was still there and could mess up the day's good work.

Intergalactic memo from $doomMetalBo

$doomMetalBo: yo yo!

Alphadomixxx: whassup man .ᢌ☉_☉?.

$doomMetalBo: you still in the blazing sky level???

Alphadomixxx: you know i ams bro

$doomMetalBo: i just got there

Alphadomixxx: ◑.◐

$doomMetalBo: have you had any luck?

Alphadomixxx: nah, i got blasted several times

$doomMetalBo: ???

Alphadomixxx: you know dude…

$doomMetalBo: T-Rex500???

Alphadomixxx: yeah, he keeps letting the fire gliders through

$doomMetalBo: (ᵒ ⊠ᵒ) FTS

Alphadomixxx: …

$doomMetalBo: i'll get ur back if got have mine

Alphadomixxx: all the way through ?

$doomMetalBo: ye…then we're enemies gain lol

Alphadomixxx: coolio (`_)乂(_')

And so $doomMetalBo and Alphadomixxx got into their respective Annihilator-X75s and flew up into the Blazing Sky area where T-Rex500 was causing havoc. The first time around T-Rex500 blasted them directly. The second time he hid behind a flaming satellite and let the fire gliders through. The third time he allied with non-other than the Swede, CyberF***ingViking himself, the very dude he'd messed up a few days ago, and surprised them that way. When xoxo.cutie13 awoke in Melbourne she would see that T-Rex500's lead had increased by more than 300 units, in part thanks to $doomMetalBo and Alphadomixxx's gullibility but also because he was a damned savage. He'd taken a defeated fucker under his wing in order to keep his competitors from moving up and, in the meantime, he'd secured The Supreme Warriors Tier lead for a couple more days, all before xoxo.cutie13, his closest rival had even logged in. What surprised $doomMetalBo the most wasn't so much that T-Rex500 would do something shitty like that. What surprised him the most was that the Swede, CyberF***ingViking, who'd talked so much shit about T-Rex500, even claiming he'd fly to Kuala Lumpur himself to beat the shit out of the little asshole, had now allied himself with his former slayer, just to come up in the game again. That was Planet War Survival III alright! The fourth time around $doomMetalBo realized he had to try something new or he'd be dropped to fourth of even fifth place, especially if r-coksF-U666 went online and took advantage of the situation. He had to take action. His time was running out at the Hollywood PC Room. He could see the drunk Finn eyeing the clock. And so he did it. Right in the middle of their fourth try through the Blazing Sky area, $doomMetalBo pretended to charge at T-Rex500, and when he got shot up by CyberF***ingViking, who was like a loyal dog to T-Rex500's, instead of displaying his protective radiation shield as agreed upon, he simply drifted away, allowing a cluster of gliders to blast his boy Alphadomixxx into dust. Taking advance of the confusion —not even T-Rex500 expected the venomous move— $doomMetalBo soared all the way to the front edge of the Blazing Sky area, gathering a massive amount of units. His message box lit up.

Intergalactic memo from Alphadomixxx

Alphadomixxx: YOU FUCKING SNAKE!

```
         ..........
.............../´¯/)..............(¯`\
............./...././/...............\\....\
.........../...././/...................\\....\
...../¯/..../´¯\............./¯`\....\¯`\
../.././..../.../.../.|_......._|.\....\....\...\.\
(.(....(....(..../.)..)..(..(.(.\....)....)....).)
.\................V../.....\....V.............../
..\...................../.........\.................../
...\............. (...........)................/.
```

$doomMetalBo: SORRY bro (口口) it was a mistake

Alphadomixxx: YOU LYING ASSHOLE

$doomMetalBo: war is war dude ¯\(ツ)/¯

Alphadomixxx: I'M GONNA KILL YOU

$doomMetalBo: survival of the fittest (■_Ĺ_■)

Alphadomixxx: ┌∩┐ (◣_◢) ┌∩┐ I'M COMING TO ESTONIA TO RAPE YOUR MOM YOU SICKENING LTTLE SNAKE> I'M GONNA BURN YOU'RE HOUSE DOWN. TALLINN INDUSTRIAL NEIGHBORHOOD, RIGHT? ┌∩┐ (◣_◢) ┌∩┐ IM GONNA KILL U AND FEED YOU TO THE DOGS! I KNOW WHERE YOU LIVE YOU DAMN RAT
┌∩┐ (◣_◢) ┌∩┐

Intergalactic memo from CyberF***ingViking

CyberF***ingViking: That's foul mate, illegal move

$doomMetalBo: same shit T-Rex500 did to u ┯┷┯┷┥(·_┝┷┷┯┷

CyberF***ingViking: my plan was to back stab him too!

$doomMetalBo: so what u complaining about?

CyberF***ingViking: YOU ALL SUCK…

$doomMetalBo: change tiers then…

CyberF***ingViking: no way, I'm staying (٩•_•)۶

$doomMetalBo: ur not cut up for this tier bro, truth

CyberF***ingViking: i'm sticking with T-Rex500 Fuck U

$doomMetalBo: whatevs…

Intergalactic memo from T-Rex500

T-Rex500: Genius move www.RE$PECT.com

$doomMetalBo: i learned from the best lol

T-Rex500: Hurts doing it tho… (ノ ̄ ̱ ̄)ノ

$doomMetalBo: right! now Alphadomixxx wants to go rape my mom lol f**ing creep…

$doomMetalBo: I know!!!!!

T-Rex500: We must collaborate in the fucha, sir

$doomMetalBo: (⊙_◎)WTH

 xoxo.cutie13 is now online

Intergalactic note from xoxo.cutie13

xoxo.cutie13: wow ᴄᴍ(□益□)ᴄᴍ

$doomMetalBo: … sorry ☹

xoxo.cutie13: thought u were straight shooter bro

$doomMetalBo: … sorry ☹

xoxo.cutie13: …

$doomMetalBo: …

$doomMetalBo: hey ya

xoxo.cutie13: wha?

$doomMetalBo: ˎ * · ♫*♥*♫· * ˎ wouldn't do it to u ˎ * · ♫*♥*♫· * ˎ

xoxo.cutie13: you dirty monkey

Current Ranking

Planet War Survival III

Supreme Warriors Tier – Alpha Quadrant

Name	Units	Status	Fluctuation*
T-Rex500	82709	Online	x
$doomMetalBo	77054	Offline	1+
xoxo.cutie13	77051	Online	1-
CyberF***ingViking	60012	Online	4+

Alphadomixxx	50947	Offline	1-

* Daily scores calculated at the end of 24-hr cycle

After all that, Artjom bought a Sprite and a bag of Doritos from the drunken Finn instead of getting more time on the computer. He felt pretty shitty on the one hand, and pretty excited on the other. He kept getting better. It's like he was discovering new ways of being within himself. But he couldn't just sit there. He had to get home before *ema* got there from the factory. He was in a good mood. He'd do the dishes and feed Mitu before she came. Then he'd check his networks. There had to be a message from Kirill by then. Even big shots at fancy startups in London had to find time to say hello to their kid brother in Tallinn, Estonia.

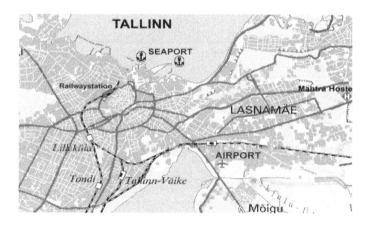

North Through the Super Periphery

Chimborazo Province

There's a church in the center of town and a cluster of crisp adobe houses by the plaza, though that's just the façade; deep Guamote unfolds past the surrounding haciendas, beyond the dirt roads, and well into the steppe, where cows, llamas, and sheep gorge on wet grass near the huts where the families live. The baby was born there, by the firewood. When she first held him, Puramama noticed he was tiny and cute (and wouldn't stop laughing) and so the name Delfín came to her. In Spanish, and in Quichua, Delfín sounds just as cute, just as *ananay*, though some might say, just as ridiculous, perhaps more so, than it does in English. After spending his first years wrapped around Puramama's back in a bright Andean shawl as she did rural chores, the tiny dolphin loosened up and wandered off into the mountains. In truth, the boy pretended to look after the animals while his father, Yuyay Quishpe, an aloof, barrel-chested man, worked the crops —onions, potatoes, corn, and some Andean produce that don't have Spanish names— for Puramama to sell at the street market on Thursdays.

But that was early on. Not even his siblings had been born then. Soon the boy began going to school. Delfín (or Fish, as Yuyay, had nicknamed him) was a soft-spoken kid, who embodied his name. He studied up to the sixth grade in a little highland school called Rudolf Clausius on the other side of the Santa Rosa trail, about forty minutes on foot, under Mr. Ibáñez, a cantankerous, auburn-haired man from Ambato, who ran it with his own funds and an iron fist. Puramama said that the teacher, who was a civil engineer from the city, had come to the highlands to cure himself of drinking. "You should've seen him when he got here, Fish. He couldn't even talk. Some say he'd lost his family in an accident. He'd drink on for weeks, then stop, then start again. But eventually he started eating with the *ayllu runa*, and spending time with us, and coming down into town with us, and helping people with his university knowledge. One day, at a church meeting regarding the hanging bridge over the rough part of the river (some *shunsho* had wrecked it getting cattle across) Mr. Ibáñez had met the mayor's sister. They teamed up and fixed the hanging bridge. Then they got the church painted over. Then they swept up the plaza. Within months they were married. Mr. Ibáñez left his hut as Minerva was never going to live in a hut, of course. She comes from a good family. Your *taita* helped them build a house and the little school. By the time he taught you how to read, the man was changed. He'd done right in coming to the highlands. Like many others, your teacher found his way by living where the *Apus* live."

Out of all his pupils, Mr. Ibáñez liked Delfín the most. He saw that the boy was clever and tried to teach him all sorts of things about the world;

some of the knowledge even stuck. Thanks to Minerva Ibáñez, who taught Spanish, and Mr. Ibáñez, who taught math, Delfín Quishpe hadn't grown up to be the rough, drunken type that chicks in his hometown seemed to fawn over all the way to the altar. Still, like most of his friends, he stopped his education at the end of primary school. Never mind his relative brightness or relative talent, a sophisticated *señor*, Delfín Quishpe was not expected to be. The boy's afternoons were spent softening the land, taking care of the cows with Chuco the dog, playing the flute, and dreaming of marrying a wide-hipped girl with a sprinkling of European blood—the type that got to go to school at the Santa Teresa Convent by the church. Every two weeks, he visited Mr. Ibáñez's, where he fixed things around the house for money. Sometimes he even got to talk about news with the teacher.

Three years went on this way. One day in May, Delfín's father, Yuyay Quishpe, got a sharp headache. It was the first headache Yuyay had ever had. It was like a knife was stuck between his eyebrows. Puramama tried to take care of him with herbs and rites, but when Yuyay started vomiting, she and her three children brought him to the doctor, which was a long way down the steppe. The country doctor got serious after seeing Yuyay had also developed diarrhea. A cropper's truck was hired to rush Yuyay to the rural hospital, but the roads were damaged by recent rains. By the time they got there, he was also feverish. Yuyay Quishpe expired hours before the sun came out. A bad strain of Andes virus was the diagnosis. The grief was as intense as the worry. The main support of the Quishpes was gone. The family also now owed money to the country doctor and to the driver that had rushed Yuyay to the hospital. As the first-born male of the house, much responsibility had fallen upon fifteen-year-old Delfín Quishpe. From dull predictability, the future had turned unstable, even explosive. The boy, for he was still a boy, didn't know how to act out his new role; he was vexed. Though he wasn't scheduled to go to Mr. Ibáñez's that day, he made the hike up and down the Santa Rosa trail, waited for the instructor to arrive, and told him all about his *taita's* death.

"Damned Andes virus. I'm sorry, *mijo*," said Mr. Ibáñez, putting his hand on his pupil's shoulder.

Both stood absorbed in the bluish shadow of the mountains.

"I'm thinking of moving to Quito," Delfín finally stated.

As with most things, Mr. Ibáñez was skeptical.

"In the capital they're going to give you one of those shitty, low paying city jobs, *mijo*, and the Third World cosmopolitans there are going to make fun of your Quichua accent, never mind the fact that their own way of speaking isn't the Queen's Castilian."

The region's hypocritical class and ethnic clashes Delfín wanted nothing to do with on instinct.

"What about Guayaquil?"

The big, hot coastal city on the Pacific was less closed-in than Quito. Mr. Ibáñez took out his pipe, which was what he did when he wanted to really think about something.

"Not Guayaquil," he said, "it will clash with your mountainous temperament, Fish. You can try, but you're not going to thrive there."

Delfín agreed. In Guayaquil they'd make fun of him too. He was too backwoods; he'd never even been to the beach.

"What if I move to the Colombian border? I've heard there's lots of commerce there."

Mr. Ibáñez turned to the side and exhaled a wave of milky smoke that stood out against the bluish greenery. He took off his small metal-framed glasses and rubbed them with his tanned wool sweater. Delfín looked at the instructor's light brown eyelashes, which remained oddly fluttering as he rubbed his glasses.

"Let's walk back to your house," Mr. Ibáñez said, putting his glasses back on, and only then opening up his reddish-brown eyes. "I want to talk to your mother."

He yelled something to Minerva Ibáñez and headed up the Santa Rosa trail with Delfín. The hill was steep and wet from the rains.

"Don't go to the Colombian border, Fish," added the teacher, as they climbed up the trail with the help of some rusty balance sticks. "I don't know if it's true, but I've heard of young *indios* getting kidnapped by Marxist guerrillas there."

Delfín didn't know what in the world Mr. Ibáñez was talking about, but he trusted the man's judgment better than anyone else's judgment, even his own. As they reached the peak of the trail, they breathed out, and gazed at the rolling hills bellow. Then they headed down in silence. In a way, hiking down the Santa Rosa trail was harder than hiking up, for on your way down you had to make an effort not to slip. The abyss was deep on both sides. The teacher was huffing and puffing by the time they got to the other side. Chucho, Chuco, and Chito, came to greet them at the entrance, waving their tails in canine excitement. Mr. Ibáñez, who hadn't been to the Quishpes' in a long time, noticed how big the dogs had gotten.

"Go get your mom, Fish," he said, exerting teacherly authority over the teen, as he kneeled down to play with the dogs.

Delfín came back after a minute.

"She says to come in."

They walked into the mud hut. It smelled like burned wood there, but it was tidy despite the scarcity. Puramama was distraught; still, she asked Mr. Ibáñez to sit down and poured him coffee. Mr. Ibáñez wasn't one to beat around the bush. He didn't know how, so he did what he'd come do to. Puramama Quishpe's eyes filled with tears. The money was enough to pay for Yuyay's medical bills as well as for the emergency truck ride.

"Yuyay Quishpe was a good man, Puramama. He had struggled with some of the same problems I struggled with when I arrived in Guamote. His body was possibly weakened when he came upon the Andes virus. Perhaps it was too many years of hard work. He was a superior worker, who worked too hard for too long. He helped me transport the materials up the hill to build my house years ago. Remember that? Minerva wouldn't have married me otherwise. I'm grateful to all of you for that, Puramama. I really am," Mr. Ibáñez said, emotion bending his voice.

They drank another cup of coffee and then Mr. Ibáñez left. The sun had set though it wasn't dark yet. Delfín insisted on hiking back with the teacher at least up to the point where the slope down began. He gave the teacher a poncho that had belonged to Yuyay and put one on himself. It would get colder still. He brought Chuco, the fiercest dog with him. A puma, which means powerful in Quichua, had been seen in the hills. Chuco would scare him away if need be. Teacher and pupil walked up the trail in silence.

"What about Argentina?" Delfín suddenly asked, near the summit.

It was clear the teen wasn't thinking of anything else but leaving. Mr. Ibáñez sat down on a rock and pet Chuco, who licked his thick fingers as if they were salty pork chops. The view below the Santa Rosa trail seemed vaster in the darkening evening.

"Argentina is like Europe (in some places) and has amazing soccer," said the teacher, "but the Argentinean president, Rodolfo Gutherman, quadrupled the size of the state, and has driven away foreign investors with 19th century economic ideas. Then he had the gall to ask the IMF for a loan. And the IMF gave it to him! Idiocy on both sides, my dear Fish. Argentina is now on the verge of defaulting for the third or fourth time in history, who knows, but when they default —and they will— shit will hit the fan all over the southern tip. We might even get a wave of Argentinean migrants in the Avenue of the Volcanos for all you know. Economic irrationality is a regional curse."

Delfín assented. It was amazing how well Mr. Ibáñez spoke. Argentina wasn't the place to go to then. Peru apparently was out of the question too.

"Peru's the same shit as Ecuador," Mr. Ibáñez said (in those terms), "except the stupid elites of both countries don't like each other. They pretend it's about other reasons, but the reality is Ecuadorians remind Peruvians too much of themselves and Peruvians do the same for Ecuadorians. It happens everywhere with closely related countries, just ask Koreans about Japan," added the teacher, smoking from his pipe. "Anyhow, dear Fish, South America is the region we have been lucky enough to have been born in: incompetent, broke, and endlessly self-deceptive."

Delfín was confused. Or maybe he was just weighed down by it all. *Taita* Yuyay was dead. His mother and two siblings needed money. And he had been born in a poor region. He was cornered by reality. Then the idea entered his head. It was like a key that could unlock all the locked doors in the world.

"What about the United States?" Delfín yelled out as Mr. Ibáñez headed down the slope.

The teacher stopped in his tracks. He took off his small metal-framed glasses and vigorously wiped them with his tanned wool sweater. Delfín pictured the man fluttering his light-brown eyelashes, and smiled. *Uncle Sam's McDonald's Republic...* Mr. Ibáñez thought. He turned around and waved at his pupil in silence. Delfín remained at the summit as the teacher descended further and further down the trail wearing Yuyay's poncho. Silence in the teacher's world, the pupil had come to know, signified tacit approval. A bittersweet sensation filled his wide chest as he saw, as if for the last time, that milky puff rising. He whistled for Chuco, who reappeared from within the mountainous gloom with a struggling orange rodent between his teeth. *Go north!* Chuco seemed to be saying with his wagging tail. *Here's my offering to the supernatural powers controlling the rain, the sun and harvest, which is life! Go north!* Delfín took the orange rodent from Chuco's muzzle and flung it with all his might far down into the black abyss below. As he headed down the Santa Rosa trail with his balance stick, he felt as though the mountains were gigantic monsters that had swallowed the little orange mammal. He flung out his balancing stick too and proceeded to run down in the dark. He wasn't going to fall, not there, for he knew every rock, every alcove, and every angle of the narrow, steep trail, like a map in his head, or rather in his heart, for it isn't only the head that records things, but the heart too, and better, closer, with a different cipher, one that lasts longer, and sees deeper, differently, from all angles, even at night, particularly at night, when thoughts don't make sense in the mind, and light cannot enter the eye. This Delfín Quishpe did not need anyone to tell him with words, for he knew it inside, with sensations, which were a greater fact, like the fact that at the end of the Santa Rosa trail Puramama and his two siblings, Güily and Karina, were waiting for him to wash themselves right, and then pray for dead *taita* Yuyay, and then eat food together, at least a little, symbolically, but whole-heartedly, with grief—the reaching hand affection lost.

Taita Yuyay's burial had to be arranged. Puramama got to talking about Jesus and the Apus, the protector spirits in the mountains. She lit up some Roman candles before a statue of the Virgin Mary, who was also the *Pachamama*. Many people arrived after lunch and they sang and prayed to both Jehovah and to the protector spirits in syncretism. Delfín knew —that's who they were— but he asked anyhow, for he wanted it said.

"One leads to the other like a tunnel in the sky," said uncle Yaku, who'd come all the way from the Cayambe province bringing a large living swine and gallons of *puntas* in his truck.

Delfín had never met uncle Yaku, whose name means *agua* in Spanish, which means water in English, but he liked him because he was talkative and had stories about *taita* Yuyay. Many others had come and not only from the Cayambe province, but also from the Cotopaxi and from the Tungurahua provinces. There was even a black family, the Carabalís, who'd come from the Esmeraldas province. Apparently, *taita* Yuyay had done his military service all the way over in Esmeraldas. There he'd befriended Pedro Carabalí, who'd brought his whole family to Guamote.

"We fought in the Cenepa war together," said Mr. Carabalí.

Delfín looked at his kid brother Güily and at his little sister Karina and saw they were floored too. Their father had fought in a war!

"Yuyay wasn't afraid of the bullets either," added the Mr. Carabalí, whose smile was the brightest thing Karina had ever seen.

The man's wife, whose name was Mabelle, looked around as if testing the waters.

"Yuyay was brave, unlike you, *amor*," she let out.

"Pedro's a nervous flyer. We had to drive here."

Mr. Carabalí was embarrassed at his wife's words. Everybody laughed. By knocking down her husband, Mrs. Carabalí, had extolled the dead man. For Delfín it was a revelation. Not even Puramama knew Yuyay had served in the military all the way in Esmeraldas, much less that he'd fought in the Cenepa War. Delfín wondered all the things he didn't know about his father. Some were told that day. Most things, however, he'd never know, for his father was like a rock. It got late that way. Time flies when you're telling stories.

"Our beautiful *taita's* thoughts belonged to the *páramo,* not to other men, not even to us, his children," Delfín asserted towards the end of the night, after having had some *puntas* to drink, which was fine, for he had to get used to being grown.

Uncle Yaku stood up and faced the young man.

"Strong men are like that, *guambra*. Hushed. Enigmatic. It's a sign of strength. Only the weak ones chirp a lot, like hungry little chicks." Delfín got quiet for a minute.

"I'm the eldest of the three here, but I'm still talkative," he added.

"That's because you're not a boy, *guambra*—you're a Fish!" uncle Yaku said, hugging the flushing teen. Everybody laughed again. It was good to laugh. "When you go through as much as your *taita* did, you will also become as quiet, if not quieter than he was. It's a kind of weight. It will be given to you one day," said uncle Yaku, and then, with much feeling, spilled a glass full of liquor on the dirt floor and then another one and then another one.

Everybody stood up. It was a sign of respect for the dead man, whose spirit was still around. They all felt it. So they stood up and exited, but not in a bad way. It was time to go get rest. Yuyay was still around. They let his spirit occupy the space quietly. People slept in different houses throughout. Some camped in tents outside. The next day, the burial took place. Flour and sand where spread around the room where the body had been. A final prayer was spoken. Then, at last, the washing and burning of Yuyay's earthly clothes was performed. His spirit had reached the afterlife. The pig was slaughtered. Burning animal hair occupied the thick air of the highlands. *Morcilla* and *chicha* were served. Everybody ate well, paid their last respects, and left. A big void hovered in the heart of the hut.

On the day before departing, Delfín was going to write a good-bye note to Mr. Ibañez, but the problem of Chuco had taken complete hold of him. Puramama and his siblings needed Chuco's protection. And not only because Chuco was fierce, but because, as grandma Tránsito used to say, *black dogs keep evil spirits at bay*. But he too needed Chuco. His Chuco! And yet, such a long trip could be a death sentence to the pooch. The real question was —he stumbled upon it in the middle of the night, in troubled dreams— who would protect *him*? Grandma Tránsito? Taita Yuyay? The Apus? Jesús? It wasn't clear. Before the sun shot up over the Andes, he stuffed things in a colorful wiphala bag that his best friends, Antay and Byron, the Guamán brothers, had gifted him on a drunken night by the San

Pedro River, and stepped outside. Chuco ran to him. Delfín pet him vigorously, as if he'd made up his mind to bring him along, but Chuco knew better. He wagged his tail lowly, reading the moment with animal candor. And so Delfín walked the long way down to the station by himself.

Some workers were already there. He waited. The bus left at 6:30 a.m. For the first day and night, as he made his way from Guamote to Ambato, from Ambato to Latacunga, from Latacunga to Quito, from Quito to Otavalo, from Otavalo to Ibarra, from Ibarra to Tulcán, and from Tulcán to Pasto, which was in Colombia. Delfín did little more than sleep and dream. The same way the bus had uprooted his body from Guamote, his dreams uprooted his mind from the road. At most he managed some glances of the extreme topography before another bus took him from Pasto to Popayán, from Popayán to Cali, and from Cali to somewhere near Pereira, where the certainty that there was no danger of kidnapping. He stopped paying attention to the names of towns and paid attention to the music instead. He was too Andean to really enjoy all the vallenato the wife-beater-wearing bus driver was blasting, and neither did he care for bachata, but when this new thing with backward beats started playing, Delfín leaned in. He particularly enjoyed the lewd rap full of Puerto Rican slang. His imagination took off. The bus got to the border with Panama, which in his mind was *The North*.

Luckily the check point was empty. He didn't have proper identification, much less so an international passport. All he had was a moth-eaten birth certificate drafted years after the fact by a Guamote authority. Panama was another dimension. He saw the beach for the first time outside of El Porvenir. The sea was alive, aggressive, the sand like gold. Delfín stared out the bus window, enthralled. Sensations were colliding inside. He'd never been so hot in his life for one. He felt sick. He felt free. And he most definitely felt hungry. And he felt scared. The bag of food he'd brought with him was not only running out, but was also going bad. He ate one last bit of home-made cheese with corn, and threw what was left out the window, onto the highway, *para los cuervos*. Eating that last bit of food was a no-no. He got diarrhea and could not take another bus for two days. He had to sleep on a bench in a triangle-shaped plaza across the way from the *Muséo Antropológico* in Panama City. The plaza was wonderful, but cars surrounded it day and night. The fumes and the noise crashed Delfín's nerves. On top of that, on the second night, he was confronted by some glue-sniffing kids. He broke his Andean flute in half to make an impromptu spike and fought back. It wasn't until a haggard *policía* on an old moped came that the felonious children left. The cop brought the bloodied Andean to a nearby infirmary (and sort of charged him for it). It wasn't technically exaction, nor was it purely good will. It was a voluntary pay off. Delfín knew how these things went; he might have been a foreigner, but he was also Latin American. The curly-haired nurse gave him pain killers for the cracked nose and rib and some cherry-flavored liquid for the ongoing diarrhea. Before taking off, Delfín looked at his face in the mirror and saw the busted nose made him look like the great Segundo Mercado, an old champ *taita* Yuyay had a poster of in the hut. Upon turning back from the mirror, Delfín saw that the curly-haired nurse was also expecting money. *Had Chuco been with me, he would've shredded those little thugs to shreds*, he thought as he drew out cash from his smelly sock. "At least I scratched the hell out of them," he said out loud, but he was failing to make himself feel better. Whatever dough the little thieves hadn't gotten from him, the cop and the nurse had. He was done with Panama.

At the end of the second day, he left on a bus. The broken bones, he didn't fuss over; he'd broken lots of bones before. But the broken flute sucked. It was Antay's gift, so he kept it, broken as it was, as an impromptu stab. Still, he was dying to play. But where could he find an Andean flute in Parrita, Costa Rica? He played Andean tunes in his head as he rode through Garabito, Grecia, Liberia, and La Cruz, and there they blended with the rhythms he'd first heard in the Panama-Colombia border. Nicaragua, he did mostly on foot plus the occasional truck ride. A *vigorón* vender near some caves advised him to the edge of Lago Nicaragua and the same at Lago Managua, always facing north. Walking had the advantage that you could catch your own food. Some trees Delfín knew. For the ones he didn't know, he looked at birds. If birds ate the fruit, the fruit was edible; if not, it wasn't. Some food he bought at markets, mostly hot-dogs, which didn't go bad. And so, by walking up and down hills, and through humid plains, and jungles, and around lagoons, and valleys, and cities, and towns, and freeways, and dirt roads, he made it through Nicaragua. Then he hopped on a boat across the Gulf of Fonseca, which wasn't free.

To keep from getting nauseous, he focused on the foam traces left on the sea by the congested boat, until suddenly drops on his head brought him back from his salty trance. A brutal precipitation was pounding upon the whole frontier coast—and he thought he saw a shark, but somebody said it was a dolphin. He smiled in silence. The whole thing was so new, so terrifyingly new, particularly the sun that emerged like an apparition. Delfín Quishpe looked around. A blanket of effervescent sea all around and the lively *cuichi* in the distance, like a slew of pigmented arrows falling upon Tiger Island. *Guamote must be over the cuichi!* he thought. But perhaps it was in the opposite direction, where a cluster of hills could be deciphered. Well, he wasn't in Guamote anymore, except for the music inside. He let his thoughts be as he set foot on land, cracked flute in his pocket, wiphala bag across the chest.

"Welcome to the most beautiful republic in Central America. The only nation in the world named after our savior and lord *Jesucristo!*" the boat's owner, a fat guy in a tight polo, let out as he grabbed the second half of the payment.

The first half had been paid before getting onboard. Because the Andean looked like a poor peasant, short, dark, and shabbily dressed, nobody paid attention to him. It was only when he opened his mouth that his mountainous accent full of heavy swooshes and dragging r's peeked out from within. But he didn't open his mouth. At first he simply followed a group of Haitian refugees, but they requested money from him, so he took off. Around Zacatecoluca, his legs started dragging like broken tree branches, so he took a bus, where he slept (as per usual, he dreamt about wide-hipped women and wealth in the form of horses). When he awoke, he saw that he wasn't worried about the future. *I could get off here and do whatever it takes.* Pulling through hardships had made his talents clear to himself. He had that baffling power of the truly rural: being utterly focused and utterly self-distracted at once. Stories, memories and songs emerged when needed to alleviate or fuel whatever hard work had to be sustained. He thought of his late father. And began to understand that silence. He felt terrific. *Yes, I could get off here or anywhere.*

But the Apus have a way. Just when you feel like a mighty condor with your wings open near the frosty peaks, they have a way. And so it was. Around the town of Lourdes, in Colon, Delfín veered off from the Pan-American Highway and somehow ended up around Volcán Izalco, which was a young and stylized volcano that seemed to have been handcrafted by lady fingers. It was unlike anything he'd seen in the equator, where the volcanoes are beyond huge – behemoth – and beyond majestic – superhuman – and certainly erected before the beginnings of the earth. In the equator, the volcanoes were all *taitas*. The Chimborazo was a *taita*! The Cotopaxi was a *taita*! The Pichincha was *taita*! Even the Sangay was a *taita*! Not here in The Savior's Land. This boy of a volcano was no one's *taita*. With its lithe and smooth body, Volcán Izalco was an adolescent like himself. It was an insight so strange, Delfín had nothing but curious tears to give, as if the apparition of this young volcano authenticated the rash fuel that had ejected him from his old country. *Getting lost is worth it,* he said, still positive, but he could've been walking in circles around Volcán Izalco for all he knew. Only after three hours did he meet a short peasant (shorter than himself!) in a straw hat, who dropped him off in the city of Santa Ana for a small sum that was also a fortune. Santa Ana was there and there he was. *I feel like a damned goat*, he told himself as he stumbled behind a steel and glass construction and allowed himself the extravagant luxury of passing out.

He awoke in the dark, city rats all around his body like cars in roundabout. For a second there, he thought it was a nightmare and closed his eyes, but when he opened them again, he got up, petrified. He couldn't take it anymore. He made his way to a motel on the outskirts. It was the first time he'd paid for lodging. But the Andes Virus, which had killed his father, spread through rats, the Guamote doctor had said, and so fear was ripping through Delfín's gut. He used a whole bar of soap in a single shower. Once showered, he came down and asked the pretty receptionist for the cheapest food around. He had enough coins for one last meal. "*Pupusas Anahí*," she said, pointing. "You'll see a patio under a ripped orange canopy, that's the spot." Delfín had no idea what *pupusas* were nor for that matter what a canopy was, but it was easier not to get lost if you had a sign—an arrow, a compass, a voice, a finger pointing *yes*.

Delfín sat under the orange canopy for a long while, so that it was impossible not to talk to the diners. Two curly-haired men who looked related (except one was dark and the other extremely pale) shouted over the Salvadorian cumbia something about the upcoming Ágila-FAS soccer match, and since Delfín did not have anything to add, they assumed he was Guatemalan or something—and Delfín, shyly or perhaps tiredly, did not dispel the assumption. The owner of the joint, a heavy woman with a silver smile, Anahí, took an instant liking of the soft-mannered foreigner. His lost puppy demeanor and exotic formality had something to do with it, not to mention the lovable name. She charged him for two *pupusas* instead of four, and gave him a big glass of local horchata, which kind of tasted like chicha to him. Delfín stayed at *Pupusas Anahí* until closing time, simply basking in the warm Salvadorian night.

"I know you're going up north," the owner finally let out as she cleaned around. "I understand how difficult this situation can be. I made the same trek when I was a young, but soon returned to The Savior's Land."

"Is that so?"

"*Cabal!* My husband got deported, so I got them to deport me too! That's what women did back then. We were so devoted. Anyhow, my daughter's going up north too, so... full circle."

"I see," said Delfín, helping Anahí move the tables to clean. "When is she going?"

"In about ten days," the woman said, "with her husband, Big Toño, and two grandparents from around here, who say they're going to meet their grandkiddies, but who knows. Oldsters get massive government pensions up there. A coyote's guiding them all, of course."

"A coyote?"

"A coyote is a man who knows his way up. True coyotes charge in the thousands. This guy's a relative of ours, something like a cousin. Real good guy, *El Gallo*. He guides people when in he's need, but mostly to help out. He's a sort of humanitarian coyote, no lie," said Anahí. And then staring at the foreigner: "You know, *mijo*, my husband, the man who got deported so long ago, was Guatemalan too. My family hated him because he was *indio*, like you."

"Seems perfect," Delfín whispered, caressing his own lips, "God sent."

"How do you mean?" Anahí asked.

"That your daughter will be going to up north so soon."

"Okay," she said and smiled. She had a good feeling and went with it. "You know, I could use a dishwasher for a few days, if you're interested. I could talk to *El Gallo* about your situation. All I'd ask for is that you look after my daughter. Her man is somewhat of a brute. Where are you staying? Come back tomorrow night. We got a little caboose in the back."

Delfín worked hard and slept well. Ten days went by quickly.

◊ ◊ ◊

The sun was about to rise. *El Gallo*, a lanky dude in a Charlotte Hornets cap, light green eyes, a rose tattoo on his neck, and a thin mustache under the aquiline nose, got out of a baby blue van. There was a white handgun nestled between jeans and belly, under his worn out Hawaiian shirt. He kissed Anahí's daughter, Sandrita, on the cheek and fist-bumped her husband, Big Toño, whom he obviously knew. At the old geezers and at Delfín, the foreigner, he nodded.

"The Guate border's on fire right now," he said, referencing some recent murders, as he struggled to slide the van's door open. "We better go through Honduras," he added. "I got some mens at the river."

The five migrants looked around in surprise. Something didn't feel right to Delfín. Going through The Country of Great Depths seemed convoluted, serpentine, even backwards. The logical thing would have been to go straight to Guatemala, which was closer.

"It's not like Honduras is safe," said the old woman, but nobody replied.

The baby blue van shot through the north-eastern edge of The Savior's Land like a burned-out torpedo. *El Gallo* blasted Salvadorian cumbia and that new music with the backwards beat Delfín liked so much. The sunroof was kept open. As per usual, Delfín put his wiphala bag on the window and knocked out. Somewhere near the border, he awoke. There was a wide, turbulent river to be crossed. Through the slimy window he noticed people struggling to swim to the other side. He also noticed Sandrita staring at him.

"It's not usually this bubbly," said *El Gallo*. "There's been rains this week. But its either this or whatever the hell's going on with the killings at the other border."

Dread gripped the Andean. He couldn't swim. Plus, Río Lempa, the longest river in Central America, was clearly much fiercer than the San Pedro River back home. *El Gallo* got out of the van, leaving the engine and the music on. He bumped fists with three men in military attire who were sitting by the shade of a guava tree. Blue and white emblems decorated their breast pockets. One took out a little cigarette and shared it. *El Gallo* smoked with them. They seemed to loosen up and laugh with their whole bodies. One of them was clearly telling a story punctuated by wild arm gestures.

After the story ended, *El Gallo* patted the story-teller on the back and fist bumped the other two. He spat on the ground on his way back, cowboy boots crushing the water pebbles.

"Off we go, *familia!*" he exclaimed, smacking his lips.

How in the holy heck are we going to get across? Delfín repeated to himself in the grips of panic. *I should have learned how to swim when taita Yuyay took us to the Cuicocha lagoon in the fifth grade. This is unconscionable.*

"There," added *El Gallo*, pointing to an inflatable military boat.

Seeing the sturdy little boat gave some relief to the Andean. Still, the wild meteoric conditions over the Golfo de Fonseca a few days prior had conditioned him to dislike water traveling. Also, too many fuckers were packed in the small boat, again. He held on to the edge with both hands.

"There's a shitload of piranhas in Río Lempa," said the young soldier who was manning the thing, lighting up another little cigarette.

"You know how to swim, right, *maje?*" asked *El Gallo* in Delfín's direction as he took the soldier's roll-up between index and thumb.

It was the first time the humanitarian coyote had addressed him directly.

"No, I don't," said Delfín, green with nausea.

"What's your name again?"

"Delfín."

"Delfín?"

Delfín nodded. It was a matter of seconds before vomit shot out.

"A dolphin who cannot swim!" exclaimed the young soldier, whose rushed Spanish Delfín could barely unentangle.

"How strange is that?" replied *El Gallo* fist bumping the young soldier.

Everybody laughed, except for Sandrita, who'd definitely been looking at Delfín. It was obvious to him now.

"How about you, *Gallo?* You sing?" asked Delfín, smiling perhaps too broadly.

People laughed, particularly the old couple. It was all in good fun.

Sandrita did not join in the laughter. A gray vulture crossed the white sky above.

"You're not from Guate, *are ya?*" she let out.

Sandrita had a strong voice like most women in The Savior's Land. Delfín froze.

"Why would ya go from Guate-land to Salvie-land if your goal is to make it to Gringo-land?" she added with a sort of bitter joviality. "Don't any make sense dood."

Delfín looked ahead, nausea curtailed.

"Leave him alone, woman," said Big Toño, her husband, who was a man of few words. "No matter where the Indian's from."

"I'm just saying," she added. "It's strange. My father was from Guate. I know Guatemalans. This boy ain't from Guate. Where ya from, dood?"

Delfín kept quiet, holding the edge of the angry boat.

"Let him be, woman!" repeated Big Toño. "What's it to you where he's from?"

"You're from Peru or Bolivia, aren't ya, dood?" she said. "You're not from Guate. It just don't add up to me."

Sandrita was getting worked up in that strange jovial way of hers. Delfín never thought Sandrita, whom he'd promised sweet Anahí to protect, could turn against him. Big Toño, the supposed brute, ironically, was the one trying to keep the peace.

"Quiet, woman," Big Toño whispered in embarrassment.

The argument was taking a different direction. Folks quietly looked on

"I don't like people who lie to my mother, *pendejo*!" said Sandrita.

It wasn't clear who she was calling *pendejo*, the *faux* Guatemalan, or her reportedly explosive husband.

"Who you calling *pendejo*?" Big Toño asked, on the threshold of fury.

The quarrel blew up in earnest as the boat made it to the other side. Lots of hills could be seen in the distance. They were now in The Country of Great Depths. The greenery was extremely luxuriant. Birds, water, heat, toads, mosquitoes, boas, parrots, tigers, lions, giraffes, elephants—pure jungle in the Andean's heart. He got off the boat quietly as the couple shouted. He tiptoed behind a tall tree and vomited. He peed too. It was a relief. Sweat amassed on his narrow forehead. When he came back, Big Toño and Sandrita were no longer shouting. In fact, and this was as incomprehensible a thing as Delfín saw in his entire voyage: they were holding hands! Sandrita's head was resting on her man's massive right shoulder. How long had it been? Six, seven minutes? No longer than eight. The Andean felt dizzy. The geezers were off to the side, laughing with *El Gallo*, who was telling them a rowdy joke having to do with angels and poop. The young soldier was cheerfully wheeling the boat back across the mercurial Río Lempa.

"*Ahí-táh,*" exclaimed Sandrita, as she pointed with the tip of her nose.

El Gallo turned around and adjusted his green and white Charlotte Hornet's cap.

"We've decided you got to go, little man."

Even Delfín, who didn't even know what drugs were, could tell the coyote was high.

"Bah! Go find some *gallinas*, man," he said, smiling.

"Seriously, you got to go, bro, you go to go."

"What?"

"We cannot trust you," said *El Gallo*, red eyes shifting.

Delfín looked around. Everybody was staring. He waited, but nobody spoke up for him, which cut him hard in the pit of his stomach. He bit his lip.

"Okay, but I need my money back."

El Gallo looked around with his red eyes.

Sandrita put her curly hair in a bun.

"No way, *maje*. You're fucking Quichua, not Quiché. My father was Quiché. You lied to momma. You ate her fucking *pupusas*. You stayed in her caboose. For ten days you got cash out of her, not only for the 'work' you said you did, but the extra dough she gave you. She felt sorry for your native ass, that's why she helped you. People always lie to her. She's good-hearted. That's her problem. Has always been. She can't face ugly truths, like the fact that you're a fucking leech. She's the eternal victim. The eternal cryer. But I gotta look out for her. That's my job, has always been. I'm *la mala*," she said, stepping forward. "The dough you paid, which isn't even half of what *El Gallo* usually gets, belongs to momma. Humanitarian coyote my ass! Those are momma's silly words. *El Gallo* has mouths to feed. Anahí Iriarte lives in a fantasy world. So, hell no! We ain't giving you shit back. It's the dough you took from us. Count yourself lucky we brought you all the way up to Honduras, *puto*."

Delfín was flabbergasted. He was a fish out of the water in the most tumultuous region of the world's periphery. The old biddy, her name was Eloisa, took pity on him. Or maybe she simply felt guilty at taking his money.

"We need that money, *mijo*…" she voiced, "I'm sorry."

Her words opened a door for Big Toño, who let go of Sandrita's meaty hand.

"Let him stay, *gente*," Big Toño said. "He hasn't caused us any harm."

Big Toño had a commanding jaw and perhaps enough pull to dissuade the others.

"Where you from, boy?" asked the old man, who apparently had a tongue.

When somebody who doesn't speak at last opens his mouth, people listen. In this case, the words that came out of the geezer's trap had the weight of finality. Everything depended on the Andean's answer. But he didn't speak. He stayed as mute as the highlands. He wasn't used to lying, and so had no sense of scale. He felt as if though he'd be admitting to treason or murder.

"Where you from, boy?" repeated the geezer, now shaking, as Eloisa held him.

Zilch. The group read the foreigner's silence as attestation of his essential untrustworthiness.

"This fucking liar *indio* could bring bad luck on to us, I'm telling you," Sandrita said.

Again, it was Sandrita, and only Sandrita, who spoke at the tensest of moments. She had something the others lacked. Delfín stayed quiet. It was crazy, but the meaner Sandrita was to him, the more desirable he found her. He simply stared at her curly hair and big round ass. But now was not the time for that. He pushed those thoughts back.

"I need at least some of my money to make it up north," he said in his accent, which was closer to whispering than to talking. "I have no money left, I swear."

The old woman shook her head no. So did her man. Not even Big Toño could help Delfín if he didn't help himself. Sandrita looked in her cousin's direction, chief-like.

"Get lost," said *El Gallo*, who had a short fuse.

Around those parts, everyone had a short fuse.

"What. About. My money?" said Delfín, with widening nostrils.

Unlike them, it took the Andean a long time to get worked up, but once it happened, he could kill. They noticed. They were rough, but they weren't idiots. It was time to act.

"Get fucking lost, now!" boomed *El Gallo*. "You fucking liar *indio*."

Interestingly, despite his green eyes, *El Gallo* was quite darker skinned than the Andean, which is neither here nor there, but it is something. That they'd called Delfín *indio* in a derogatory way was at least incongruent, but Delfín had gotten used to that kind of treatment. Unlike most Latin Americans, he'd kept his roots, which irked many, perhaps even most, Spanish speakers, whom he sometimes called *half-breeds*. Ire surged in his chest. He took three steps forward. *El Gallo* pulled out his handgun. It was unlikely he'd shoot. Still, a gun pointed at your chest by a coyote, humanitarian or not, in the mossy backwaters between The Savior's Land and The Country of Great Depths commanded a certain, shall we say, tension. Delfín stopped in his tracks.

"Let's go!" Sandrita ordered to the rest of the group. "He's a little fag."

Delfín took one last look at Big Toño. *He's going to hurt her tonight,* he thought. *El Gallo* might have had the handgun, Big Toño might have had the muscles, and the geezers might have had the years, but Sandrita Rosales had that wonderful *locura. What do I have?* Delfín asked in his head. Suddenly he felt his body charging forward like a bull. *El Gallo* reached under his Hawaiian shirt and fired at once. Delfín plunged to the ground. *El Gallo* fired again. Delfín crawled behind a bush with no feeling in his body. He knew that if he poked his brain out, he'd join *taita* Yuyay in the Hanan Pacha, under the Great Illapa (*taita* Santiago) lord of thunder and lightning.

So he hollered instead:

"Your momma's a saint, but you're a darn *carishina*!"

Sandrita had no idea what Delfín had said, but charged forward nonetheless. Big Toño held her by the wrist. It was nothing to him even though she was a powerful woman.

"I hope that giant brute beats you senseless tonight!"

"Alright *puto*!" cried Big Toño as he himself headed towards the bush.

"*¡Aguanta!¡Aguanta!*" shouted *El Gallo*, firing straight at the bush.

Three shots. No movement perceived.

"*¡Vamos! ¡Vamos!*" he added, putting his gun away.

The migrants rushed towards an old red truck that was parked in the Honduran distance. Two minutes later, someone flung a colorful rag out the window. The livid, nearly ghostly Andean sprang through the bush, scratching his arms. Just like before, *El Gallo* had shot slightly off from where he thought Delfín was. The aim was *not to kill* (he must have been something of a humanitarian after all). Delfín kept running. The red truck had seemed closer than it was.

A tall dark figure stepped out from within the foliage.

"Hey, that shit's mine!" yelled the Andean violently.

He was ready to kill for that half shredded wiphala bag of his. Also, maybe, just maybe, his money was in there.

"You must have Atahualpa's gold in here, comrade," hollered the voice.

Delfín looked up at the backlit figure, laughing in the swirling glare of Honduran sun. The white of his eyes radiated like two violent moons. The scar on his cheek was like the fossil of a comet's trail. The figure stretched his hand forward and handed Delfín the bag. There was no money in it.

"Where you from, comrade?"

Delfín dusted himself off.

"My name is Delfín Fernando Quishpe Alulema. I'm from the town of Guamote, in the Chimborazo province, Republic of Ecuador, spiritual and geographic center of the world," he said, close to tears.

He never wanted to lie about his place of origin again.

"Ah, the center of the earth! I once trained a guy from *Alfaro Vive Carajo!*"

Delfín had no idea what the man was saying. He was so ignorant about so many things. And yet, his almond eyes gave away honest curiosity. He trailed the man into the backwaters. There the man, whose name was Abraham, discoursed on and on, hypnotically and labyrinth-like, until dozing off mid-talk. *I wonder what Mr. Ibáñez would think of this man?* Delfín thought, as he pushed his foot on a tree, rocking the hammock where he lay. Turning the day's tumultuous memories into the easy foam of dreams happened easily in the busy darkness of the bush. But there seemed to be no room for dreams in that thickness. The morning was there again almost at once.

"Care for one?" hollered the old man, peeling a green coconut with a machete.

"*No gracias*," said Delfín, rubbing his mosquito bitten arms near a calm arm of the turbulent Lempa. "I'll find something, *señor*."

"Don't call me *señor*, comrade! That's a nasty bourgeois convention. I'll take Uncle Abe, but not *señor. Vení!* Let's go see if we can go catch something besides upriver trash hahahaha!"

Delfín checked his shoes for spiders. At the riverbank they washed themselves and fished. Delfín was not good at fishing. Abraham caught four trout and cooked them with plantains. The sun got intense. They went to the shade at noon. It was in the after lunch lull that the tales begun.

"The 1957 Cienfuegos revolt was almost it, but the tyrant's forces slaughtered over a hundred of us. I got away by a hare's breath," Abraham said, revealing the scars on his torso. "I got no ribs, comrade, but an accordion that plays German tunes whenever I fart, hahahaha!"

"I've never been in a war," Delfín said, too enthralled to laugh. "My father fought in the Cenepa war, though we didn't find out until after he passed."

"Every man is given a war. This is yours. The Sierra Maestra was mine. It's a beautiful place, the same as the *Merendón* mountains here," Abraham said, widening his eyes. Then he pulled out a book from his pocket, and then an old photo from within the book. "I'm the stud on the tanker truck, and the feral beardo bellow is none other than the man himself. We had captured that pretty bounty earlier that day. *El Comandante* actually stated I had Chief Lempira's spirit living in me. *Mirá.*"

Delfín turned the photograph around.

> *For my Garifuna comrade, Abraham Benguché.*
> *With fondness, strength and respect — Fidel Castro.*

"I was there for the whole thing, rifle in hand. After January 1st, 1959, I did farming in the countryside, but farming wasn't for me. I was young. Like Che, I'd caught the revolution bug. Once you catch the bug, my brother, be it art, revolution, the bottle, or love, no power on earth can hold you back. I got happily sent to the Congo, where I spent six months fighting and two months as a POW. That's how I got the kiss of the train tracks on my mug, hahahaha! Upon returning, I became a Cuban national and flew to Vladivostok on a scholarship where I met a golden haired *babushka*. I also picked up the words, though she ended up learning more Honduran than I did Rusky. Our language sticks more easy. I was happy, but the bug was still in me, comrade. Lyudmila saw and divorced me. I came back and turned advisor to undercover Boricua secessionists in Panama. Then I worked with the Zapatistas in Chiapas. I did it for free because I basically love how Mexicans talk! I don't feel bad about not making money with all my skills. I do feel bad about collaborating with the Colombian guerrilla. They were more about kidnapping and dandruff dealing, than about Marxist liberation, so I penned a column detailing my views. The column came out in Venezuela under Carlos Robledo, my *nom de plume*. Sounds like a sickly bureaucrat hahahaha! The Venezuelan newspaper editor betrayed me. Bitter subordinates paid him off. They claimed I was a CIA agent. *Pura mierda!* I was wanted by the CIA. How could I work for them? Anyhow, by then most of the pals I'd fought along with in the Sierra Maestra had been replaced by nasty bureaucrats. I was stripped of my Cuban citizenship and branded *anti-revolutionary*. No worse label than that, comrade. I was deported to the Country of the Great Depths and my Russian kids were forbidden from writing to me. I did time at the San Pedro Sula Penitentiary. That's one beautiful castle hahahaha! Terrorism, insurrection and treason were the charges. Silly stuff. Laughable. Had the death penalty been legal... I did 131,400 hours at San Pedro Sula before they let me out partly because I'd got old, but mostly because I had no bite left in me. I was toothless! *Bobos* couldn't see I still had one big molar in the back, take a look, it's still there hahahaha!"

"What about your Russian family?"

"They melted into the snows of Vladivostok. Poof! I met a good woman in jail, the guard's sister. We got married. I gave her some kids. All girls. But I never did see my Russian boys again. I still hold out hope they'll come try our delicious *Ayote en Miel* someday. It's worth the transatlantic trip.

They got to come here. I can't go there. Old bones crack in the snow, ya know, hahahaha!"

Delfín laughed with his host, whose laughter rumbled fully formed, like he was laughing about all the silliness in the universe, and the little things in it too, including his own personal tragedies.

"Let me tell you something about your own war," added Abraham, before yawning. "City folks can't survive the trek up north. I've lodged a few in here. But they never last. City folks need restaurants to eat in. Screens to look at. Maps to travel with. They don't even know how to shit in the bush. It ain't like that here. Here you gotta learn the right leaf to wipe your ass with. The *Merendón* mountains aren't a trip to the mall, *mijo*. Only folks like you have a chance. You're a country boy. A real *campesino*. That's an asset, Quishpe. Take it from a country boy who took a bullet or two with Che Guevara in Cuba and with Patrice Lumumba in the Congo."

Delfín's host was suddenly asleep again. The Andean followed suit. It was easy to sleep in the humid humdrum of the woods. Three hours before sunset, they woke up again and went hunting in the hills. At night, they made a bonfire and ate some fire-roasted mammals. Neither was squeamish. One couldn't be. Abraham picked up the conversation. He was in a melancholy mood now and talked about how everything gets corrupted in the end, even the flesh. The old man's learned words were tough for Delfín to understand, something about the preservation of heroes. "I dedicated my life to fighting for others, comrade," Abraham said, eyes like wild moons again. Then, holding up a roasted whatever-it-was: "Now I count myself lucky if an *Alfaro Vive* Samaritan helps me catch one of these wild *bichos* for a gourmet feast in the wild, hahahaha!"

At dawn Delfín left. He was soaked in sweat and did not slow down when the rain developed, but when lightning burst, he had to seek refuge. His own war. Abraham's words echoed in the eerie gas station where he rested: *The harder the storm, the faster it goes.* No one had ever talked to him like that: *Time is long but full of lulls.* Beautiful abstractions. He found a small machete and a hand-drawn map in his bag. *There's goodness in The Country of Great Depths and richness in poverty too,* he said to himself, as the storm began to subside.

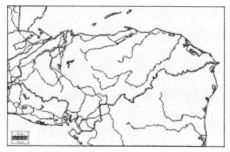

Honduras, Rivers and Roads

Now two countries, Guatemala and Mexico, stood between the United States, economic core of the world, and the super-peripheral Andean. Something terrible happened in Guatemala that he buried deep in his mind. The event was so vividly traumatic as to erase his impressions of the landscape itself. Not many details can be given. Suffice it to say that sometimes you have to use the tools at hand. Delfín's tool, in this case, was Abraham's machete. In truth, he hadn't seen the other man die, but he'd hacked him right at the juncture between shoulder and neck. He'd heard him wail and seen him fall, much like a bull falls when a bullfighter's sword traverses its spine. It's not the cut, but the inability to handle his own weight that brings a sack of flesh and bones to the ground. It was the same then. He'd done it. And then he'd turned around and walked away, pale with murder, immersed in a sort of dreadful liberation. The other was older, bigger, shrewder and through lies and deception had gotten Delfín into a dark corner: a terrible room with terrible materials he did not want to remember. As if that weren't enough, Delfín had had the clear feeling that the man had manipulated countless others into going there. Money was money, a thing, its physicality, which you can recover, but your kindness, your sense of goodwill, fingered, messed with, by way of shamelessly faked gentleness and metropolitan politeness, the softest, kindest manners dexterously employed to fool an uninformed countryside teen, that was wrong. So when Delfín looked up and realized that he'd been had, particularly when he realized with a sudden gasp what he'd been brought to that foul place for, it was like seeing the actual fucker himself, *el diablo*. The hair on his nape pricked like barbwire. He was white as a sheet and also oddly exposed. Fear, certainly. But there was a sadness within, an embarrassment, he had no words for. The Good Samaritan turned out to be a villain. And the decent home he'd promoted with superfluous verbiage, a rat den. Everything was wrong. The obscurity. The stench. But bleakest was the sense of intricate manipulation the Andean teen had felt —witnessed, really— as the liar smiled, either oblivious, or just detached from his earlier performance. And when confronted, the liar's sugary mirth had turned into foul smugness (as if his young guest had no choice but to join in the activities), and when further pushed, the smugness had turned into violence, or was about to, and the Andean knew this because he'd seen it in animals before, the gathering of vile a snake displays right before charging, say, or the circling of the victim birds of prey perform before plunging. He felt it deep in his core. So the strike hadn't been a thought-out decision but a reaction, or an anticipation. He struck the manipulator at the base of the neck, as it has been said. Blood bounced from the gash as the other fell to his knees, and it was likely that life itself bounced from his body soon thereafter, but this, Delfín Quishpe had no way of corroborating, for he himself bounced from that awful place, as if ejected by the blow. Which is what he wanted, to be ejected at once, like blood from a wound. He did not belong there. One thing's for sure, he would rather think of it as an honest murder than live with the murky hope, which was too close to self-deception, that somehow the corrupt other had survived. It was a nightmare of sorts, in which Delfín had clashed and prevailed. Then he'd chosen to push the whole incident to the bottom of his memory, and it was okay, it was nice, it was good. In fact, from a geographic perspective, the country was the most beautiful of all. In Delfín's vague recollection of landscape, it had been impressive. And the people, all the others, good. Many *indios* like himself, though they spoke languages he knew nothing about. Unfortunately, Delfín was in no mental place to make connections. He traversed stunning Guatemala in a detached haze. He couldn't even say what he ate or how he got through to Mexico.

All he knew is that his feet were swollen. And his cheeks were peeling. And he must have smelled; he hadn't seen a bar of soap since The Savior's Land. He could've been mistaken for a pan-handler, though he would've rather starved to death than beg. He was surviving. When mammals became hard to hunt, he made an impromptu sling with rubber from an old tire and a tree branch he found somewhere between the towns of Matías Romero and Acayucan. As old Abraham had predicted, Delfín Quishpe was better than most at surviving under harsh conditions.

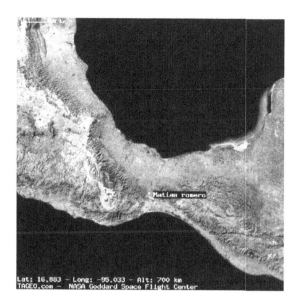

Around Veracruz, he befriended two Honduran boys of about eight and ten. He shared with them the breast of a bird he'd struck with his sling. The meat was awful but it was food. The boys and the Andean stuck together. The problem of survival demanded teamwork. Pickpocketing wasn't out of the question. Pedro and Simón were good at it. Delfín wasn't. He was good at hunting. It all flowed until they reached the church-heavy city of Puebla, in east-central Mexico, where they got wrecked by two bad *policías* who demanded lots of dead presidents from them. *Mordida* is what they call it down there. After the beating, sitting in the shadow of the *Basílica Cathedral,* cursing in Quichua (which the boys found astonishing) the *policías'* harsh edict "go back to your shithole country! " echoed in Delfín's head more than the blows. Martínez was the large one's last name, Alcazar was the other. What did it matter?

"If they hadn't found my blade, I would've pulled it…" said Delfín, stretching his legs on the broken sidewalk.

"Shoulda chopped their noodles off, *jefe*," said Simón, the eight-year-old, rubbing a black eye that occupied a quarter of his round face.

"They would've dropped us then," added Pedro, the ten-year-old, spitting in a crevice. "*Puuuta*," he added in pain as spit rubbed his wound.

Pedro's lower lip was so busted you could see right through to the gums.

Delfín was simply waiting for the adrenaline to subside, but it was the adrenaline that was keeping him afloat. When it finally wore off, he grabbed his ribs and gaped like a guppy. The upside-down *Basilica's* cross over a whirl of shadows was the last thing he saw. He woke up in an infirmary or something. Things happened extremely quick then.

"You okay?" whispered little Simón, who now had a large patch over his busted eye.

"I think, yes," said a drugged out Delfín from a small bed.

"*Aguas!*" added Pedro, handing him his clothes. "A Haitian said they turn minors into the agencies here."

Being turned in to an agency meant deportation. Anything was better than deportation, even death. Delfín got dressed as best he could. He had trouble breathing but it had to be done. They managed to grab a bunch of stuff (utensils, clothes, a small stereo) from the church's shelter —that's what the place was!— before hitting the road again, where north was north, south was south, and clarity would be sought. With the cash they got for the stolen goods, they managed to achieve what had seemed impossible before: avoiding the monstrous *Bestia*. They got on a cushiony bus instead. The Ecuadorian claimed the window seat as always, but not for the views. He laid his head on that dusty wiphala bag of his and dreamt the road away all the way to Tijuana.

They hung out all day at the heart between two seas. First at a park, with many other migrants. Then at a *taqueria* on the fringes where they got to talking to a drunken *tijuanero* who claimed to know the best way across. He wanted coins, of course. Could have been a waste. It didn't matter. The kids were sort of elated. Writing stuff down was out of the question. Each memorized a portion of the directions. "Seven kilometers to the east, turn left, avoid the hills, do not enter the red valley..." repeated Delfín as Pedro and Simón repeated theirs. When darkness fell over the last Hispanic city in the world, they walked. Turns out, the actual border was not close. For miles they basked in funny Quichua phrases and the outrageous images painted by Honduran slang. Too drained to attempt a crossing that same night, they sat by a tree, under a shaving-of-moon the clouds had left untouched. The young boys dreamt of a green Centaur who was also their father. Delfín dreamt he got rich playing the flute in a silvery subway in Berlin. Then the night wore off, as if hurried. Clearly the tide had turned the next day. Enemy number one, the heat, was subdued. A white blanket held it back with aplomb. Delfín called it the breath of the Apus; the boys looked on in innocent gladness. To put a complex situation simply, the three migrants slipped through the desert like ghosts in a trance. They weren't caught. A hill turned into a slope and then they caught the opening vista of that which —they all felt with dizzying certainly— was not a country, but a self-contained sphere, a continent as deep and as ebullient as the one below. And so they crossed.

.

Several years later…

The Furukawa Sisters

The Furukawa sisters hippety-hopped into The Sunset Florida at 4:15 in the afternoon. Little Eimi had had a whatever with her babe back in Los Angeles. It was always like that with Mamadú, he refused to plan stuff so that, as they made do, he got to manage things. All of the missed chances of the year (the Izakaya thing, the London soirée, the anniversary bash, the hair appointment for their pooch) had burst in her mind as the summer broke in. Mamadú had reacted as always—blasé at first, cantankerous latter. This time, though, when things got rippy, Little Eimi had slammed the bungalow door. In theory the Furukawa sisters had moved to Los Angeles for two reasons. One was that their little *mano*, Yusuke, had become a star in Japan. It was something to be proud about —*mochiron!*— still, the state of affairs in Tokyo had become sort of rarefied. Paparazzi took to tracking them around. Photos were snapped at the worst of times: when Little Eimi had a big pimple on the cheek, say, or when Kaori was hammered, or when Yukiko had hooked up with an ugly Yakuza. And when Yusuke's fangirls spotted the sisters online, it all soared. The release of *Kingdom Journey*, a flick based on a huge comic, would probably turn Yusuke into the top male star in Asia. Yukiko was used to getting attention from her ballerina days. She wanted to be at the Toho Cinemas in Roppongi Hills for the premiere, but Kaori and Little Eimi needed a break. Besides giving the Tokyo craziness a break, learning the world's language, without which no girl (or boy) could call herself a full-fledged citizen of the cosmopolitan world, was the second reason to go to L.A. And so they'd moved. Fumihiro Otah, their *mano*'s right hand, had helped them get situated. The change would be good for Yusuke too. Perhaps he could try out his hand at Tinseltown?

Within a month in the US, Little Eimi, who was teeming with raw power (or given to spontinudity as her sisters put it) had enrolled in Make Up School and, most importantly, started a situationship with a solemn, and really tall, Liberian real estate investor, Mamadú Anderson. Three months later they'd gone Photogram-official. By the sixth month they'd moved in together in Santa Monica, the *kawaii* but overpriced city by the beach. Her older sisters had stayed in the Miracle Mile. That was quite alright. Between dating, shopping, learning to drive, and soaking-in both L.A's sun and Shakespeare's tongue, they had plenty to do. So a year into their American adventure, the trip wasn't just an escapade after Little Eimi's quarrel. It was a chance to put their hard-earned English to the test. And, unlike Okinawa, Honolulu, and Bali, South Florida wasn't in the Furukawa sisters' sun and sand map, so there they were.

The Sunset Florida was three blocks away from the beach. The ocean could be seen from their seventh-floor room. They were drowsy from the coast-to-coast trip and took a siesta. After about an hour and a half, Kaori woke up and rubbed her stomach: *onakasuita!* Yukiko said to get ready first. It gave the car time to be delivered. And so, one of the typical Furukawa sisters' circular beauty scenes ensued. It was a ritual that went back eons an, as such, had been honed to perfection. Little Eimi, who was in her early 20s, had always been good at eye shadow and rouge, but now at Make Up School she'd learned all sorts of risqué skills she tried out on her sisters. Kaori was a whiz at coming up with unique nail designs. She worked at the Catherine

Schuster Salon in Beverly Hills and was happy that no one knew who she, her family, and most importantly, Yusuke was. To them all she was just another dutiful nail girl. Had they seen the car she drove, they might've wondered. But Kaori parked it down the street. Yukiko was not a hairdresser, but a former ballerina, who'd danced in the Ballet of Japan her entire life, until recently. But she was good doing big, party hair. She also knew color and cutting techniques. There was a chance, if she didn't decide to go into ballet coaching, she might open up her own salon. And so the Furukawa sisters turned their Sunset Florida hotel room into a catwalk's backstage. Yukiko cut Kaori's hair, while Kaori painted little Eimi's nails, while (lord knows how) little Eimi put purple eye shadow on Yukiko's lids. They achieved a flow and then rotated. Little Eimi did Kaori's make up, while Kaori did Yukiko's nails, while Yukiko (lord knows how) did little Eimi's hair. Then they rotated again, and again if necessary, until all three were primped up and sparkly. They hadn't drawn the curtains. It'd been a spectacle to behold.

Sometime after 9:00 p.m., they hoped into the white convertible Tesla Roadster (with tiny back seats even by Little Eimi's standards) and went to eat Peruvian food in South Beach. Kaori had seen pictures of the restaurant on Photogram. She was going through a Latin phase, which included Álvaro, or Alvo, as he liked to be called. After dinner, the sisters went to a place called *Zombie Tiki* by the beach. Some guys tried talking to them, but they were bearded and sort of beefy, except one called Charlie, but Charlie was into Little Eimi, whose heart was set on the tall Liberian back in L.A. They stayed for a bit anyhow, moving their bodies from side to side to a reggaetón song. As they drank a second zombie, a crazy idea came up.

"Why not?" said Kaori. "We're on vacation!"

They drank a third zombie and headed out. Charlie and his beefy boys were left behind. That was a big part of vacationing; you got to flirt with random guys and then leave them behind like paper napkins on a stool. The sisters' minds were elsewhere now. Planning was half the fun! After brunch the next day they rented pink chairs and parasols (The Sunset Florida provided the towels) and collapsed like woozy chameleons on the beach. It was just what they needed. Other than failing to communicate with a group of Italians from Milano, who in their useless English managed to ask them to come hang out that night, not much happened. They drank coconut vodkas, listened to more reggaetón (upon Kaori's request), and then African rap (upon Little Eimi's request) and did their first real tanning session of the trip. Well, Kaori and Little Eimi tanned. Yukiko couldn't stay in the sun for long because she turned red. After showering back at The Sunset Florida (they refused to use the beach showers) and taking a quick dive in the swimming pool —which was not heated— they got pretty (er), and did dinner at Boca Grande, the most Photogramed eatery in South Florida. The Brazilian-Vietnamese fusion spot in Fort Lauderdale had been Yukiko's pick. There was a colorful mural in the patio. The photos were great, but the food was sticky. They headed over to a rooftop party at the W. The guys there were extremely attractive, though perhaps too attractive. At one-point Yukiko, who most thought was the prettiest of three (though Kaori was the sexiest and Little Eimi the brightest) struck a conversation with Jeff, a tall, muscular Hugo who looked like a model, and was indeed one. Soon they disappeared amongst the summer bodies. Kaori and Little Eimi stayed by the pool.

"It's not that he's not good for me," Little Eimi said. "But I do get fed up with him..."

"Did he push you again?"

"Um, yes, but I pushed him harder. But that's not the real problem. Mamadú never makes plans, except for work. Like, he can't make plans for fun stuff at all. And he eats meat, though less now. We moved in too soon, I guess. We see the world differently, which is great in some ways. Sometimes we laugh like crazy. We show each other how ridiculous we are. And the sex is like wow."

"Wow?

"Ha!"

"Does he know you came to Miami?

Little Eimi answered with a wide smile.

They both laughed. Kaori's phone lit up. It was the Italians.

"Where's Yukiko?" asked Little Eimi.

"With that model guy."

"He's gay right, no?"

"I don't know."

"She'll find out for herself…"

Two guys came up as they laughed. They offered to buy them drinks.

"I want a piña colada, please," said Kaori.

"Whisky on the rocks for me," said Little Eimi.

The guy's nice but too young, Yukiko texted back. She was at a bar next door. Kaori and Little Eimi used that as an excuse. They met out on the street.

"Where's the hot guy?"

"He's *kichigai*!—let's get out of here."

At 12:17 a.m. they got into the white Roadster and sped back to Miami Beach. The Sunset Florida valet parking was closed. Parallel parking wasn't easy for Kaori. She ended up scratching the thing on a red Jeep with a mile-long bumper. There were no cars like that in Tokyo. Kaori texted Alvo in desperation. The Jeep had no damage and there wasn't much to do about the scratched Roaster except report it the next day. They left it on the street. The question, then, became what to do next. Yukiko wanted to go meet the Italians. Little Eimi wanted to go to the beach. Kaori was shaken about the scratch and didn't care either way. They agreed to mix plans like one mixes a cocktail. First, they'd go buy beer, then they'd walk to the beach, and finally they'd text the Italians. They could join if they wanted to.

"I really want to turn Mamadú vegan," said Little Eimi, picking up the previous conversation, as they walked to the liquor store, "even if we end up breaking up."

Yukiko and Kaori chuckled. Little Eime had always been the most experimental one. She was always on the lookout for the next level of self-improvement, be it yoga, meditation, dietary changes or, like, dating.

"Look," added Little Eimi, in clear English: "I just want to give-it-a-shot."

"Oh, *give-it-a-shot*," said Yukiko, in Japanese, "she's already talking American."

"You better do vegan here," said Kaori, "because in Japan, it's going to be hard."

"It's not going to be hard," said Little Eimi, crossing her arms.

"Not hard… impossible!" said all three in drunken merriment.

It was a truism. Whenever things got complex, or whenever a dude acted out, the Furukawa sisters became an even tighter unit. They fused their heads together, making a super head. Little Eimi's messed-up love equation was there to be solved. But so was Yukiko's: the fact that she was actively looking for a serious relationship. It was like Yukiko didn't know the landscape, not even the role she was supposed to play. She lacked a map (or was holding the wrong map, or not even a map, but a different tool, like a flag, which is worse) to navigate the turbulent waters of contemporary love in America.

Jeff, the tall, muscular Hugo who was a model, had seemed perfect in many ways. Green eyes, brown hair, and tanned body. He'd seemed funny, polite, and well-dressed. Yukiko's only doubt had been his sexual orientation. He was just so dishy. Well, that hadn't been the issue. Perhaps it'd been soon, but what the heck, she'd had a couple of drinks, so they'd liplocked as the electronic beats had surged. That's when the blond truth had come out of a corner. Blond and perky and waiving from the bar, like a puppy waiting for a cookie. "That's my girlfriend," Jeff had said, whispering in Yukiko's ear. Yukiko had pulled her moist face away, thinking that it was a language issue. *These people call their lovers girlfriend or boyfriend*, she thought, *but also their friends*. She'd become suddenly angry, not at the situation, but at the culture itself. *Why couldn't they come up with two separate words for such different relationships?* It was maddening, as if they were looking for the confusion. Yukiko's face had turned pale and then suddenly vermilion. The stupidly hot girlfriend had kept waving and bearing her bleached white teeth. The Hugo had kept babbling. *And had the girlfriend been about to come over. Oh God. The loud beats were marching on.* Yukiko had been certain that a non-Japanese girl would have been able to disentangle herself. But she wasn't built like that. She wasn't non-Japanese. She'd stood there as model Jeff explained the word threesome to her. And not only the word, threesome, which she'd readily understood when he'd replaced it with *mènage-à-trois*. She'd lived in France during her ballerina years, but that had been neither here nor there, the point had been that model Jeff had gone on to explain to her the mechanics of this particular arrangement as if she'd already acquiesced. The waving goldilocks had, as it turns out, actually devised the liaison *as long as Jeff found the right girl*.

"They'd been looking for regal or whatever…"

"Ew!"

"OMG! That's you!"

"The weird thing was having his girlfriend there." Added Yukiko." It was like I was saying no to both at the same time!"

"Oh, so you turned it down Yukiko-nee-san…" Kaori said facetiously.

"Funny, middle sister," said Yukiko.

"Would you do a woman?" asked Little Eimi point blank.

"That's not the problem," Yukiko said.

"What was the problem then, Yukiko-san?" asked Little Eimi.

"It was weird," she said, "like done in a creepy way. I said, thank you, and left."

"So you thanked them!"

"I mean, it was sort of nice of them…"

They all laughed.

"So, um, …" added Kaori.

"*You* wouldn't?" asked Yukiko, guessing.

"No way!" said Kaori, making a face. "I like rough, ugly, *men*."

Drunkenness allowed them that kind of freedom.

"I like manly men too…" said Yukiko, "but…"

"But…?" asked Kaori, surprised.

"I don't know " said Yukiko. "How about you, Little Eimi? Would you try *pussy*?"

"OMG! You must be drunk," exclaimed Little Eimi. Then quickly: "If she was vegan!"

They laughed and then exhaled as if sending their laughter into the black ocean.

"Let's go to the water!" said Yukiko, who felt breezy.

The water was warm.

"It would be nice to live in Miami," said Kaori.

At that point —it was well past 2:00 a.m.— two of the Italians from Milano showed up. Maurizio, the hunkiest one, was missing. Still, the Furukawa sisters felt obliged to hang out with the other two, Sergio and Giovanni. At first it was tough to talk as neither the Furukawa sisters' English nor the Tortelli's English was fluent enough, but words became unimportant after a couple of puffs. Sergio Tortelli, a graphic designer and a scuba enthusiast, was okay, though maybe it was the time and the breeze. He got along with Yukiko best. The problem was Giovanni, who was rather fattractive, especially given his green eyes, but acted a little too Ambercrombie and bitch with his unending talk of dough, as if the Furukawa sisters didn't know what dough was! He was into Kaori, and pretty soon started getting touchy. Kaori, who, like Yukiko, was ghastly at saying no, navigated Giovanni's touchiness as best she could, for she thought he behaved like that either because he was Italian and drunk, or because he really liked her. *Japanese men are much more polite,* Little Eimi thought. Unlike her older sisters, Little Eimi was so good at saying no that sometimes she had to say no for them all. She waited for a sign to step in. The problem was that the nice Tortelli and Yukiko were getting along. A little more time was needed for them to establish something if something was to be established. But all of that went to hell when Giovanni tried to go for a kiss, and Kaori subtly turned it down (too subtly!), and the brat tried again.

"Time to go," Little Eimi said loudly in English, and then in Japanese, "*hayaku, hayaku!*"

Kaori, a formerly accomplished volleyball player, saw an opening, and was on her feet at once, an action which took Giovanni Tortelli a few seconds to perform. And so the Furukawa's began to pack. Too bad for Yukiko. She smiled at Sergio who smiled back.

Then Giovanni had the gall to ask if they wanted to go hang out at the hotel.

"No Way!" said Little Eimi, as her sisters watched on.

Where had this fireball come from? They thought. Little Eime was certainly made of different stuff. Sergio was embarrassed by his cousin's insistence. It was 3:56 a.m.

Still, unbelievably, Giovanni kept at it: "*per piacere, per piacere.*"

He even put his round hands up in a prayer-like clasp. He was almost charming and was about to get away with it.

"Under no circumstances," interjected Little Eimi, reading an idiom from her phone. "Kick rocks dude!"

Giovanni opened his arms as a sign of defeat.

Little Eimi walked up to Giovanni and gave him a hug. He closed his long arms around her tiny body. When the hug became too long, she hit him with her sharp elbow in the gut. He could've gotten mad, but upon seeing how little she was, and how she put up her tiny arms like a boxer, he couldn't help but laugh. They parted amicably.

The three sisters made sure not leave their phones buried in the sand, which had happened before. The Maldives trip had been a mess without phones. That little machine came in handy in every latitude; it was like having an extra brain for an appendix, except when reception was off, which was like getting brain fog.

ITALIANO (kakkoii)
S: Sorry *bella* ☹ ...
young cousin douche bag
now he's almost passed out
by wather lol
He will wake up to this photo online
(drunken photo of Giovanni)
hahahahaha
That is my payback!!!

Yukiko was too drunk to make any judgments. The next day, or the day after, or the day after that, she might reply, if she felt like it, and her sisters approved. She needed their guidance. They all did in the United States. It was a zone where none of their knowledge applied, where everything had to be learned anew. The next day they snoozed until past midday. None of the Furukawa sisters remembered their dreams. It wasn't something they did. They got up, peed, brushed their teeth, put their Zeagoo swim wear, Estée Lauder make up, and Clinique sun-screen on, and took the elevator down to the pool. Little Eimi ordered vegan brunch. Yukiko ordered Starbucks. Kaori did a somersault straight into the deep end. The lifeguard looked the other way. Yukiko and Little Eimi were talking about cruise options, when they heard their middle sister scream from the pool. The lifeguard rushed from under his white tent. He'd seen people break their neck diving like that.

"*Kuruma*! *Kuruma*!!" kept yelling Kaori from the deep end.

Yukiko and Little Eimi rushed out of the Sunset Florida. So did Kaori, who splashed pool water all across the mahogany lobby. The lifeguard was left at a loss. Out on the street they saw the Roadster wasn't there anymore. They looked up, trying to decipher the parking signal.

Meanwhile Kaori starting jumping around like a tap dancer. "*Atsui, atsui, atsui!*"

Her sisters laughed.

"*Venga pa' acá*," said a deep, cigar-roughened tone from the shade.

The sidewalk was too hot to walk on without flip flops on. Kaori knew that *venga* means something like come here from Alvo, her boyfriend.

"Very nice car," said the Cuban sidewalk vendor as he shook his head. "Probably you can get it back today. It happens almost every weekend here. Call this number, *señorita*. Would you like to buy some cantaloupe juice? It good for you."

As a thank you gesture, Little Eimi bought the overpriced cantaloupe juice. They walked to The Sunset Florida, well, except Kaori, who hopped like a bunny. Two Haitian employees were drying the mahogany floor in the lobby. Back at the pool, the lifeguard, a tall, tanned boy, whose name was Maxwell, came up to them. He said they couldn't dive, run, nor leave their things unattended.

"That somersault was pretty kick ass, though," he added, winking at Kaori.

Had Kaori been the type to blush she would've blushed.

"Thank you," she said.

"I can tell you're an athlete. I play water polo myself. Where are you girls from?"

They talked to Maxwell for a while, and then went back to the chaise loungers, where they instinctively divided up the tasks. Yukiko looked up things to do that night; Kaori looked up cruise options; and Little Eimi, whose English was best, found out where the white Roadster had been taken, and how to get it back—all from their phones, of course, while sipping, munching, and tanning, except for Yukiko, who had to lie by the shade, lest she got lobster-red.

This is what each one had after forty-seven minutes:

Furukawa Yukiko – Things to Do at Night

1. Private yacht party with two deejays spinning 70's disco and vintage hip-hop. Valet parking, entrance fee, and an all-you-can-drink bar included.

2. Bash at Donald Trump building in Sunny Isles Beach, featuring a performance by local South Florida hero Tim Hopper, of Dancing with the Stars fame. Drinks, parking, and entrance tickets *not* complimentary. Dress code, *seashore chic*.

3. Wango Tango by the River. Down in Key West. Big two-floor club shaped like a barn. Country music and classic rock played both live. Line dancing (whatever that was) on outdoors deck. Electric bull-riding and wet-t-shirt competitions from midnight to 2:00 am. Two-for-one Budweiser and tequila specials until 11:00 p.m.

Furukawa Kaori – Four Cruise Options

The Disney World Cruise – safest choice. Mickey, Minnie, Pluto, Donald Duck, Tinker Bell, Pocahontas, Captain Hook and Prince Charming on board. Movie theater, roller coaster, swimming pools, ice-skating rink, retro-futuristic arcade, and paint ball arena featured. Satisfactory theme-park-buffet according to reviews. Clothes: polo shirts for men and summer dresses for women encouraged. Family-oriented. General design, including cabins, which are tiny, mirror Disney theme-park style. Passengers may request Disney World Cabins™ for a fee. Goofy or Minnie Mouse may be requested as servers for additional fee (limited availability).

The NBA All Star Cruise – Michael Jordan as Captain. Well, co-Captain. And not the flesh and blood Jordan, but a giant hologram. Other interactive hologram stations with players like Magic Johnson, LeBron James, Wilt Chamberlain, and Kobe Bryant peppered around the ship. Cruise not huge on theme-park attractions, but features world's tallest water slide, The Slam Dunk ™, which leads to a gigantic basketball-shaped swimming pool with artificial waves. Go-kart racetrack on deck. Each go-kart features different NBA franchise logos and flags. Racetrack itself shaped like a basketball court. Live music performances done daily, most of which tend toward contemporary R&B. Physically rotating, favorably reviewed soul food restaurant perched high on superstructure. Main attraction: real-life cameo by former Miami Heat star Shaquille O'Neal, who sings in confetti-laden grand finale.

The Reggaetón Cruise – Multi-platinum star Patuma Baby scheduled to perform but, after relapsing rumors, replaced by other Latin stars. Cruise centered around reggaetón, mixture of hip-hop, pop, and Caribbean beats. Four restaurants: chill Tex-Mex inspired "taco lounge," fancy Michelin-starred Peruvian bistro, Brazilian churrasqueria, and pan-Hispanic buffet featuring Spanish *paella*, Dominican *mondongo*, and Chilean *empanadas*. Cruise not encouraged for minors. Several cocktail bars and not-so-secret "edibles lounge" on faux-marble deck. Pool party with Italian influencer-deejay Gianluca Vacchi, spinning global hits. Survival Portuguese lessons at foaming Jacuzzi by Brazilian juiceheads and curvaceous cherry bombs. Speed-dating party in which matches share private capsule in 437-feet Ricky Martin Ferris Wheel ™: $25 per round, no questions asked.

*The Animal Planet Cruise – Could be called Noah's Ark. Only cruise in the world to feature full functioning zoo on board. The Floating Zoo™ is divided into separate microclimates with different animal populations. Rocky Mountains section holds bears, bald eagles, deer, and mountain lions. Amazon rainforest section holds anacondas, wild boars, parrots, pumas, pink river dolphins, and piranha ponds with live feeding demonstrations (*You get to feed the piranhas!*). Indian subcontinent section holds lion-tailed macaques, red pandas, golden langurs, rhinos, plus of course, tigers and elephants. Sub-Saharan section holds zebras, giraffes, gigantic mountain gorillas, water buffalos, flamingos, and tigers. Arctic section holds seals, narwhals, penguins, musk oxen, arctic wolfs, and polar bears. (*Catch 'em before they go extinct!*). Safari chic dress code. Other features: casino, slot machines, and live jazz band. Ship painted lima green color in support of global bio-diversity causes. From public comments: "As a warning, this

---

* The Animal Planet Cruise is intentionally short on sea animals. Germany-based premiere cruise corporation, A-18T64 Enterprises, is currently building a sea animal cruise in tandem with SeaWorld Entertainment Inc. This new cruise, which is planned to debut next year, features all kinds of seafood restaurants, water slides, thermal water pools and, of course, the largest floating aquarium in the world.

cruise attracts older folks, children, and back-packer types. If you're looking to party your ass off, this cruise is not for you. Great buffet though."

Kaori didn't look into the islands the cruises were set to visit. Every island, she figured, would be new and cool. The cruise, on the other hand, had to be carefully chosen.

Furukawa Eimi – The White Convertible Tesla Roadster

Little Eimi phoned the Miami Parking Bureau and sat through a muffled pop song for forty-two minutes and twenty-three seconds before a nasal-voice gave her another number to call. She called the new number and waited for seven minutes and ninety-six silent seconds punctured by an intermittent beep. Good news! The white Roadster had been recovered by Luxury Rentals. It was all taken care of, except for a recovery fee. Despite her usually strong, confrontational personality, Little Eimi did not inquire about the fee. They were on vacation.

And then it got late, and the Furukawa sisters found themselves at Wango Tango by the River, a giant barnyard in lush, soggy Key West. Yukiko could boast a dancer's sense of rhythm from her ballet years. Sergio Tortelli, the architecture student from Milano, who'd joined them *sans* uncouth Giovanni upon the ballerina's request, had two left feet though he also had the unselfconsciousness of good looks. That also meant Sergio Tortelli was slightly vanilla, though it wasn't a big deal (a blandish guy was good for a change to mark the end of her roaring 20s). So Yukiko Furukawa and Sergio Tortelli were on the dance floor, white cowboy hats on. Kaori and Little Eimi were live-feeding the craziness from the bar where they were half talking to Maxwell (yes, the lifeguard) and Nathan, Maxwell's University of Tallahassee sidekick. Given Yukiko-nee-san's body language, it was becoming clear that she and the *ragazzo* were hooking up.

Dancing honed the chemistry. Photogram lit up. As it has been said, Sergio Tortelli's English was deficient. Yukiko's English was not as good as Kaori's, and not nearly as good as Little Eimi's, but they managed. The atmosphere took care of itself. The odd perky dance on stage was a phenomenon, as if they were all trapped inside an ethnographic documentary about American culture, not the multi-ethnic bazaar they'd found in L.A., which in many ways, was so similar to the multi-ethnic bazaar they'd found in London, Hong Kong, or Sydney. This was like a cowboy movie. The lifeguard and the University Tallahassee boy were tall and honey-hued, and as such, part of the ambiance. American realness! Bags of social media followers in Japan went nuts at the Photogramed feed. Exoticism turned people on. It went both ways. *Kimono-wearing* girls in Kyoto and *kariyushi*-wearing boys in Okinawa always attracted foreign eyes. For the Photogram viewers in Japan, it wasn't just golden Maxwell and Nathan, it was also the all-you-can drink Budweiser, the chicks in jean shorts clinging to a robotic bull with their heavy thighs being flung, boots up in the air, and then falling on the floor, faces cherried with beer and laughter, while something like Sweet Home Alabama was played over again by a band of mullet-haired guys who talked in curled-up clusters that must have been words. All that sweet confusion, urgently alive in digital simultaneity, *was the American event in itself*, its core, the pixels and sound bites, exploding like little atoms on their followers' screens to experience, digest, and most of all, *like*. And like avalanches of candy, the Photogram *likes* shot across the earth through the wireless networks (from phone to satellite, from satellite to phone) and accumulated in heaps for the sisters to gather and dive into right then and there, or the next day, if they felt like it.

"Ya'll interested in dancing?" asked Maxwell, the lifeguard, college buddy by his side.

Kaori looked at Little Eimi for cues.

Little Eimi leaned her phone against a Budweiser bottle, allowing the Photogram feed to go on by itself. And even the un-held feed was *liked by her followers*. Indeed. What was not to *like*? The Star-Spangled Banner kept majestically waving above the contorting crowd, baby, yee-haw!

About two hours later, as they walked out of Wango Tango by the River into the balmy Florida night, having danced to one too many Southern-rock songs, and in Kaori's case, having ridden the bull (twice!) and won an *I Love Florida* t-shirt, each of the sisters had something different to worry about. Yukiko had told Sergio Tortelli that they were going on a Caribbean cruise, and now there was the possibility that the *ragazzo* (and even his cousin Giovanni!) would come along. Yukiko was afraid she'd blown it. Perhaps bringing this new guy on the cruise would make her sisters uncomfortable.

Kaori's problem was different. In the hot, wet excitement of the night, she'd let the lifeguard kiss her and now she was freaking out. Álvaro had texted her five times during the night. He must have been texting her even as she allowed the lifeguard to come closer on the dark side of the dance floor. The night's momentum had led her there. *Shit, shit, shit.* Even worse: she'd let the lifeguard add her on social media! Maxwell Eastman was now a "contact" on a complex network of mirroring platforms, and, surely, an endless network to come. That's how the self-reproducing amoeba of social media functioned. If you allowed someone in, they could start replicating their avatars into eternity. Even as you chopped their heads off, time and again, these "contacts" could stick to you, like digital leeches for good. *Focus. Focus.* The *kissing* had been the wrong, not the virtual *adding*. To think she didn't even like the lifeguard that much. She liked Alvo, her boo. *Yarakashita!* Little Eimi's problem was smaller than either Yukiko or Kaori's, though more pressing. She'd smoked with Maxwell and Nathan and now her head was spinning and it was a matter of minutes, perhaps seconds, before she puked. The all-round humidity worsened things. So did the neon lights and the craziness outside. Strangers were roaring all around.

"Where we goin'?" asked the one named Nathan, blowing pot smoke into the night.

Little Eimi leaned on a random beige Volvo and unloaded all the six chewed-up vegan wings, and at least half a pound of the sweet potato fries she'd ingested earlier that night. Lots of vomit got on the side of the luckless Volvo. Yukiko and Kaori gathered around their little sister in a panic. Sergio Tortelli rushed to go get some water. Maxwell and Nathan, who were just as drunk as Little Eimi but hid it better, stood around, swaying on the shifting ground with other partiers. A girl puking on the street. Nothing to fret about. Nathan ventured a snarky remark, meant to be edgy, or something, but it fell flat, except for Maxwell, who couldn't restrain a chuckle as much as he tried. Kaori had no idea what exactly the dig had meant, but she knew it was about her puking sister, and most importantly, she'd seen the lifeguard react. The afterhours plan was scratched right then and there. An Uber was called.

When Sergio Tortelli got back with two bottles of Perrier and a handful of napkins, nobody was there. Almost twenty minutes later, he got a text from Yukiko.

YUKIKO (*ragazza giapponese*)

Y: SORRY BRO!

Sister sick ☹ ☹

had 2 go…

See ya soon Cerjeeoh!

good nite: 🌙

Yukiko was tough, he saw, and hesitated. But then again, how beautiful she was! Her clothes were classy, her movements regal, her skin pearly, and her features so ...well, *kawaii*. Of course, he'd call her the next day. *È una pazzia!* He'd come from Milano to Uncle Sam's country dreaming of a summer fling with a blond bombshell and was now falling for a Japanese dancer. If she let him, he'd come along the cruise with them. *È una pazzia!* He drunkenly sauntered along the Riviera Canal behind the bars and shops in Key West.

Some people were gathered along the way. He got close. A cluster of baby caimans were hanging out in the canal bellow. Locals were throwing Flaming Cheetos at them. Sergio leaned on the guardrails and, like the others, recorded the baby caimans as steadily as he could. He posted the video on Photogram (#soFlorida) and got hundreds of likes back in Italy and a few in the States. Three of the likes came from Miami Beach. One of those likes was by one @ballerinalove. He clicked on the profile and saw her photos on the way back to Miami.

The next day, from the Sunset Florida's Jacuzzi, Kaori called her boyfriend. She felt guilty about the night before. She also wanted to hear his opinion on something. Little Eimi had vetoed the Animal Planet Cruise, calling it *crazy cruel*. The NBA Cruise had also been ruled out as it fell short in Photogramable vistas and Photogramable vistas were half the trip. They were torn between the Disney Cruise and The Reggaetón Cruise. Perhaps Alvo could help.

"You know more about reggaetón than I do, *mi amor*," he said, lowering the music.

Wind could be heard on the phone. He was coasting the Pacific Coast Highway on his way to Santa Barbara.

"Everybody's playing reggaetón here in Florida."

"Who's playing in the cruise?"

"Some guy from Ecuador."

"From Ecuador... Really?"

"That's what the website says."

"I've never heard of any famous Ecuadorian musicians."

"Viral guy. More followers than Deejay Vacchi. The site says he's scheduled to do Xtreme Fest this November."

"In what universe have I been living?"

"In your tennis universe, bro."

"Who's the Ecuadorian artist?"

"The Twin Towers guy!"

"The Twin Towers guy?"

"Delfín Quispe."

"*No puede seeerrr!!!*"

"Whaaa'?"

"He's a complete joke."

"So we shouldn't do the Reggaetón Cruise?

"No—you should *definitely* go."

"Whaaa'?"

"Go, go, go!"

East Through The Core

Álvaro Garzón was teaching a lesson at the Beverly Hills Tennis Club when he got a call from Tokyo. It was Kaori's teen brother, Yusuke. The words were frantic, but the urgency was communicated so that Alvo dropped the green balls on the court, excused himself from Ashley, ran down the stairs, jumped into his Camaro, and sped-up on Sunset Boulevard. The gate at the Vista Gardens in West Hollywood always took forever. Alvo nearly scratched his ride. He parked, flung the door, and ran up the underground stairs, not waiting for the elevator. In the hallway mirrors he caught a glance of his own sunburned face. Several pearls of sweat were making their way down to his neck by way of his beard. He attempted to dry himself with his own t-shirt (the hand towel lay at the court) but the t-shirt itself was drenched. He opened the side door and was hit by a rush of air-conditioned air. He stepped in. White light occupied the space. Mamadú Anderson, Little Eimi's six-feet-two-inches-tall boyfriend, was waiting in the middle of the foyer. They shook hands, avoiding each other's eyes.

"Let me put my rackets away," said Alvo, who looked like a barrel in comparison to the gaunt Liberian. Everyone did.

Mamadú followed Alvo into the elevator.

"It's all over the news-menh."

"We got to get ourselves to Florida."

"No planes to Florida now."

"State Department, eh?"

A Spanish-style patio could be seen from the elevator above.

They walked into an airy place overlooking the Hollywood Hills. A large pink portrait by famed Venezuelan artist Billy Botero hung over a broad beige couch. Alvo put his tennis rackets away and poured the Liberian some Perrier.

"Ice?"

"No thanks, bro."

Mamadú looked around.

"Live by yourself?"

"Kaori's décor—all her doing."

"Great real estate."

"I work hard."

"What do you do?"

"A bunch of stuff. *You?*"

"Liberty Investments," Mamadú, said, pulling out a card.

"Real estate's hard right now," Alvo said, pouring more water in Mamadú's glass. "You need major liquidity."

"I'm backed up—thank God."

"*Muy bien*," said Alvo Garzón. "I'll be right back. Help yourself to anything you want."

When Alvo came out of the shower, Mamadú was browsing his phone.

"What's the situation?"

"Real fucking scary," said Mamadú.

Alvo hesitated, awkwardly standing in his own apartment as if it weren't his.

"How so?"

"American terrorists. Or so the news say…" said Mamadú.

Alvo looked at the Liberian. This was no time for half-baked political statements. He walked out to the balcony; the sky was intensely blue above the Hollywood sign. He looked down at the cigarette box on the wooden table outside and decided to quit smoking on the spot. He took a breath and turned around. Mamadú was browsing his phone again.

"Can you drive stick shift?" asked Alvo, almost confrontationally

Geographic Positioning System: 2,743 Miles to Miami

0 - 230 Miles, Blythe, California

After 50 miles of traffic, the radio had nothing new to say, so Alvo turned it off. A stretch of about 200 miles of near silence ensued. The landscape was rough and parched at this juncture of the American West. They stopped at a gas station near the Arizona border. The Liberian woke up from a light sleep. Alvo got two Gatorades, some roasted peanuts, and Ecuadorian bananas. He filled up the tank.

"I'll chip in for the dinosaur whiskey."

Alvo shook his head.

230 - 380 Miles, Phoenix, Arizona

Arizona was sizzling hot. From 110 degrees at the lowest end to 118 at the highest. Luckily, the Camaro's AC worked as it should—rigorously crisp.

"I used to drive a banged-up Cherokee," Alvo said.

"Six cylinders?"

"Eight"

"Gas guzzler?"

"Oil guzzler."

"Oil guzzler?"

"Burner."

"Shit."

The Arizona landscape looked like a lizard's skin, which awoke something inside people. Alvo sped up to 120. It felt like an airplane the way gravity pushed you into the seat.

The Liberian put both his hands on his knees.

Alvo let go a bit.

"80 mph," he said, "that's a good speed: above the speed limit, but not stupid fast. 120 is stupid fast. When I was young, I loved going stupid fast, but what for? At high speeds you miss out on the road. 80 mph is good: faster than average, but you get to enjoy the road."

He sped up again. 120 MPH… 123… 127.

"What are you doing, man?"

"It's good to know you can go real fast if you really need to, as a concept, *ya know*? But now and then it's also good to go stupid fast."

Alvo went further. 127… 130…138…142 MPH.

"Alright-o," said Mamadú, hands back on the knees.

"It's good to know you can, then can you get back to normal," Alvo said, letting go again. "You know, several years ago I had a bad accident coming down the Hollywood end of Mulholland Drive. I almost died. I'll tell you about it someday."

A few hours went by. At night they stopped at a parking lot mall near Phoenix. It was windy. Swarms of mosquitoes crowded the yellowish streetlights above as if the lights could keep them from the wind.

"I hope to God our girls are safe," Mamadú said, discarding the burger wrap from the red tray. "It's such a terrible fucking situation."

Alvo assented with his bearded face.

"You wanna drive?"

380 - 650 Miles, Lordsburg, New Mexico

Some miles past Phoenix, rain broke in. Near Lordsburg, the rain intensified into hail until it became too blurry. Mamadú drove so carefully it was almost funny. Almost.

"Out! Out! Out!" Alvo suddenly yelled out, discombobulated.

That stupid yellow car meant so much. It was proof that he could survive without his parents' keeping. Mamadú exited and parked under a bridge. A cop car pulled up. The Liberian started fidgeting with his wallet. But for no reason. The cops waved and pointed at the sky.

"Gotta look like a puppy," said Alvo, waving back with a smile worthy of a North Korean stage performer.

"Ya'll live in an alternative reality-menh."

"Who do you mean?" asked Alvo, pulling his seat back, hands behind his head.

"You-menh, and the Furukawa sisters…" said Mamadú, as he glazed his words with an idiosyncratic laughter that was both impossibly sarcastic and impossibly open at the same time.

What the Liberian did not say —what the Liberian could not say— was how reassuring it was to be driving across these United States with such a naively overconfident companion. It was the same thing with Little Eimi and the Furukawa sisters. That blissfully ignorant aura rubbed off. Mamadú couldn't generate that type of aura himself. But it was good to be held by it, as if by a shield. Whether it was real or not was a different thing. But now wasn't the time for doubt. They weren't even halfway through the American map. And Alvo needed sleep. Lot's a of sleep. Alvo awoke sometime after 4:00 a.m., his back numb. The yellow Camaro wasn't made to be slept in. His head was spinning. The car was moving. *It had been moving!*

"Two hours-ya," said the Liberian with the broadest smile.

650-770 Miles, Las Cruces, New Mexico

When the sun had come out, but the road was still wet Alvo commented on the Liberian's ability to function with no sleep. Mamadú shrugged his shoulders with a smile.

"Once, while spotting ghosts in Guinea bush, I had no shuteye nor pizza for a week."

"I think you're *spotting ghosts* now, bro—*calmado*!"

"True thing, *amigo*. It was ku-ku. A clan fed me bushmeat and palm wine."

"You coulda circled the drain…" Alvo said, but his tone said otherwise. *Este huevón no es capaz de matar una mosca,* he thought.

"Have you ever fought off warlords?" asked Mamadú after that caustic giggle he had.

"A Head Graphene's the only warhead I've ever needed, *ñaño*."

It was a tacit draw followed by silence. Neither the Liberian nor the Ecuadorian knew it at the time, but that uneasy silence had its beauty. In fact, decades later, as they recalled their North American trip from different hemispheres, it was that pure wind and engine sound across the South West which had impressed them the most, and not in awkward uneasiness but in luminous hindsight.

"Hey, can I ask you something?" said the Liberian after a long while.

"Shoot."

"How did you get into that big accident?'

"I rented a Ferrari to front a Belorussian model."

"*Red*?

That caustic giggle again.

"What do you think?"

"Chee-chee-polay."

770 – 876, Esperanza, Texas

It was an odd feeling, driving along the Mexican border on the 10-East. They couldn't simply approach the edge where The Periphery begun, as if nothing were there, because there was. A metal fence, a Mexican flag in the wind, vendors, dusty roads, decrepit buildings, sensual colors crashing eye. *The other side!* It was like shaving the edge of an emotional abyss. Like peeking into the word from whence they'd emerged, like a womb. The Liberian felt it too, but at the end of the day, Mexico was utterly exotic to him. To Álvaro Garzón, however, Mexico was the beginning of the earth known as *Latinoamérica*. Part of him wanted to cut a sharp right at once and plunge deep into the wet, bloody bowels of the Hispanic tummy. A sharp feeling accosted the air. But not a word was said. Both men had traversed vast swaths of space-time in their day. This border was but another swath. Another abyss. And then, at some point, it was over. The long, sensuous kiss between the northern edge of the Third World and the southern edge of the First was done, lovers parted, union un-established. A weight was lifted. The trepidation dissipated. The whole thing seemed instantly preposterous.

"How about a slushy?" asked the tennis player.

"Okay," said the African.

Another RaceTrac, another snack. The landscape, unchanged.

"Liberia, Liberia…" muttered Alvo, sucking on a blue slushy from his place at the filthy gas-station table where they had sat. "Isn't that where George Weah's from?"

"You know King George!?"

"*Concha de su madre!*" said Alvo, faking a heavy Spanish: "I'm not an ignorant!" and laughed, but as he breathed-in, he caught a nasty whiff. "Let's go, bro. It stinks in here."

A trucker who was exciting a near-by toilet shot them an angry glance.

They laughed as soon as the trucker re-entered the store.

"In my country women aren't usually truck drivers," said Mamadú as they walked back to the Camaro. "How about in yours?"

"Don't be an itinerant sexist pig, bro."

"Bah! You Mexicans invented that shit!"

876 - 1207 Miles, San Antonio, Texas

As they left Esperanza behind and got closer to the heart of the Lone Star State, the idea of driving straight from Los Angeles to Miami began to seem like a pipe dream concocted by two desperadoes with no idea of what to do to help their formerly sheltered Japanese girlfriends immersed in a bloody global emergency. They drove on. The road was like a snake above the flatness with a peppering of small hills but not a single curb. The Ecuadorian made a point of driving faster than the Liberian, which was a breeze. But it wasn't just about that. Thinking at high speeds took on a different shape, as if the thoughts themselves got caught-in and stretched-out by the passing landscape. *Mamadú's and Little Eimi's altercation*: the catalyst for the Furukawa sister's steam-blower escapade. A flung Grande Latte on her end, a shove on his. Alvo's thoughts became abnormally drawn out, but it was a slippery subject, so he allowed the thoughts to lengthen and break into separate sections like sweet, elastic *melcocha* as he powered through the black freeway and saw himself and Mamadú step into agoraphobia (no matter how close the motor got to 100 the car seemed to stand frightfully still in the expanse). Was this The Core's geographic center? Was it Americanness, the center of which was everywhere and its circumference nowhere? Perhaps the secret of the USA was nothingness. A nothingness so wide you could see from side to side to both edges of the earth. A transparent monster.

"It ends!"

"It does not end!"

It did not matter. They were two-minute dots in a projectile of minimal propulsion hovering over the ceaseless blast of Texas sun. The landscape didn't help of course. It seemed to demand one address serious things. Like existence. Or desire. Or God. Yes, the blasted landscape seemed to yearn after God. But the African and the South American did not yield. They drove on absorbed in dead silence for countless miles until the night surreptitiously took over and San Antonio lit up in the incandescent GPS—like the Aleph of science it actually was. They parked somewhere. The minute Mamadú saw the bar was full of whites, he felt something could go wrong, and Alvo felt it too, not because they thought whites were particularly aggressive or harmful, quite the opposite, whites tended to be polite and helpful, if naive, but because of the incendiary mood the country was in, exemplified in the Reggaetón Cruise awkwardness. Alvo and Mamadú were sweaty, smelly, and like the rest of the country, moody, broody, and ready to snap. But they pushed on. The Liberian with wide steps and a gawky way, and the Ecuadorian with short steps, consciously uppish every time he walked into places like this, where he didn't know people, and that was the case here, the difference, both between each other (the real tall Liberian in his wrinkled red shirt of loose, fine fabric, polished orange-brown leather shoes, and that impactful gold watch over his exceptionally even-hued skin; and the shorter brown-bearded Ecuadorian who passed for an Arab, with his posture and his Hawaiian shirt displaying the Saint Bartholomew pendant he'd got at Placita Olvera, where Nuestra Señora de Los Ángeles was founded) and in comparison to the others, the suburban Texans, who were in their untarnished territory, still, Mamadú Anderson and Álvaro Garzón Villacís pushed on, feeling the translucent eyes on them, and sat a table towards the back, by the jukebox, and ordered beers, and then whisky, and then mescal, and it was okay (it wasn't 1955, for God's sake!) but then at some point, much later, after the wish to talk about normal things had returned, and they had talked about how it was dating Kaori and Little Eimi, who were so alike and so unlike each other, and how easy it was to make money in America in comparison to West Africa and the Andean region of South America, after a lot of that and a bunch of other stuff, which neither of them would remember the next day, perhaps something about *il calcio italiano* (and King Weah's Milano goal against Hellas Verona and Kaviedes' *chilena* against Barcelona) and a little about *Dumboy* and boiled yucca, which both ate, and Ferraris vs. Lamborghinis, and the shape of African women versus the shape of South American women, and maybe, just maybe, about the emergency at hand, though maybe not, the drink had got to them, mostly due to the heat and the road, but also due to the lack of proper food and sleep—and most of all, though they didn't know it then, *pendejos*: water!—after they had talked about all of that, and drank even more, which nipped-off the pronging tip of the crisis, after all of that, towards the end of the night, something had happened, and it wasn't clear just what, perhaps something to do with the jukebox, or some pink round girl who smelled like baby powder, and had seemed flirtatious at first, who knows, something had happened, perhaps it was their fault, though maybe not, the thing is a punch or two had been thrown and the word *niggers* had been uttered, though they weren't sure, maybe yes maybe not yada, yada. They left the establishment before the cops arrived and slept on the open grass somewhere, and up above, the black Texas sky felt like an actual Van Gogh. There wasn't a lone star there but a million tiny ones so high-up your innards spun. The next morning, they bought coffee at a doughnut shop. *Decaf isn't for real men,* said Alvo, followed, as predicted, by the Liberian's acidic giggle. *Shut your front door-menh.*

1207-1601 Miles — Baton Rouge, Louisiana

> **Sugar Land
> I-10 East**

"That's a good place to go, just based on the name."

The Ecuadorian nodded and drove on.

The urban hum got so loud, it occupied every bit of emptiness, even the inside of the car.

Houston

I-10 East

There was a hill there, in the distance. Alvo thought of Margarete. They had seen the 4th of July fireworks from that same Houston hill years ago. He thought of all the fireworks with Margarete. Fireworks and Tchaikovsky by the Onondaga lake. Fireworks above a dark country road as they ate corndogs by a California vineyard. The candied apples she'd make in the summer. The red, white, and blue veins of America had made inroads in his core, he knew, looking at the same Houston hill smaller now, already behind.

It's the hangover, he said to himself.

Mamadú was elsewhere. More signs came and went.

Sour Lake

I-10 East

"Sour Lake! Sour Lake!" Alvo suddenly yelled out.

"Whut?"

"My grandfather discovered oil in the Amazon back in the 60's!"

"Okay."

"Are there any cities in Liberia named after American towns? American Texaco was founded in the tiny town of Sour Lake in 1901. An Ecuadorian city named after Sour Lake was founded in the 60's. My grandpa, who started off land surveyor for Texaco ended up becoming one of Lago Agrio's first mayors, just as the town was booming. He built an airport, three roads, a high school, and *Cine Oriente*, the only movie theatre in our neck of the woods. I saw Rambo there for the first time."

"An old school bossman-ya."

"Who? Rambo?"

"Your founding father, bro."

"He *is* Rambo to us."

The yellow Camaro was now flying on a lengthy raised structure above the Atchafalaya Basin: the muddy banks of the river below, the lush of the foliage above. The weather had changed again. The flat Texas blaze had given way to an intensely layered Caribbean warmth.

1601- 2,022 Miles — Mobile, Alabama

"Humidity makes you more alive," said Alvo.

Mamadú shook his head.

"I'm into the chill at my parents' in Portsmouth."

"Portsmouth?"

"New Hampshire."

"I thought your folks were in Liberia."

"My American parents, man."

Somehow that impacted Alvo.

"Adopted?"

"Indeed-ya."

"At what age?"

"Sixteen."

Alvo turned the radio on. That gave him room to chew on things both big and small. There was a tornado warning. He changed the station. They tried to listen—it sounded like "Kiss from Rose" by Seal, and then some classical music, and then maybe Prokofiev, and then Daddy Gato, which was a lot to take—but all of the stations were warped, except for the tornado warning, which sounded crisp, tactile really.

Alvo turned off the stereo.

"What are the odds?"

Mamadú played with his phone until he got a wisp of reception.

"Most tornados are like 50 yards wide-ya."

"The Tornado Alley does snatch up drivers now and then..."

"On March 18, 1925, the tri-state tornado," said Mamadú, reading, which thickened his accent, "swept through the Midwestern and Southern U.S.A. killing 625 people."

The wind picked up.

"*Puta madre,*" said the Ecuadorian, holding on to the wheel.

"We can pull over."

"No way. Let's push through."

"Cold dry air clashing against warm wet air, that's all."

"Most tornados are harmless."

"Exactly."

"Are there tornados in Africa?"

"First world problems, bro."

"Tornados are first world problems?"

"Absolutely. We got bigger problems than that."

"What's Liberia like?"

Alvo wanted to keep the conversation going; it kept him from fear.

Mamadú saw that. So he talked.

"Picture Switzerland in your head."

"Wow… okay… okay…"

"Liberia is the complete opposite of that."

Laughter broke-in, liker rain in the desert, and it lingered in booming mischief, until the Liberian got suddenly serious though Alvo thought he might be playing around.

"Liberia —the oldest republic in Africa— started as an American experiment in racism and utopia like 200 years ago. What do you expect-menh?" he added, fixing his golden watch.

"Didn't we all?" said Alvo with a chuckle.

"Who's *we*? You're not African," said Mamadú, settling into moodiness.

"I guess, for me, Hispanic republics, all twenty one of them. Ecuador in particular: Our first president was Venezuelan! Can you believe that shit?"

"To me, all of you is the same, bro," said Mamadú. "And… you guys are really fucking Switzerland compared to us, just so you know."

"Who is *us* to you?

"Heart of darkness folks…" said Mamadú with a smirk.

The literary reference went over Alvo's head like a loop over a net-rusher.

"What?"

"They don't teach you that in school, huh?"

"Who's *they*?" asked Alvo, getting annoyed.

"The ungrateful beneficiaries of all they despise—trade, capitalism, and colonization."

The Ecuadorian intuited where the conversation was going and wanted to cut it at the root.

"Fine," he added, "I just have one point to make."

He looked at Mamadú straight in the eye.

"Shoot?"

"Fuck Switzerland!"

"Whut!"

"I don't know, just fuck Switzerland, bro!"

Alvo had never sounded so annoyingly Californian to Mamadú, who couldn't help but chuckle. In some ways the two were similar. In some ways, they were like a Martian and a Plutonian crossing over Neptune in a trance.

"I guess I see what you're saying…" said the Liberian.

"Don't you *agree*!!??"

"I guess, *amigo*, I guess."

Two hours to Mobile, enunciated the robotic voice in the Geographic Positioning System with its digital orange lines that stood for freeways, and its blue lines that stood for rivers —with French and Choctaw names— and its thin grey lines, like little serpents, that stood for country roads.

"This shit's just like a videogame," said Alvo, looking at the dynamic board, which was like an extension of his pixilated childhood filled to the brim with Marios and Luigis, and princesses and boxers, and F-1 cars, and street fighters, and inter-galactic warriors.

"This shit's just like a videogame," he repeated, thinking the Liberian had not heard him.

It didn't occur to him that perhaps the Liberian had gone silent on purpose as he was traversing a map of his own.

2,022 - 2521 Miles, Orlando, Florida

The platform was stabbed into an Alabama hill. Except for the baby blue and vivid pink in the distance, the landscape was intensely yellow and then suddenly gray. It poured down for fifteen minutes. They switched seats and took off again. The hills had darkened except for the yellow flowers, which seemed to have retained the day's light. Alvo felt a heaviness in the belly.

He hadn't pooped since he'd left the Beverly Hills Tennis Club. It added to the lack of sleep.

"Why didn't you stay in your country?" asked Mamadú from the driver's seat.

It was a question he liked to ask all other migrants. He wrote the best answers down on a cowhide book he'd gotten in Bong County.

"Because I would've turned into a criminal," said Alvo, thinking that'd do it.

The Liberian's big golden watch shone in the dark. *If not fake, that shit's worth thousands*, thought Alvo. The Liberian caught Alvo's eye. To him, the Ecuadorian was faking nonchalance. Something in him wanted it broken.

"And just what turns a mayor's grandson into a criminal?"

"I did not turn into a criminal," said Alvo, putting his feet up on the dashboard and his hands behind his head.

"You said you could have..." said Mamadú, holding on to the wheel.

The other looked out into the inscrutable distance. The American road, if there indeed lay a road underneath —because it was also possible that there was no road underneath but the rough Alabama turf shredding the chassis into rubbish— went on darkly, but for the looming headlights, which drove Alvo to oscillate within, until in a sort of rare (to him) somersault, he came to a rest.

"Had I stayed in Guayaquil, bro—*claro.*"

The way the Ecuadorian had said *Guayaqui*l was different. Like he'd pulled the word out from within the mangrove swamps of that ancient river: a gem in the mud of lexicon. The Liberian pictured the river, which the other had talked about. Dark, sweet, and heavy; perpetually seeking the ocean's salt to the west.

"Looks like you got a good education."

"Private academies, yes, of course," said Alvo, lifting his slight nose.

"Good for you, man. I really mean it."

Two big headlights materialized in a row, then dissolved into the dark.

The minutes didn't necessarily drag on; they turned concrete.

"There's more to childhood than good schools," said Alvo, pulling on his brown beard.

"I know that."

"People here are obsessed with relative advantages..."

"But variables do play out..." completed Mamadú, who agreed with the other.

"Exactly," said Alvo, intuiting a sort of voyeurism from the refugee. "In my case there was a particular tennis coach, who slapped me hard in the face after a junior match. I couldn't speak up when I was little. Maybe twice. Maybe he slapped me twice. Could have been three, though definitely not four. *That's a variable.* I would've killed him had I stayed in Guayaquil. Little kids do grow up, you know? There's your answer."

The yellow Camaro entered a dark tunnel, but once inside, the tunnel wasn't that dark. There was a light twister in there, which was hard on the eye.

"Did that ruin your childhood?"

"That's a fucking violent question, my man," said Alvo in that hyper-relaxed California way he'd mastered to the point of parody.

This time Mamadú did not giggle. "Is that right?" he asked.

"Speed up a little..." said the Ecuadorian, who was going from annoyed to irritated, fast.

The Camaro shot out of the twirling tunnel like a bullet in the night. No cops in sight.

"My childhood...." he said, with the funny glint of well-earned madness. "Summer trips, shrinks, grandpa's *Cine Oriente*, tutors, and camps for all kinds of stuff—pretty standard."

"Pretty standard, huh?" said Mamadú, slowing down to get through a curve. He wasn't suicidal. Quite the contrary. He was a committed survivalist. "How about your folks?"

Alvo crossed his fingers behind his head and yawned.

"Pretty standard, *ñaño*," he enunciated, seeing it got to the other. "Two stylish college brats who were too self-consciously modern to be straight-out parents. My folks come from a generation that wanted both: a big family like their folks, and, like, whatever you called the sophisticated lives that came out in *Miami Vice*. We get it. Felipe, Macarena, and I, I mean. That was *precisely standard* for our folks' in-between generation. We get it. We're not *irrational*."

"Standard. Is that the verdict?"

"Is this fast for you? You drive like a fucking turtle, no offence, bro."

Mamadú stepped on it— "There..."

Gravity pulled their bodies back like a plane.

"That's right, *mijo. Como macho!"*

Mamadú, who deeply believed once people came to America, they should speak English, and leave their other languages behind, simply squinted.

"Who was gonna take care of us? *That's the verdict,"* Alvo went on, comfortable in a racing car. "In a sense there was a team of people. Most of them amazing. Lots of sports: water polo, baseball, golf. Gifts galore. Plus, the people. The employees! A parade of personalities. Some of them important, I mean, like, spiritually. I remember Chico, a sort of wall cop for the property. He'd been a fire breather in Portoviejo. Dude could hold fire in his cupped hand. Drove us around. Took us to the fair with his own kids. Played soccer with us. Dude could do *la culebrita.* Do you know *la culebrita?"*

"What does that mean? You know I don't speak your language."

"The meaning is that some fucking *tarado* slapping me in a way I did not understand (once or twice or whatever!) and my parents' failure to see it for whatever generational circumstance, did not ruin my childhood, man. It estranged me from myself. It created a sort of crack at the base. But much of my childhood was absolutely glorious. I mean it from the heart. As for *la culebrita...* I'll show you once we get a hold of a ball."

"So, what's the problem?"

"What do you do mean *what's the problem?"*

"Is that it?"

"I can't make shit up to satisfy whatever it is you're after. A lot of it was *glorious!"*

The Liberian stoically held on to the silence until the other went on.

"Maybe the problem is now..." added the Ecuadorian. "Felipe, my brother, Chief Petroleum Engineer at Petroecuador —best job in the country— still banks on grandpa Rambo's connections. Okay, that fine, but he claims not to like sports anymore. It's one thing not to do sports, but he won't even keep up with the Grand Slams. Doesn't watch the World Cup. It's fucking disgusting. Made up. Artificial."

"And?"

"Papá found his true self in tree hugging. Instead of business trips, he does spiritual retreats now. Got in touch with his feminine side. Owns a purple mat and all."

"How about your mother?"

"My mother's Ecuador's representative to the World Health Organization. Still married to my father on paper. Helps on the holidays."

"How about your sister?"

"Macarena's doing architecture in Rome. Huge Photogram account."

"You *do* have a great family. Álvaro. Amazing."

"And yet, I'm sort of stuck. I sort of can't stop fantasizing about going down there and obliterating the asshole who disrespected me so long ago. It's like I can't move on in life until I do that. Like an obsession."

"So why don't you?"

"I'm sure he's a good, caring, Catholic retiree by now."

"What's his name?"

"Why?"

"What's his name?"

"Why the hell do you want to know his name for?"

"Trying to help you, cousin. Don't get vexed. Ain't no palaver."

"Juan Manuel Córsica," said Alvo with a shaky voice. "That's his name."

"Juan Manuel Córsica," repeated the Liberian, adjusting his gold watch.

It was as if he were saying the name of a dead man. Alvo smiled at the pronunciation.

"Listen, cousin, I'ma tell you. You go down there, look up this Córsica, don't kill him, but get the shitballs out of your system. I mean, *really*, do what you have to do. Break the hand he slapped you with. Nobody's going to mess with you there. You got connections. If he's already dead, spit on his grave. Move on. Also, while you're at it, tell off your parents if you must. Do so as a child would. Then come back to the US, marry Kaori, and then move to Tokyo, or wherever you want go."

"Ha, you just solved my life," said Alvo clearing sweat from his brow.

"I'll help," said Mamadú, feeling the tart taste of adrenaline for the first time in ages.

"Mr. Garzón, former tennis champ, gone transnational thug…" said Alvo, sarcastically.

The Liberian stepped on the breaks violently. The yellow Camaro almost lost traction before coming to a stop. After a three long seconds Mamadú spoke, as if addressing a crowd.

"I've killed people, you fool. "

"*Eh?*" said the other, too worried about oncoming cars to be shocked. "Fucking drive!"

Mamadú started driving slowly. No, he had never been suicidal. He was simply a taciturn man who could become violently assertive at critical times. It had helped him survive.

"What you wanted to avoid," he said fixing his gold watch again, "I am."

"Please drive fucking faster, bro. We're going to get smashed."

"In Liberia I am a criminal."

"You were a child!"

"I was a teenager."

"Nonsense!"

"*Nonsense,*" groaned Mamadú, as he penetrated his own mental map. "The rebels put shit in Seagull's coconut. He was a boy too. A friend of mine. But he had recruitment in mind. I saw it."

"You're telling the truth. You did it to save others."

"The truth can also be an excuse for criminal actions. I was a criminal."

"No child's a criminal, ever. That's impossible by definition."

"I wanted to show myself I could do damage too," said Mamadú. And then, shifting his tone: "*Was it your choice to move here?*"

Alvo felt the full brunt of irritation now. He considered knocking the other's teeth out.

"Are you daft? I told you I grew up on Nintendo, water guns, and Hulk Hogan. My folks hired famous clowns for our birthday parties."

"So what?"

"You don't get it, do you? I took my first English class at four. I did summer school in Cambridge while my parents worked out their reconciliation. What do you mean by *move* here?"

"Was it your fucking choice to move to the United States of America?"

"You mean *summer school?*

"Sure, okay."

"People like me never *move* to the U.S. because we're born with half a foot here. By age ten I'd been to Disney World three times. We're in between places—it's not bad."

"Liberty Investments is worth lots of money," Mamadú said, fixing his watch, "but I bring the war with me wherever I go."

"I don't know war, bro. I don't know what the hell you're talking about."

Mamadú played with the car lights. After a while, he spoke, much more subdued.

"How about a video game where things are blowing up, women are getting raped, children are getting abducted, viruses are spreading, and a whole nation's infrastructure is collapsing at your feet. Even *you* can identify those videogame terms, *amigo*."

Alvo didn't need any more darkness. All his life he'd been trying to go the other way. It was as if the Liberian was trying to drag him down with him. He was done.

"You know, Kaori and I saw a documentary once... a trashed-out beach where people take shits on the sand. Could be a beautiful beach if you guys cleaned it up a bit."

"I've seen that film. Vice. Pure Western masturbation. You should know as a Third World man yourself."

"Was it real or was it fake?"

Mamadú closed his eyes, though he was at the wheel.

"Back then war was spreading like a zombie apocalypse," he said, opening his eyes. "But even don't try—some levels of sin you just can't. The mind stops for self-protection."

"Is you watch real?" asked Alvo, brutally.

Mamadú kept playing with the car lights.

"My American father made real dough in HFT's. As an investor he was a ruthless bossman, but as a father he has the purest white heart."

"You're going to break my car lights, dude."

Mamadú turned the headlights off. Alvo was ready to strike.

"I was a child once too, you know," said the Liberian, disarming the other with his gentle tone. "Except my relative advantages were not too, shall we say, advantageous. The horror... it had a habit of swallowing things up then: men, women, children, animals, the landscape. Big rocks that you got used to seeing on your way to the river would just disappear quick-quick. Or they'd appear somewhere else, but in a heap, obliterated. Poppa was gone first. Momma carried us deep in the bush. The horror spread there too. That's when the foggy years began. It got unspeakable, like a child's scribbling on a book. We went through the eye of war, landed somewhere, Sierra Leone maybe. There were no sounds of war there. But Bobby, Latoya, Tito, and little Sammy knew the horror was coming, small-small but coming. You know how some Native Americans put their ear down to the ground? You could almost hear it like a rumble. Momma started behaving. *High up above*, she chanted, *high up above*. To some she said goodbye in the flesh, others she appeared to in trances. Lady Cheapoo was washing her clothes at St. Paul's River near Haindi when momma shoot up from within the depths, and stood in the current, like Jehovah, before plunging, no splashing. When Lady Cheapoo looked down, she saw that the wet clothes had no hue. Hold word! We didn't see these apparitions. All we heard was momma. *High up above*, she chanted, *high up above*. Some yelled she was cracked. But she wasn't cracked. Her skin got too hot that week. The Action Against Hunger folks said it was dirty water. They sent messages out. Early the next day, an elder we called Bob Marley because of his hair said a demon spirit had told him the roads were blocked. They called him a bad-heart, devil messenger. *High up above*, momma kept chanting in the hut. They wouldn't let us in. We stood in the bush."

"I'm sorry."

"It's facts, bro. Poppa was a fact. Momma was a fact. The war was a fact. The bush was a fact. The bad water was a fact. We ourselves were small little facts. Facts can't be helped, can they?"

An Alabama truck passed the slow Camaro in anger, but the Liberian and the Ecuadorian were in their own realm with migrant dreams.

"The ambulance got there thirty-six hours and twenty-three minutes *after* the fact. I counted up minutes because that's the thing with facts: they're hairy definite. Beyond horror, really. Well, the ambulance got there. It had a big ass red cross on the door and a big ass UNICEF sign on the hood. The medics went to the chief and said they had to bring momma's body *for sanitary reasons*," Mamadú said, letting out his caustic giggle. And then, as if snapping out of it: "Hear me out, cousin. This is for you. What do you think *we* did?"

"I don't know what you did, Mamadú."

"Word—you *don't* know," said Mamadú. "I told you how I killed my friend Seagull."

"You stabbed him."

"I juked him in the back. That's a fact. Hear it, man. I lost part of my soul then, but I learned something too. It's always like that. I learned the value to a well-placed crime."

"What?"

"When they tried to take momma's body *for sanitary reasons*, I knew what to do. Nadia helped. Even the little ones helped. I knew it'd be good for them too. We smashed the ambulance's windshields, slashed the tires, ripped the doors out. Nadia got diesel from a stove. We fired up the fucker, sirens, lights medical equipment and all. The nurses got a good shaking too. Which helped. You understand? We did it. You know why?"

"To avenge your mother."

"No! It was about us. If you let bad-hearts brew, it gets heavier and heavier cuts you inside. You know what I'm talking about. Hear it, man. Sometimes people break free by going against legality. We let our hatred out then. It was healthy. People saw. We got away with it. That's a fact," said Mamadú, as if changing into something else, even the voice.

To Alvo the Liberian seemed suddenly young, obscenely so.

"*Chucha*," he babbled, stunned at the mutation most of all.

"We didn't allow nobody there. No casket, no tomb, but a heap of wildflowers, and two little twigs for a cross. We burned the body and buried the ashes on the outskirts, by a black pepper bush."

Alvo extended his arm in a reflexive gesture. But there were broken down colors within that Monrovian eye that were not meant for the Ecuadorian to see.

"Stay away, motherfucker," said Mamadú in a voice so cavernous, it had to have come from the belly. "I could slash you in two in a heartbeat... and you wouldn't even know it when I drank your blood off the soil."

There was a hot surge in the chest. Alvo's entire world view told him to knock the shit out of that crazy *prieto*. But he didn't. As delicately as he could, Alvo withdrew the arm from the other's shoulder. No, the arm withdrew itself, reflexively, just as it had gone there. It wasn't cowardice. Nor was it daring. It was something else: the outskirts of friendship, perhaps.

A shaking Mamadú put the window down. Hot Florida air rushed in, obliterating the air conditioned cool. That was it. The two peripherals had cut east through the whole contiguous country in counter Manifest Destiny: 2,357 miles on the I-10 before going down the I-75 South. After a while, the Liberian softly turned off the engine at the edge of Disney World, which was off too, the whole park, quiescent but breathing, like a massive organism collapsed on the ground. The sizzling Camaro snugged in as into a mothership. Her sweet bosom, fiberglass and steel.

2521 - 2746 Miles— Miami, Florida

Alvo drove through the *City Beautiful* in the muggy morning. He had accepted Mamadú's apology and was in a good mood; he retracted the roof and all. It was like stepping into a time machine. Disney, SeaWorld, Legoland—so many childhood trips! *We should bring the Furukawa sisters here once this whole thing's over*, he thought, *because it will be.*

"Are you hungry?" he asked, instead of sharing his plan.

"Like a wolf," replied the Liberian, followed by his acidic giggle.

They pulled over at a RaceTrac and got four vanilla-frosted Cronuts, a bag of Lay's potato chips, two Big Red Roller hot dogs, Grannies apple juice, and two Folgers coffee cups (one decaf and one not) to go. They ate on the fly because the closer they got to Miami, the more the crisis demanded their attention. Fifty miles from ground zero, Alvo tuned into CNN Radio and set it at an insufferable volume as if to make up for his previous indolence. The terrorists had posted a statement. Mamadú grabbed his phone and downloaded the entire document.

TWO

The U.S. Army's Summer Program for Teenage Developers

Three years after becoming the youngest defending champion of Planet War Survival III at the Supreme Warriors Tier, Artjom Pärn, was officially invited by the U.S. Army to join its Summer Program for Teenage Developers. The U.S. Army prohibited its summer program fellows from being contractually tied to any outside entities, and Artjom, or rather $doomMetalBo, had ongoing commitments with Smith&Ferrer, a war-game agency. As reigning champion, $doomMetalBo's role at Smith&Ferrer was that of Public Relations attaché at fairs and conventions throughout Europe. It was a fun post where he got to show off his skills in live demonstrations as well as giving autographs and taking pictures sporting Smith&Ferrer gear. The pay was substantial for a high schooler. Plus he often got to travel to England where he got to hang out with his older brother, Kirill Pärn, who brought him into the company's London headquarters. Kirill and his team developed facial recognition applications in the Chinese auto industry, the private jail industry in South Africa, and (this was Kirill's focus) the theme park industry in South Korea. Kirill wasn't happy with the kind of work he was doing; to him it was a drag. He wanted to do something more exciting, with greater repercussions than just making sure kids don't swap passes at Seoul Disney. Still, Kirill was making money. He'd bought an apartment in London and was sending enough remittances back to Estonia so that their *ema*, Marija Pärn, didn't have to work in a Tallin factory anymore. As a matter of fact, Marija had left her job and started taking Yoga classes instead. Her plan was to become a part time yoga instructor for seniors. As for young Artjom, now at the last stage of his formerly aggrieved adolescence, life had become much more composed. Neither his older brother nor his mother worried about him anymore. His attitude towards school had changed. He was going to graduate high school early. Most impressively, he was making money as a gamer. The only issue since he'd set up his own state-of-the-art gaming station at home was his weight, which had ballooned, since he no longer needed to ride his bike to the Hollywood PC Room in Kalamaja. Also, he didn't have a girlfriend. He was shy around women. His big brother felt that joining the U.S. Army's Summer Military Program for Teenage Developers would be a step towards solving those problems.

"It's time you start branching out from gaming, *vennas*," Kirill told Artjom one day over Skype during the half time break of a Premier League game in Old Trafford. "If I were you, I'd move to North Carolina."

Artjom had concerns about his contract with Smith&Ferrer.

"Just end it, *vennas*!" added Kirill.

As to Artjom's concerns about school, Kirill said a diploma from an American high school would be a strength, even if it took longer: "Better your English, *vennas*. All big industries work in English or Chinese. You can work on your Mandarin later."

Artjom laughed through the phone screen.

"I'm serious, *vennas*," added Kirill, who had a father-like influence over his brother. "Now's the time for you to set your career up in a way that you can soon be at the heart of something exciting. Life and death stuff. The forefront of the high-tech world. Those kinds of jobs do exist, *vennas*. They're in the shitty BRIC countries —Brazil, Russia, India, and China— but those places aren't going to be shitty for much longer. Of course there'll always be the U.S, which is both shitty and developed at the same time. The vanguard. That's what I envision for you, *vennas*. Don't get stuck managing trivial projects in Estonia. Europe is the past. Take the leap. Go to The Core, work on significant shit. Hell, I might even join you one day. You could be my boss. I don't mind. Think about it, *vennas*, old chap."

"Alright I'll think about it, *vennas*."

"You're a good man, a really good man, *vennas*. Take care of *ema*, please. Tell her not to overdo the yoga, yeah? Anyway, the teams are coming out. Rooney got a red card at the end of the first half. He elbowed a defender right on the nose, broken, lots of friggin' blood. Manchester City's looking to tie the game! You got to come see the Premier League with me. It's slightly better than the Wuote.

"Don't shit on Mother Estonia, you dirty monkey foreigner!"

"Flora Tallinn 'til death!"

"That's more like it."

"I'm bringing you to 'The Theatre of Dreams' next time you're in England, *vennas*."

"Put it on paper."

"I'll put it on text. Pet Mitu for me. *Hüvasti* bro!"

That same day Artjom talked to Marija. They called a lawyer and the lawyer said there would be a significant loss of money, but that the Smith&Ferrer contract could be unilaterally terminated. And so it was. Within a month Artjom Pärn, the gaming champ, had moved to Raleigh, North Carolina. It was summer, but he enrolled in Booker T. Washington High School to take English classes. There he met lots of Mexican kids whose parents had come to work the land in The Core. The Mexican students had crazy stories about crossing the dessert and running from the authorities just to get where they were. A hyperreal videogame. In the quad he met some white and black American kids who were taking remedial summer classes. Artjom gravitated towards the so-called rejects, both Mexican and American. In general, Raleigh had more metalheads than Tallinn. He made friends. Before he started the Army's program, he was invited to a show by a band called Evil Incantation. The sound was like traversing a castle made of speakers and medieval screams. Back home Artjom hadn't paid attention to black metal. That loud, static rumble made him feel sedate. It was so unlike the rushing cavalcade of thrash metal back home. Thrash started sounding childish to him. Between his new buddies, the new scene, and the bong air like a gong in his temples, Artjom Pärn didn't pay any mind to the Army stuff, nor did he call home. He'd found a new way in Raleigh, including the secret YouTube channel he'd started. Not that it was a secret for long. Artjom's gaming fans —and some of his tireless detractors who spread the sophomoric rumor that Pärn had somehow killed T-Rex500 in real life— found out who he was within a few days. The Estonian accent, the red and gold SF 49s cap, his round silhouette, the long hair, and his unorthodox "dirty" gaming style gave him away. Within a few days the Estonian revealed his identity: $doomMetalBo – YouTubing from The Core.

The channel took off. $doomMetalBo showed glimpses of the metal scene in Raleigh and short clips of himself eating French fries at a parking lot with Tookie10, a whacky Oaxacan skater who spoke no English, or hanging out with the theNeverwhöre, who had green hair, a pierced septum and pushup bra who talked to his fans, or more accurately, rambled on almost incomprehensibly about all the dicks and assholes she encountered in her daily life. $doomMetalBo mostly laughed, though he got serious when it came to gaming advice. More and more kids started following him. Artjom didn't know if the U.S. Army would give him trouble for having a YouTube channel. He tried to hide it. Had he known how critical he was to the growth of the Military Arcade Center (M.A.C. ™) at Raleigh's Carousel Mall, he wouldn't have cared. Not only did the military consider the Estonian critical; they actually knew of his YouTube channel. And not only did they know of his channel: they were secretly promoting it. The mushrooming number of followers was no coincidence. The U.S. Army's goal was sowing and reaping fresh data about potential recruits from the gaming channel.

Within a few months the M.A.C. ™ materialized. The "Army of One" campaign, which had appealed to pride and civic duty, took the back seat. This was different. The speakers were turned up, the lights dimmed. It was a club of sorts. All sorts of screens with video game versions of war glowed on the wall. The Arcade Officials ™ were modeled after Abercrombie And Fitch ambassadors; that is, they were young, muscular, friendly and keen on excitement. At the M.A.C.™ the kids got to feel the weight of real machine guns (unloaded), try on parachute back packs, and play Army-developed video games that incorporated hyper-realistic artillery. This last element — the Virtual Reality Warfare ™— was king at the M.A.C.™ It was also the aspect where $doomMetalBo had the most influence. He told army contractors that kids loved to pretend to fly planes that had seen *actual combat*. They did a focus group. It was a revelation! Actual plane parts were flown in from combat zones in Afghanistan and Iran. The Virtual Reality cabins were more real than real. It wasn't virtual reality, it was hyper-virtual-reality. $doomMetalBo's last idea was genius. Metal plaques and photographs attesting that the parts had come from formerly war-active aircraft were put up on an actual pedestal. A slightly blown-up facsimile of the U.S. presidents' signature lay at the bottom of the plaque, as if sealing the deal. A young intern from Samoa had thought of that.

As to the actual games, $doomMetalBo pushed the idea of competition. The bosses latched to his every word:

"The Military Arcade Center shouldn't just show teens what it's like to fly planes. Teens don't care about dry learning as much as they care about checking their skills. Teens wanna be challenged. Teens want real action. We wanna compete against others. You should set up a points system kids can access at home—that's key. Think chat rooms. Think tier systems like in real games. These should be real video games. Players should be able to come back and play over and over. In fact, you should charge the crappy players and let the good players play for free. Also, make the blasts louder. And change the sky graphics from day to night. Teens come in during the day, right? Give them something that takes them away from where they are. If its day, make it night. If it's night, make it day. Follow that as a principle. I'd also buy the rights to songs like Judas Priest's 'Breaking the law' or Metallica's 'Fight Fire with Fire.' Also there's this new band I've been getting into called Evil Incantation. They have a song titled 'Heart of Darkness.' Kids would flip on that shit, *vennas*. Yes, yes, throw in lots hip-hop too, but make it the aggressive kind. Wait. *Do not have the music play during the war action*! Blast it before and after the action. The Virtual Reality war action should be as realistic as possible. And did I say competitive? Don't forget competitive. Here's the bottom line, *vennas*. Give the real feel of war short of pain: One last super key thing, the buff Arcade Officials™ are cool and all, but try getting hot chicks in there. I don't know how you're gonna do that, but you got to get hot chicks in there. These are horny, adrenalined-up teens we're talking about. Hahaha.'"

To think Artjom had said all of this while stoned out of his mind. He'd done it in the $doomMetalBo character, using the same tone he used to give videogame advice online. The contractors and the military bosses knew the Estonian was gold. Gold for the Army. Gold for the nation. Gold for the teens who would get a shitload of shots. A shot at fleeing the ghetto, a shot at a career, and a shot at money for college. Indeed. The first M.A.C. ™ at the Carousel Mall in Raleigh, North Carolina opened to overwhelming success. It recruited more people than all the local college fairs put together. There was some backlash in terms of press but whatever. It was recruits the

Army wanted. The press could go to hell."

Within months, three additional M.A.C.s ™ went into development. One in Roanoke, Virginia; one in Chattanooga, Tennessee; and another one all the way in South Tucson, Arizona. Artjom Pärn or $doomMetalBo went from Army intern to senior advisor in record time. He started traveling up and down the Appalachia spine and, as the project advanced, west to Arizona. Unbeknownst, himself, he'd become the key player in a recruiting revolution for the mightiest military on earth. And he wasn't even out of high school yet.

The Coalition of the Eager

PDF download successful!

> *Dear American reader:*
>
> *If this communiqué has reached you, The Coalition of the Eager has been successful in bringing attention to the dire situation in the Gulf of Mexico, even if our patriots have perished at the hands of the so-called government. The Coalition of the Eager will use this missive to lay out its demands in relation to the ongoing <u>Operation Righteous Cruise Raid</u>. First, however, allow us to address:*
>
> *A). The urgency of the situation.*
>
> *B). The patriotic coalition's how's and why's.*
>
> *A. Too often has the notion of urgency been brought up for counterfeit motives of vulgar power and underhanded deceit, all in aggressive detriment of the plain-spoken, good-hearted, and historically freedom-bound American. In particular, the notion of urgency has been abused by the executive branch of our government with mass media cooperation for pernicious reasons, including: pointless wars that have sullied our sacred military; the mass-migration of non-whites that in compassion's name has irrevocably distorted our nation's make-up; the economic lies put forward by neoliberalism and its tools exemplified by*

free trade agreements such as NAFTA, elite-serving international banking institutions such as the World Bank, illegal government rescue measures to giant corporations, and unfair tax rates that squeeze the hard-working middle class while unfairly assisting scores of foreign Malthusian families and voracious billionaires; the international (always international) sanitary scares without any basis in science or reality such as the most recent L-37 Malaysian flu that was apparently going to wipe out a quarter of the heartland's population, but which did nothing but give the government carte blanche to inoculate millions of innocents with God-knows what goal in mind; the environmental emergency, which in a sense is the most deceitful of all because it is an actual emergency in terms of animal extinction, resource depletion, and human loss of life, but also a fraudulent one for the lying government uses it to boost its pro-global purposes, while ignoring nature. The American people have seen through the manipulation for years. And we can't take it anymore. For that reason, The Coalition of the Eager has been formed. There will be no more waiting around for those in power to fool us into addressing ghost crisis. There will be no more lies.

B. The Coalition of the Eager is composed of four disparate groups that have found in the dire state of matters a uniting cause. We have set our differences aside to step into the arena of direct confrontation. It must be stated that none of our four organizations has primacy over the others. Members of all four organizations are participating at every level of the affair, from inception, to development, to execution, to communications (including the drafting of this document), to viral practices, to potential negotiations, and lastly, to post-event objective-success appraisal. Though there have not been talks of the establishment of a permanently collaborating body, that is not ruled out. It all depends on the outcome of this particular operation. As an exercise in reciprocity, we can say that if the criminal globalist agenda, which also contains disparate members, has for decades managed to strengthen (with our government's money and in our very land!) the organizational structures that give their scandalously criminal aims a varnish of legality, there's no reason why there shouldn't be a permanent body of collaborating American patriotic organizations despite our differences.

If the globalized world has the United Nations, which is a permanent thorn in our side, shouldn't America have a permanent organization designed to strike back?

For now, a permanent body remains a dream. But then again, that's how we started: notions and dreams. While none of the four independent organizations that make up The Coalition of the Eager has power over the others, it should also be known that the original idea behind it belongs to a single woman, whose name shall remain hidden, but whose vision will be presently apparent. For obvious security reasons, and for organizational reasons having to do with the coalition's intra-democratic process, the name of the organization which this patriotic lady directs shall remain confidential as well. The criminal FBI will have to wrestle with that one. As to the group identities of the other three organizations, we shall proudly provide them.

The organizations that make up The Coalition of the Eager are:
- *Blood and Soil America (BSA)*
- *Earth Rescue Brigade-USA branch (ERB-USA)*
- *Nonaligned Federation for Neoliberal Termination (NFNT)*
- *Fourth Group Classified (FGC)*

Blood and Soil America is concerned with the ethnic distortion of the North American genetic pool. In particular, it reacts against the criminal change that took place in the United States after The Immigration and National Act of 1965 unlatched the flood gates to non-European aliens. In less than fifty years since that law –perhaps the most important law enacted in the history of the United States – and probably influenced by the pernicious aftermath of the Civil Rights Movement, the United States has gone from a majority White Republic to a soon-to-be majority Murky Republic. The BSA's focus on the White/Murky dichotomy isn't merely a skin tone affair, though it is also about that (see T. R. Thompson Jr.'s article on the lawless Mestizo South-West takeover on our site). It is a metaphorical juxtaposition between the White vision in terms of freedom, civics, and morality and the Murky world vision brought over by Hispanics, Asians, Arabs, and other invading aliens. We consider it our duty to preserve our race and worldview as pristine as possible. The Immigration Act of 1924 should have remained in place and must be reinstated.

Unlike the BSA, Earth Rescue Brigade-USA, is part of an international organization. However, due to the crisis in the Gulf of Mexico, the international chapter's unwillingness to take action, and the American chapter's limited resources for wide-scale confrontational actions, the ERB-USA has decided to go against its own international organizational precepts and join The Coalition. This does not mean that the ERB-USA renounces its goal of saving the environment, but the recognition that a new phase in that critical fight began when the Gulf of Mexico's plastic island was located on July 28. That a plastic island larger than Puerto Rico was found in the Caribbean by an unrelated dolphin-preservation NGO was critical enough, but the fact that the government was coercing said NGO to hide the truth, compelled the ERB-USA to go rogue. In a related matter, it must be known that ERB-International's request that the environmentally preposterous cruise industry halt all operations in the Gulf of Mexico was met with derision. Anger and frustration ensued. These conditions have forced Earth Rescue Brigade-USA to pursue environmental justice at home. ERB-USA abhors violence, but this is self-defense.

The Nonaligned Federation for Neoliberal Termination is the oldest organization in The Coalition of the Eager. It is also the organization with the most law-abiding, non-violent record in our group. For over twenty years the NFNT has grouped together concerned individuals from the left, the right, and the center brought together not by political ideology, but by the certainty that the neoliberal economic policies enacted by all American presidents starting with Ronald Reagan constitute thievery. Free trade as practiced by neoliberal cronies has been the worse illness to strike the United States of America in economic terms since the Great Depression. The NFNT sees the direct link between neoliberalism and the looming national debt, the shameless auction of our government to China in the form of bonds, the loss of manufacturing jobs in the heartland, the trade deficit with lesser developed economies, and the evil deregulation of Wall Street in detriment of the poor, the middle class, and even the law-abiding *affluent. The NFNT joined The Coalition because of the Cruise industry's immoral practices <u>against the American worker</u>. First of all, these are not American companies. These companies are registered in tax heavens such as Bahamas, Panama, or Venezuela, though they operate mostly in Florida and traverse American waters. In addition to not paying taxes, cruise companies hire mostly foreign workers (typically Filipinos), thus mirroring the criminal practices of all neoliberal corporations who make money in the USA, rip off American culture (see their cruises' so-called themes), and shamelessly poison our waters, while not even hiring Americans. A single cruise can produce, for instance, more smog than 700 trucks or a small town, not to mention the tons of toxic sewage dumped into the ocean, among other environmental wrongs. Now, <u>the NFNT is not an environmental organization</u>; the NFNT is an anti-neoliberalism organization. But in all of the environmental damage, of course, as in all of the economic damage, there's a lingering stench of rancid neoliberalism. We are fiscal pragmatists and as such believe in environmental taxes. International cruise companies poison our air and water and yet do not pay environmental taxes, fail to hire American workers, and won't even consider environmental reparations. As an American patriot organization, the NFNT is finally choosing to take a stand.*

The Fourth Group, as stated before, shall remain classified for security as well as for management reasons. Suffice it to say, that there are other unmentioned ills that the cruise industry perpetrates against historically disenfranchised segments of the population. Perhaps more will be communicated about this subject in the future.

There are negotiable and non-negotiable aspects to Operation Righteous Cruise Raid.

The negotiable aspects include:

- The possible release of all <u>American</u> passengers in the Reggaetón Cruise.

- The possible release of all private property belonging to <u>American</u> passengers.

- The possible release of all international passengers <u>in a country other than the USA</u>.

For the above listed concessions to be made, the following non-negotiable demands must be forthrightly met:

1. That all cruises out of Florida are immediately halted for a period of three months.

2. That Norwegian, Celebrity, Royal Caribbean and Carnival register their corporations in the United States effective immediately.

3. That the above-mentioned corporations pay back taxes in the US for a retroactive period of five years.

4. That all major cruise companies post The Environmental Damage in the Cruise Industry Report (<u>click here</u>) on each of their individual sites and keep it posted for six months.

5. That a mandatory number of American-born crew members in each ship equal the percentage of American-born passengers in that ship with a deviation no larger than 10%.

6. That the industry pay living wages to its crew members. No crew member, American or foreign born, should make less than twice the Federal minimum wage.

7. That the environmentally terrorist practice of waste dumping in the middle of the sea be outlawed immediately (a legally binding contract has been emailed to the largest cruise companies as well as to the press). <u>This contract is at the heart of our current operation.</u>

8. That from now on women, born or transitioned, make up at least 51% of all crew leadership roles, including that of ship captains.

9. That the escape route be absolutely respected. The meaning of this item shall soon become apparent.

10. That all major American news channels and newspapers link to The Coalition's <u>live video feed</u> from the Reggaetón Cruise. The live feed shall become available on our various platforms when The Coalition of the Eager considers it safe to do so.

Again, for the negotiable aspects of Operation Righteous Cruise Raid to satisfactorily unfold, the non-negotiable aspects must be met. <u>The Coalition of the Eager will not capitulate in any of the non-negotiable aspects of the operation under any circumstances</u>. We cannot emphasize this enough. Any attempts at dissuasion will be met by increased speed in the execution of key targets. Be advised to interpret *our words judiciously. Subsequent messages as well as the above-mentioned live video feed will follow.*

Together in harmony, strength, and eternal good will:

Blood and Soil America

Earth Rescue Brigade-USA

Nonaligned Federation for Neoliberal Termination

Fourth Group Classified.

Pluribus est Unum: The Coalition of the Eager

Somewhere in the contiguous core of the United States of America

The Turbulent Waters of Honduras

"I know that *cipote* from somewhere," Sandrita muttered to herself as she eyed the television screen on the light blue wall.

There had been many changes since Sandrita had taken over *Pupusas Anahí* after her mother's injury during a robbery years ago. For a few days after the robbery, Sandrita had considered selling the joint. Her mother, Anahí, couldn't run it anymore. But the offers were meager (*putos trying to take advantage of someone else's tragedy*, as Sandrita put it) and so after two sleepless nights, she decided to keep the business rather than feeding it to the neighborhood hyenas, who were probably the very ones who'd nearly slaughtered her sweet mother. Sandrita had invested her every penny in the venture. First she'd bought a shotgun, which she kept loaded under the cash register in case one of those animals dared to come back. They hadn't yet, but Sandrita was vigilant. Then she'd thrown away that horrid orange canopy and put up a solid barn instead—bones, tin sheets, tiles and all. Then, she'd thrown away the half-rotten wood tables and replaced them with plastic IKEA ones (the first IKEA in Central America opened in Santa Ana the same year Anahí was attacked) for if she was going to take over her mom's joint, she'd make it her own. She'd also painted the inside walls beige, and then in a sudden fit, light blue. In her mind beige was *fee-fee*, which Sandrita hated, because it was pretentious, and she abhorred pretense. She'd failed to see, though, that light blue made the eatery look like a hospital waiting room, or worse yet, like the public restrooms at *Estadio Cuscatlán*, the national soccer stadium of El Salvador, to which she'd only been once, as a child, with her cousins, and she hated soccer, for she deemed it a ridiculous circus for meat-headed machos and their whorish broads. It was funny how Sandrita just hated certain things passionately for random reasons. Funnier still were the convoluted self-explanations she came up with for her colorful prejudices. She was full of those. They made her charming. It's not like people asked her to explain herself. Most liked her somehow. Plus, she had a shotgun, and on top of the shotgun, she had a temper, which like the shotgun, was loaded and cocked and ready to fire obscenities, or punches, or Coke cans, or even cheese pupusas, if tried.

Above the plastic IKEA tables, Sandrita had placed a big ceiling fan. In truth, she hadn't put the fan up herself. Jimmy had. Jimmy was a very thin man, several years her junior, who lived with her, and whom she was considering marrying. Jimmy didn't talk much, but he could fix things. The twins, Petra and Gladys, adored him. He was good with academics and that was becoming important for the twins had started school, and Sandrita had only done up to grade five and remembered almost nothing from school. Jimmy worshiped Sandrita. There was an undeniable undercurrent of eroticism in her bossing around of all kinds of bad *hombres*, some of whom would kill if talked to like that by any other, but not Sandrita, because, as they themselves said: *Everybody knows Anahí's daughter is explosive as hell.* Not to mention how she pushed *him* around, yelling, cussing, shoving, even slapping. For Jimmy, it was strange. The more beastly Sandrita got with him, the more acquiescent he got with her. Of course, during sex the roles reversed. The fire in him ignited and he was somehow, time and again, able to wrestle down that big brown woman right in the kitchen or in the shower, which is what she liked best. The pale, scraggy, repairman was crazy about Sandrita's wide hips, the thick, unshaven legs, the way the breasts spread to the sides like jelly when he undid her brassier; it was like entering a wild mountain of sorts, meeting that woman in the flesh, the ups and downs of her structure, the hair, the smells, the sweat, unpredictable. He was certainly ready to marry her.

Her temper must be stressed. It was constantly and unrelentingly horrid. Her clothes were constant too. She never wore anything else besides tight-ass jeans (or tight-ass shorts in hot days) with a rotating range of either flower-print blouses or single-color tank-tops. She never wore high heels for she was naturally tall, and she had stopped wearing make up to hide her acne scars after Big Toño, the twins' father, had died as they tried to make it to Uncle Sam's when she was pregnant. Everybody knew Sandrita, who was already tough, had hardened after the accident. Jimmy knew of Sandrita when she was married (he knew her as an attractive older woman) but he didn't get to know her until after Big Toño's death. When she'd come back to Santa Ana, literally crushed—car, bones, dreams, and soul. He knew Big Toño was a violent man, who on more than one occasion had blown up on her, even breaking her nose once. He also knew Big Toño was the love of her life. Sandrita had adored Big Toño the way Jimmy adored Sandrita. That's why, perhaps, *el finado* had been an asshole to her. And also why she'd tolerated it so much.

"Sandrita used to have a hooked Indian nose like her Guatemalan dad," her mother, Anahí, used to say. "Now she has an upturned Spanish nose, like mine. Her man's gift, hahaha."

It wasn't mean spirited. The way the old woman said it, her tone and mannerism, tapping Sandrita's nose, with her index, could even be said to be sweet. You'd have to have been there, in those powder-hot Salvie evenings. You'd had to have been through what these two women had been through together to begin to understand the sweetness behind the vile.

It was always like that.

"Our Lord *Jehová* took him for a reason," Anahí would say about Big Toño, feeling the glint in her own eye.

She never spoke like that when Sandrita or the twins were around. The glint was too dark, the tone too mocking, and the mannerism too biting. It mattered not that the name of the Lord was uttered through her lips: Anahí hated Big Toño as much as she adored Jimmy. She hated Big Toño for the way he'd treated her daughter, but also, more than anything (as if Big Toño could have helped it!) for when and how he'd perished. Anahí had seen the change in her daughter, who never ever talked about her late husband, not even to Petra and Gladys, and tried to un-stiffen her with kisses and hugs.

But that was before the *cusucos* had beat her to a pulp for a few coins in her own joint, confining her to a wheelchair. After that, Anahí let her daughter be as tough as she wanted to be. "Perhaps that's what it takes to survive in The Savior's Land," she'd say. As to her own self, Mamahí, as some called her, could not become bitter, even after the assault. Bitterness simply wasn't in her. Gladness was. Plus what kind of ungrateful person could fall into bitterness when she had Petra and Gladys to brighten her days at home? She was happy letting Sandrita take over the *pupusería* and glad to see her granddaughters grow up. Even in a wheelchair, Anahí cooked and washed clothes and cleaned around the house, singing old cumbias day and night.

As for slim Jimmy, he could do no wrong in Anahí's eyes.

"Marry him, girl, he loves you like a puppy," she'd say to Sandrita. "I want to see you married again before I drop dead one of these days hahaha"

But Sandrita dismissed her mother with a grin, as if Jimmy, her lover, stunk of shit.

Jimmy did love her like a puppy. As to the *barrio* rumors that after Big Toño's death Sandrita's sexual taste had taken a turn for the fairer sex, Jimmy couldn't care less. He knew there was some truth to the rumors, but so what? In many ways Jimmy was as close to the idea of a delicate woman as a man could get. Except in bed, as has been said, when he turned into a skinny, pale domineering bull. Anyhow. The point is that to Sandrita, Jimmy had seamlessly become an indispensable part of the new landscape after her husband's death. Plus (and this was perhaps the main point) unlike most other things in the universe, Jimmy wasn't a tragedy. He was much like her daughters: simple, solid goodness. Marriage could be a step. Despite her foul reactions, she was considering it.

For now, her focus, *their* focus, was keeping *Pupusas Anahí* afloat. After taking over, Sandrita had increased prices to pay for the expensive changes, which only Sandrita considered improvements. The hike had driven out some old patrons. But the main challenge, besides the matron's retirement, was that Sandrita had put up two television sets in the joint, which she obdurately kept on, despite the fact that most customers liked Anahí's cumbia records better. Patrons had to tolerate the trashy *crónica roja* crime reports if they wanted to eat there. Sandrita was hooked. Most of those trashy news shows weren't really news; and they didn't focus on El Salvador or

Central America. They were packaged out of Miami, and hosted by a bunch of hot, pin-headed North American models of second of third Hispanic descent who couldn't even pronounce the Spanish language all that well. The focus was on Mexico, Colombia, Cuba, and Argentina, the larger countries. On the rare occasion that The Savior's Land was mentioned, the Miami shows made Salvadorian lives seem tougher than the patrons already knew them to be. Anahí's cumbia was nothing like that; it was a celebration of life. But Sandrita didn't care for celebrations, and thus disliked cumbia. Her utter love for the Miami shows were a symbol of her rebellion against the naive happiness her mother clung to for dear life despite all of the terrible shit that had taken place in their lives. To Sandrita there was something obscene about her mother's uncritical gladness. So *crónica roja* it was. The joint might still be called *Pupusas Anahí*, but Sandrita was in charge now.

"We got plenty in town," she would tell patrons, particularly the drunken ones, which, unlike her mother, she kicked out mercilessly, sometimes even drawing out the loaded shotgun (to Jimmy's outward dismay but deep erotic ecstasy).

Most patrons kept coming back. Perhaps it was the mural of her mother's face with the words *Doña Anahí, Forever Walking in Our Hearts* written in cursive red, Sandrita had Jimmy paint on the outside wall that got to customers, many of whom were touched by the old woman's story. Jimmy's mural wasn't accurate, nor was it completely proportional. In fact, the mural made sweet Anahí look like some sort of intergalactic Hollywood alien. And yet, there was an element of the old woman's liveliness, which Jimmy, who was not an artist, but was unable to say no to Sandrita's requests, had been able to capture. It was in the eyes, or in the eyelids to be more accurate. And it had made all the difference. It had been seven years since Big Toño's death and five since Anahí was confined to a wheelchair, but business was still going at *Pupusas Anahí*. It generated enough dough to feed everybody: Jimmy, Sandrita, Anahí, Petra, Gladys, and even the two guys who helped out at the kitchen.

"I know that *cipote* from somewhere," Sandrita repeated to herself, glancing at the petite man in white cowboy boots and the oversized leopard-print jacket on the screen above.

"Excuse me?" said Ana, who was a regular.

"Nothing," Sandrita said, "what do you want?"

"Eight cheese pupusas," said Ana, looking back at her four children. "And two large Coca-Colas."

"Alright. Eight cheese pupusas and two large Coca-Colas!" yelled Sandrita to Jimmy, who was in the kitchen.

Before calling on the next costumer, Sandrita made a mental note to look up the petite man in the leopard-print jacket after feeding the twins that evening at home. To think Sandrita had fought Jimmy on getting an internet connection at home because to her it was a waste of money.

"What for?" she'd asked.

"It's like you're nowhere without it nowadays," he'd whispered.

"You're at home, eating, shitting, or watching television," Sandrita had said, getting worked up. "I don't get it."

"You will see. It's like you're in two or three places at once. You're here in Santa Ana, El Salvador, but you're also wherever the website might be, and then you could be there as well, but also wherever it might take you, like a chat room, or a person's profile. It's multidimensional."

"What?"

"A profile inside of a chartroom inside of a website."

"Sounds like a description of hell."

"Just try it for a month, *corazón*. I'll pay for it."

"You want to waste your bread, *muje*—your deal. But I ain't payin' for it."

A few days in she'd seen what Jimmy was talking about, though she didn't say it. That was a year prior. Now she was all about the internet. The several places at once. The multiple territories. And it wasn't just another television, but a compliment to it. Sandrita had a method. Whatever caught her eye on the television at the restaurant during the day, she usually went home to look up online in the evening.

This time, however, it was more intense.

She knew that *cipote*.

Like every night Sandrita played with Petra and Gladys before dinner at home. Petra and Gladys were the only ones that got sweetness out of her. Then they all ate the *Sopa de Pata* Anahí had prepared, while a Mexican soap opera about a poor maid who falls in love with a blond hypocrite played on T.V. Then Jimmy went to play video-games with the twins as Sandrita helped her mother wash herself. After that Anahí rolled her wheelchair outside where she sucked on her two daily cigarettes, while Jimmy did the dishes and Sandrita put her daughters to bed. Then Jimmy went to his corner of the house and worked on a neighbors' decrepit stereo. Jimmy was good with electronics and fixed peoples' things for cash. Sandrita undressed in the bedroom, gazed at herself in the mirror, and went to shower. The water heater had broken again, but she didn't yell at Jimmy as she usually did. She was thinking about the *cipote* in the oversized leopard-print jacket. She jumped out of the shower. Jimmy was still in his corner, tweaking machines. Sandrita considered going to bed, it was after 11:00, but got online instead. The thing was nothing short of miraculous: a door of light, and on the other side, the infinite cosmos, Borges' Aleph.

One click and there he was, Delfín Quishpe! She read an entry about him. An Ecuadorian who had become a world musical sensation after posting a ridiculously original homemade music video. The memory washed over Sandrita like a large sea wave, not only soaking her up in old sensations, but dragging her into that cursed border-crossing trip, where so many had lost their lives. But not the petite Ecuadorian Quichua, whom she had kicked-off the group for claiming he was a Guatemalan Quiché. And she was right. The little man wasn't Guatemalan. It was so long ago… She'd thought he was Bolivian or Peruvian, but he wasn't, he was Ecuadorian. *Same shit*, she thought. *He bullshited so I kicked him out*, she whispered, as if trying to assure herself. It was like God himself had helped that fucking *indio*. And yet, it was like she had cursed the whole group with her harshness, her sinfulness. *But he did lie*, she repeated to herself. *He did lie*. Still, it felt wrong, so she left that thought alone and focused on the *cipote*. Not only had the little fucker made it to the United States. He'd become famous. *Holy shit*. Another wave surged all around Sandrita and dragged her out with the force of the sea. But it wasn't a memory. Or not just a memory. It was the memory of the impression, live and raw, of the trip where her husband had perished.

Yes, yes, that (Sandrita held her emotions in mutherfucking check), but it was also like viewing somebody's parallel destiny unfolding in a compressed way (through videos) right before her eyes from the vantage point of the trip (the past), or the woman she was then, and also concurrently, from her here and now, the woman she had become. Multiple territories. Multiple levels. She felt her future shifting. Sweat. Fear. Vertigo. She could have shrunk back. Pale Jimmy had walked into the room and had asked her to come to bed. But she didn't. Sandrita wasn't like that.

G o o g l e

> *Delfín Quishpe...*

Thousands of videos popped up.

First and foremost there was *the video*. That is, the viral epicenter of the thing: an electro cumbia song with hints of EDM. Sandrita clicked. There it was, something like a phenomenon: the same Ecuadorian *cipote,* wearing a white shirt and jeans, in his humble living room, his actual living room, watching television.

Suddenly, as he changes channels, he sees the 9/11 terrorist attacks.

Two planes crashing into the Twin Towers.

The towers collapse as he screams in an overly dramatic tone: *No puede seeerrr!!!*

He takes his hands to his head. Not exactly Marlon Brando kind of acting.

The beat picks up. It's a hellish mash of electro-cumbia and Andean flutes.

He gets up and dances and sings an impossibly naive and impossibly catchy love song, which narrates, a story of love, migration, and terrorism:

When I went to see you/ I couldn't believe my eyes
The Twin Towers were on Fire / Full of black smoke
And you were there/ Good God! Ayayay!

(The electro beat with Andean flute picks up)

From Ecuador, South America/ Delfín has come right in!

(Starts singing)

When I left to the Big Apple/ I planned to meet my sweetie
She lived on that island/ And worked at the Twin Towers
I got a phone call/ Goodbye my love, is all she said!
What a terrible thing to go through/ Terrorists had killed her

(Spoken)

Who did the attacks? God knows.
And why, oh why?/ Good God! It cannot be!
Lord help me!

(Singing)

Trapped between flames and clouds.../ Not money nor church saved her
And now you're left buried there/ Underneath the Towers' rubble
I wanted to hug you so/ Had no idea you'd die,
leaving a goodbye only tears will answer.
Good god, it cannot be...!

(Spoken)

This is an homage/ To all my countrymen
Who lost their lives / In the September 11 attacks
Seeking the American Dream/ Ayayay!
To all my homies in the U.S./ Listen up!
Be strong compadres!
All the amorrr.../Comes from Ecuadorrr....

Delfín has come right in!/ Adieu my guaguas!

It isn't clear to Sandrita whether the song tells of true events. It doesn't seem to be in jest, but there's jest in there. And drama, real drama. The attacks are real, Quishpe is real, the dance moves are real. He's suddenly wearing *the outfit*. The oversized leopard-print leather jacket is real, the white boots are real, and the white cowboy hat is real. The beats, terrible, infectious, unforgettable, ecstatic, and very nearly traumatizing: a daring pastiche of the most post-modern and most ancient motifs. Sandrita feels a renewing vertigo. She's tapping her foot. There's a close up of Delfín's face. The eyes, the nose, the mouth. Jesus! He could not be any more *indio*. Sandrita suddenly understands why she'd hated the little *cipote* so many years ago. It wasn't about the lies he'd said. Everybody knew he wasn't Guatemalan. Sandrita had hated Delfín Quishpe because Delfín Quishpe had reminded her of her father, who was Quiché: the same reason why her mother had taken an instant liking of the guy. At once Sandrita understood with ruthless clarity one of the key questions of her life: how exactly opposite she was from her mother. Sweet Anahí and Sandrita were exactly the same, but in opposing —or complimentary— ways.

Sandrita stopped the video.

Millions and millions of people had watched it. Many more millions of people than there were in The Savior's Land, many more millions than there are in Honduras, or in Ecuador, or in Bolivia. All those peripheral republics. It wasn't clear whether people hated the song, and were making fun of it, or whether they loved it and were celebrating it. It wasn't even clear whether the song was terrible—terrible music, terrible singing, terrible taste, terrible timing, terrible clothes, terrible images, terrible everything—or whether the song was great—great music, great singing, great taste, great timing, great clothes, great images, great everything. It didn't matter. It was both. The flip side of something can often be the closest thing to its opposite. Like her mother and herself. Like everyone else, Sandrita laughed. And she laughed so loud and so much from within that she cried and suddenly she was laughing and crying like she never had laughed and cried before, like a bitter-sweet juice that emerges from within, a bitter-sweet juice that had been dormant at the bottom of her being (those poor people in the Twin Towers, the poor *indio*, her poor father, and Big Toño, the twins' father, vanished for good from the earth). Sandrita bawled without concern. Not even at Big Toño's funeral had she bawled like that. She felt new and instantly saw the pure, joyful idiocy of the Ecuadorian *cipote*. The video was so fucking awful dear Jesus! She cracked up like crazy. Delfín Quishpe had linked up (weaved-in, really) a melodramatic Andean love story, such as you hear in the mountains, with the most important world event of the last hundred years. He had mixed in simple mountain melodies with electronic music. It was genius, genius! She hadn't laughed like that since she used to play with her father as a child. He used to tickle her so much. He used to tell her stories. Animal stories. Mountain stories. Such a strong presence that man was in her early years. And then nothing. What had exactly happened to him? She crossed a void of sorts. There had never been an explanation. As much as her mother, Anahí, was all sweetness and all love, she had never given Sandrita an explanation for the most important event in her life. The trite, *your father was indio and my family didn't accept him* didn't do it anymore. It never had. There was something else there. She'd always felt it. Funny. In all of her outlandish strength, Sandrita had never had the guts to ask her sweet mother about her father, the Guatemalan. She hadn't even had the guts to inquire within herself.

When the feelings subsided, and a kind of understanding settled in. She didn't know the ultimate meaning of the insight, or whether it would hold the next day. All she knew was that the *cipote* had, God knows how, caused her, the toughest, harshest, most callous bitch in the history of The Savior's Land, to cry. She'd been moved. And with a crappy-ass, homemade viral video with a phone number at the end. It was surreal. The internet itself was surreal.

She almost called the phone number right then and there, but it was the middle of the night in New York. Delfín Quishpe in New York! And a famous man! What would she tell him? *Sorry about kicking you out of the group in The Country of Great Depths seven years ago. Can you please send me an autographed poster?* Suddenly an idea occurred to her.

Google

Delfín Quishpe...El Salvador

Indeed. The little dweeb had played at the Cuscatlán Stadium in El Salvador.

And at the Azteca Stadium in Mexico City (where he'd opened for Vicente).

And in Barranquilla, Colombia (where he'd recorded a salsa version with Patuma Baby).

And in Caracas, Venezuela (where he'd played Hector Sánchez' birthday bash).

And in San Juan, Puerto Rico (where he'd done the popular jungle house remix).

And in Guayaquil, Ecuador (where he'd received the National Medal of Honor).

And in Lima, Peru (where he'd been named Ambassador of the Indigenous Federation).

And in Santiago, Chile (where Miguel Littín had shot a documentary about his life).

And in Buenos Aires, Argentina (where he'd partied with Diego Armando Maradona).

And in Curitiba, Brazil (where he'd raised cash for local favelas).

And in Ibiza, Spain (where he'd guest-deejayed with Steve Aoki).

Not to mention the United States. He'd played in Los Angeles, Chicago, and New York, where he'd done the Puerto Rican parade. And in Miami, where he'd done the *Calle 8 Festival.*

There were other places which excited Sandrita Iriarte's imagination to a feverish pitch. Delfín Quishpe had played at the Performance Art Festival in Cologne, Germany. He'd played Fuji-Rock in Niigata, Japan. And Dubai's Electronic Music Extravaganza. He'd also been asked to go play in North Korea alongside former NBA star Dennis Rodman, who'd seen the Ecuadorian in Dubai, but Delfín had turned down the offer, and lots of money, *due to irreconcilable differences in human rights matters.* Much had been made of that decision. Bloomberg News, Al Jazeera and RT (formerly Russia Today) had done segments on the matter. Due to all of that press, Tele-Amazonas out Ecuador, had spread the rumor that Delfín Quishpe was being considered for the Nobel Peace Prize. "If Rigoberta Menchú got it, I don't see any reason why our very own Delfín Quishpe shouldn't get it," one of the panelists had said. Another panelist (a blondish man of Bulgarian roots) had laughed and had in turn been denounced all over the internet as "a racist prick." Social media warriors had made such a fuss that Tele-Amazonas had had to declare the blondish man, and former media darling, *persona non-grata*. There was a video of the blondish man —whom Sandrita had found hunkylicious— begging for forgiveness on Photogram. Sandrita braved the strong pull to branch out into this parallel universe. You had to watch out. Online currents could drag you into different territories, just as a rip current can pull you away from shore and far into the sea. Such was the nature of the thing.

She wrote the blondish man's name down and stood her ground. There was the Miguel Littín documentary, *The Precipice of Glory*. Sandrita had entered the twilight zone and went on clicking. Somehow she paid for the documentary on a Chilean site. God knows what time it was. With Andean flute music playing in the background, and a sentimental narration, *The Precipice of Glory* showed Guamote, the little Andean town where Quishpe had been born. It showed images of cows and llamas pasturing, a dirt road, the hut he'd come up in, a street market, lots of corn fields... They interviewed Puramama, Mr. Ibáñez, Yaku, Byron, Antay, and a busty lady who eagerly claimed to have been Delfín's first. The documentary touched upon the death of Delfín's father in a melodramatic tone. Then they cut to footage of Delfín playing in concert with commentary by one Américo Tomassini, president of the *Los Delfinos* fan club in Chile. And then to clips of an interview Delfín had done with prominent interviewer Oprah Winfrey at the Dancing with the Stars Studios™. With Oprah, he'd talked about getting jumped in Panama, and back-stabbed in El Salvador, and about meeting a wise Garifuna in Honduras, followed by huntin', pinchin', and bustin' through Mexico before meeting a saintly wino and then high-tailin' through to the other side on a cloudy day he labeled "the luckiest, happiest, most blessed ever."

"I got a surprise for you," said Oprah, and smiled.

One of the Honduran boys who'd crossed the border with him, Pedro, walked into the studio. He was a man now, father of three, who worked at a vegetable canning factory in Watsonville, California.

Delfín smiled broadly.

"How about your brother?" he asked Pedro.

A dramatic pause, masterly cued in by the Oprah's production team, followed.

"Simón's in jail," said Pedro, and went on to tell the story of how his little brother had got in with the wrong crowd.

The Precipice of Glory cut to video of the New Jersey State prison followed by graphics of incarceration statistics broken down by ethnicity and gender.

Delfín's eyes filled with tears.

"I promise you, Pedro, I will visit Simón in jail, and I will do all I can to help him out," Delfín said, honestly but also in full celebrity mode. "Simón was a good kid," he added, allowing the tears to come out. "I'm going to get him the best lawyer possible. Everybody deserves a second chance."

"*Buen hombre*," said Oprah. "Let me ask you something. What was the first thing you thought about when you made it across the border?"

Delfín put his hand on his chin and breathed in.

"Legal or illegal, here I am!" he yelled out. "Yeehaw!"

Oprah's crowd went crazy. Delfín, who'd become an experienced crowd master, waited for the clapping to subside, which took a while.

"The thing is, dear Oprah," Delfín said, putting his hand over hers in a stately way. "Crossing the border is a kind baptism, a fire baptism, isn't that right, Pedrito?"

Pedro's eyes filled with tears, though he didn't cry.

"It changes you," Pedro said, nodding.

"Absolutely," repeated Delfín, hugging his old friend.

The American TV audience clapping resumed.

"*Gracias, gracias, yupaichani* everyone!" added the Ecuadorian, taking his hat off.

This cipote *could barely put a sentence together in Spanish back then*, thought Sandrita, who was having trouble keeping her head up. *Now he speaks English!* Indeed. Out of all the things she'd seen, the one thing that impacted Sandrita the most about the *cipote* was the fact that he spoke English. She didn't care how bad it was (nor could she tell). The man spoke English and that was a damned triumph. A warm feeling radiated inside her. She had no name for that strange emotion. She thought about Petra and

Gladys, her twins. It wasn't necessarily pride, but it was close to pride. They had crossed the river together. *The fire baptism.* She also knew.

By the time the Chilean documentary got to the "dark side of viral fame," Sandrita Iriarte had resolutely, like only she could, taken the Ecuadorian's side. He was no longer *that indio. Au contraire!* In Sandrita Iriarte's mind, Delfín Quishpe had turned into an *ángel de Dios*. Though she had no idea what *cultural appropriation* was, Sandrita yelled out *damn right!* when Delfín's manager blamed Hollywood in general, and Lady Gogo, in particular, for cultural appropriation (apparently, Lady Gogo had sampled *Twin Towers* without the Ecuadorian's permission).

"Why is that ho' ripping off Delfín's music?" yelled out Sandrita.

"You alright, *corazón*?" asked Jimmy, half-asleep from the bed.

"Don't mess with me," said Sandrita. "Go back to sleep."

He did.

Two minutes later, Sandrita approached Jimmy and shook him gently awake.

"Sorry *amor*," she said.

Jimmy couldn't believe his ears.

Sandrita wasn't one to apologize. Ever.

"Are you alright?" he asked.

"Yes," she said. "I have a question, baby."

"Are you alright?"

"Yes, yes," she repeated. "What's *ironic*?"

"Huh?"

"What does *ironic* mean?"

Jimmy tried to explain the meaning of *ironic* but the truth is he wasn't sure what it meant, particularly at four forty something in the morning.

"I should have fucking finished school," Sandrita said to herself. "I'm a goddamned ignorant. And then to Jimmy, kissing him on the forehead: "It's alright. You can explain tomorrow, baby. Go back to sleep now."

Sandrita's uncharacteristic sweetness made Jimmy think he was dreaming. He fell back sleep at once. She went back to the computer. By 5:20 a.m. she had assembled a complete and satisfactory narrative of the last seven years of Delfín Quishpe's life. She also had taken another view of her life. It was only then she got sleepy.

"One of the first viral videos," she heard a Spanish media expert saying as her consciousness transitioned into the realm of dreams. "Total accidental sophistication. Incredibly, this naïve Andean peasant turned globalization inside out, all with a homemade music video."

Cerote... Sandrita could hear herself thinking in her head, for while she could not decode the meaning of the Spanish critic's words, she could feel the contempt behind them, and said more violent things, but by now she was in the world of dreams, looking through another window, that of subconsciousness, and she was back on that boat, crossing over those wide, turbulent waters in Honduras, The Country of Great Depths, with Big Toño, *El Gallo* and the others, when she saw a gray bird crossing over the white sky above, and turned to *the little indio* because she knew he was there, but when she looked, *the little indio* was no longer there, and suddenly she realized that the boat was filling up with black water, and that the bird was a sign, not for *the little indio* who had swam to shore, like a true dolphin, and did not need any heavenly signs, and was now waving his tiny reddish hand, but a sign for them all, the fools, the idiots, who thought themselves so much better than *the little indio*, but by then it was too late, the turbulent waters had reached unmanageable heights while the *cipote* had been made Cultural Ambassador to the United Nations.

No Puede Seeerrr!!!

   Yukiko, Kaori, and Little Eimi have had a blast. They have danced to reggaetón. They have slid down the giant Fiesta Water Slide™. They have shopped at the Zara, Pink's, and Benetton boutiques. At the Tropicana Bar™ they have had margaritas, and daiquiris, and piña coladas. And at the Old Madrid Bar™ they have had tequila and Coronas, and pisco sour. They have gotten intensely tanned (except for Yukiko, who has gotten a full-body exfoliation, followed by a goat milk and raw honey skin treatment instead). They have been to the on-board casinos, and won cash, and then lost cash, and then won cash, and then misplaced the cash. They have laughed like mad and they have eaten *fish ceviche* (except Little Eimi, who has had jack fruit *ropa vieja*, where the jack fruit supplants the shredded pork). They have laughed at the Venezuelan waiter (so *kakkoii*!) who has compared *sashimi* to *ceviche*. And they have swapped Photogram accounts with him and the other and agreed to hang out on land. But who knows, for being in a cruise is like being in Disneyland or in Las Vegas. It's unreal. A feeling heightened by the bizarre islands they have seen, and by the cruise's Wi-Fi which comes and goes in the middle of the sea because nobody lives in the middle of the sea, obviously. It's so trippy, being left unplugged like that. Good thing Sergio Tortelli has come along (sans Giovanni) as planned, and after the goat milk and honey skin treatment, which has left her feeling soft, while Kaori and Little Eimi were getting toasted by the pool under the Caribbean sky, Yukiko has brought the Italian into the cabin. And now it's after 7:00 pm and the sun has begun to drop. They're all gathered by the stage, listening to Deejay Vacchi, spinning tunes they all know, and singing, and dancing the same, and it's like all these persons from all over the world belong to the same tribe, a grooving village on the Reggaetón Cruise which feels like a platform that reaches up to the blue sky with orange and pink tints, and no language is needed except the universal one of deejay music, which is in essence love —what else could it be?— and the beats and scratchings start to reach a pinnacle, boom, boom, boom, and just before the pinnacle there's a kind of plateau, and from the middle of the stage a second higher stage emerges, where the one and only global star dressed in his signature white pants, white boots, white hat, and oversized leopard-print jacket stands with open arms and an open smile, as confetti's shoots up from the sides, and subsequently falls, in colorful smithereens, and the beat starts morphing into the global hit everybody recognizes and loves and cheers to in absolute orgiastic glee, piercing straight through irony, right into adoration, as the only global Ecuadorian star articulates his signature *no puede seeerrr!!!*

Gigantic screens and club lights glow behind and above the star as the Fanta-colored sun sets in the fizzy ocean, and the original viral video plays, except two giant roses have been photo-shopped in place of the Twin Towers and bubbling hearts in place of the planes. And everyone gets that the message is one of love, and not one of mocking as some bitching critics have stated —for, again, what is music if not love!!!— and everybody gets it, and some weep and others cheer, aided, perhaps, not by mere endorphins.

And just then, out of the blue, the speakers blow up.

The star gets flung off the platform by the force of the blast.

He falls on his back—nuked.

Mayhem ensues.

Bunches of armed terrorists creep in from all sides. They're all wearing green. Yukiko and little Eimi, and hundreds other tourists, have unwillingly live-posted part of the attack. Kaori too, but in the sudden impact of the crazy crowd, she drops her phone, which gets trampled. As does her body when she reaches down. By the time she manages to get up, her sisters and Sergio Tortelli are no longer there.

"Everybody calm down!" says one of the terrorists, who has climbed up on the stage where Delfín was. "We're not going to kill you."

People freak out worse.

Shots get fired into the air.

Only then do most passengers stand still, though some rush with light steps in the edges like frightened little animals.

The green terrorists start dividing up the passengers into separate large groups and spreading them across the deck.

"You're to turn in your cell phones," announces an older man with a bullhorn.

Unlike the other terrorists —most of whom are college-freshmen young— the man with the bullhorn has a calm, subdued demeanor. His graying beard, the thick framed glasses, and most of all his diction, are those of a sophisticated college professor.

"We're separating you into groups. Again, we're not here to hurt you. If anything, you should come out of this situation improved. That is, you'll be aware of the horrible damage your senseless actions are causing our fragile world. So do comply, please, as we genuinely do not wish to use lethal force on anybody, but will... we will *smoke* anybody who steps out of line."

Suddenly, and very quietly, a drunken shirtless guy in Bermuda shorts emerges from the highest point of the Fiesta Water Slide™ located near the stern. Nobody notices him. But then he knocks down a half-empty coconut vodka bottle, which falls several feet, and shatters on the rails. The noise scares everyone, including the beardo professor-terrorist, who spots the guy at the top of the water slide and shoots him in the chest. The shirtless guy plummets down the water slide. People look aghast as he tortuously glides down the serpentine slide right into the swimming pool. Most have slid down there themselves earlier in the day.

The body floats in the water.

"He *had* been warned," the beardo professor states, caressing his chin, as if on the verge of a smile. "That was unnecessary. But we're not playing around folks, no, no, no. Do turn in all devices at once, *por favor.*"

Groups of green-clad terrorists move around the clusters of passengers with burlap sacks. One by one, including Yukiko, Little Eimi, and Sergio Tortelli, who are in one cluster, drop in their cellphones.

The same is done at different clusters throughout the platform.

"I dropped my cellphone on the floor," mutters Kaori, from another corner of the ship, as a freckled-faced girl, who seems hardly an adult, places a bag like a big-mouthed fish before her. "I promise."

The freckled girl smiles at Kaori's cute accent and walks on. The rough cloth of the bag rubs against Kaori's forearm, and the sensation of rough cloth against her forearm feels intensely rougher than it should. The feeling seeps into her core (and will cause her nightmares in the future).

Slowly all cellphones are collected into the burlap sacks. And then the sacks bursting with cellphones and their pictures, and their videos, and their open windows, and their songs, and their texts, and their passwords and their pixels (what indeed is a cellphone but a dead brain?) are bundled together at the base of the cruise's bridge. It is at this point that the true weight of the situation kicks in. Most passengers reach into their pockets for their cellphones even though they know well that the little devilish gadgets are no longer there. They're no longer tourists but captive seafarers.

Meanwhile, the body of the guy in Bermuda shorts has floated on to the center of the pool and has begun to ooze blood made pink by contact with the chorine water. One of the young terrorists whispers into the leader's ear; the beardo raises his head and then slightly lowers it. A couple of minutes later, the body is dragged out of the pool, wrapped in white bed sheets, and hastily flung overboard, where glistening Caribbean sharks welcome it with open fangs. The passengers sit down. Kaori keeps looking around for her sisters, and they for her. The leader steps away to the inside of the cruise. The mostly Filipino and Venezuelan crew, and the European command, including the Norwegian captain, one Thomas Hylland Eriksen, who looks shocked, or drugged out, are spoken to in the harshest terms. Captain Eriksen is brought to the deck and pushed onto the stage, where he's put on a chair brought in from the Ritmo Caliente Dance Floor™, and handcuffed. All of the deejays and reggaetón performers follow suit. The rest of the crew's kept inside. A small group takes over the navigation bridge. Then, it seems to dawn on all the green-clad terrorists at once. *Who's got the viral star? You? Me? Obliviots!* Three youths run behind the stage to retrieve Quishpe's body, except that Quishpe's body's nowhere to be found. A squadron is deployed by the beardo professor. To kill is the order.

A Landscape by Cézanne/ Random Acts of Senseless Violence

Yusuke Furukawa, their girlfriends' famous brother, was instantly recognizable. Tall, bleached-haired, and no older than seventeen. Garzón honked and waved with a smile. Yusuke grabbed his Givenchy bag and jumped into the yellow Camaro. They drove in near silence to the Trump Hotel in Sunny Isles. Warner Music Japan had gotten the presidential suite as a show of support for their A-lister. It was supposed to be a secret. Still, somehow, the media had found out about Yusuke's arrival. TV Trucks from all over Asia were camped out in the hotel's surroundings. Rumors circulated that the young star would address the media.

"I will absolutely not talk to them," said Yusuke, looking out the window of the presidential suite, which was on the highest floor. "I do not want any interaction with them. They're responsible for my last break up, and the one before that. I do not like them in the least. At the airport they asked me about my upcoming album. *Can you believe that?* It is not the right time at all. Please don't talk to them, guys. The Japanese press will certainly approach you. My fans might try to add you on Photogram."

The Ecuadorian and the Liberian shook their heads yes from the wide suede sofa where they had sat. Here was the star brother at last. Both Alvo and Mamadú had seen the guy's movies and media appearances, at first prompted by their girlfriends and then of their own accord. J-pop, it was a strange world for them. They couldn't think of anything to say. The seconds added up uncomfortably. Alvo thought about bringing up Yusuke's latest music video, but decided against it. All he could think about was how oddly formal the teen star was.

"You got, like, a British accent," mumbled Alvo.

"Australian. My English coach is Australian," said Yusuke, looking at his phone.

Mamadú stood up and moved around the presidential suite. It was quite a contrast to the Motel 6 where he and Alvo were staying: "We got to create a plan-ya," he said, pausing to look at a painting that could have been a Cézanne (Mont Sainte-Victoire seen from Bellevue?) though it could also have been a bad copy. He didn't really know about 19th century art. It was all possible at this juncture. "Perhaps we could use the media to our advantage," added Mamadú.

"I see, I see," said Yusuke, now looking at the glittering Atlantic in the distance.

"Whatever our plan is," said Alvo, pretending to fidget with his phone, which had gotten cracked in the Texas brawl that seemed ages ago. "We need to execute it, not just yap about it."

It got quiet again.

Mamadú continued to scrutinize the improbable Cézanne painting as if it could offer him some way out. For some odd reason, the painting reminded him of his first home near one of the arms of the Mesurado River, east of the People's Bridge. The one where things had been alright for a while before the war burst. Perhaps the painting reminded him of his old home in how different from it was; that is, in all that it wasn't. And yet, there was something there that was the same. He kept looking.

Alvo Garzón who'd gotten in an incredulous mode of thinking, took the extended silence as proof that they were wasting time. And even if they did something, he thought, they were at the mercy of the crazy green-clad terrorists.

"This country has gone to complete shit," he blurted out, putting his Court Lite sneakers on the marble coffee table. "The USA is gone, gone, gone, *a la mierda.* I can't even recognize it sometimes. I played tennis in Sweden for a while in high school. I should've stayed there."

Yusuke looked at Garzón with barely hidden contempt. The sudden display of annoyance was rude in his eyes. Not to mention the sneakers on the table.

"When Kaori comes out of this mess, I'm taking her down to South America," added Alvo Garzón as a joke, and in retaliation for the look, but neither of his companions laughed.

"Brazil?" asked Yusuke, trying to hide his disdain.

"Ecuador," said Garzón

"Oh," said Yusuke. "I thought you were from Saudi Arabia."

"No," said Alvo "I'm from Ecuador, center of the world. And I'm going to take Kaori there. Or to Chile, which is better off. Or to Colombia, which has better music."

"We got to get them out first, *amigo,*" said Mamadú.

"We're not getting them out, bro," said Alvo.

"Why not?" Asked Yusuke.

"We're not," said Alvo. "The terrorists are."

"Or they're not," said Mamadú.

"That's right, or they're not."

The suite's phone rang. Yusuke told security to let up whoever was calling.

"We need to go to the damned cops. That's what we need to do," said Mamadú, turning around from the improbable Cézanne.

He was suddenly aware of how utterly pointless scrutinizing an old European painting was. A probable fake one on top of that.

"What are *they* going to do?" asked Alvo.

"Might be able to guide us somehow," said Mamadú.

"Piss in the wind-menh," said Alvo.

"Eh?" let out Yusuke.

"He means it might *backfire* on us," said Mamadú.

"Backfire?" asked Yusuke.

"The cops might call immigration on us."

"You said you was a US citizen…" said Mamadú.

"Aha, but you're not," said Alvo.

"Let *me* worry about my legal status, asswipe," said Mamadú, stepping up.

"Wait, wait, wait," said Yusuke. "It is not a proper idea to go the police yet."

The teen's deep, well trained voice annoyed the Liberian, who felt it was fake.

"Or at all… think about it. The police, the Navy, and the CIA know what's up," said Alvo, noticing the others' shit-sandwich expression. "*What?* You planning on stealing a motorboat and pull a Soviet ambush on the Reggaetón Cruise? You don't look like Ethan Hunt or Jason Bourn to me, with all due respect, bru. Anyway, the news say they shut off the ship's GPS. We don't even know where they are. So why not drop the white knight baloney, and think of something useful instead."

"You callin' the kettle black, bro."

"How?"

"You the one who said to drive to Miami like some type of fuckin' *Fast and the Furious* ho."

"Well, you agreed, asscaptain," said Alvo, stepping up.

"Wait, wait, wait," interjected Yusuke, looking out the window. And then in his trained voice: "Perhaps… I could use the media to send some type of message."

"Exactly," said Mamadú.

"I thought you hated the media, bro," said Alvo.

"Not as much as you love the police," snapped back Mamadú.

Yusuke turned away towards the Atlantic again. The Liberian and the Ecuadorian struck him not only as sweaty but also as terribly rude. He'd introduced Kaori and Little Eimi to so many top notch men, and yet they'd come to America and gone for these two… outliers.

There was a knock at the door.

It was Fumihiro, Yusuke's manager who, upon entering, bowed. The Ecuadorian and the Liberian awkwardly bowed back. Much was said at lightning speed. Alvo, who prided himself at having mastered basic Japanese through Kaori, couldn't catch a word. The conversation started getting heated. Mamadú pointed at his cell phone.

"Excuse me," said Alvo.

Neither Yusuke nor Fumihiro turned around.

"Excuse me."

Nothing. It was as if they weren't there.

"Sumimasen!" yelled out the Ecuadorian in a heavy Spanish accent.

Yusuke turned round, deeply ticked off.

"Yes, my good friend?" he said coolly.

"Can we please turn on the T.V.?" asked the Liberian politely.

"Yes, yes, my good friends. Make yourselves at home," said the J-pop star, turning back to Fumihiro.

Alvo and Mamadú made their way to the suite's media lounge. It felt like the Oval Office or what they imagined the Oval Office would feel like. There even was picture of the 45th president up on the wall. Mamadú turned on the news.

Jen Cornell, a blond anchorwoman in a red dress, was reading The Coalition's announcement.

Due to our strategic actions in The Gulf of Mexico, The Coalition of the Eager foresees that the organization will be blamed for this morning's shooting of Sir Antoine Ruggeri in Sarajevo, Bosnia. In fact, ill-intended rumors are already being spread by the wicked corporate media. They are all lies. The Coalition of the Eager does not condone random acts of senseless violence, even if they are perpetrated against the enemies of the people. The Coalition of the Eager is not a terrorist organization. Our aim is not to terrorize, but to bring about change in specific areas related to the evil cruise industry in the Caribbean. As stated prior, these areas include: the cruise industry's destructive environmental policies, the cruise industry's destructive economic policies, the cruise industry's senseless stimulus of disastrous globalism, plus a fourth undisclosed goal. Needless to say, The Coalition of the Eager would like to see a change in paradigm everywhere on this sick earth, but for now we are focusing on the Reggaetón Cruise. Our demands have already been stated. We shall not free any passengers unless our demands are fully met. More information about that matter shall soon be communicated. For now, let us be clear once again about the unfounded accusations being raised against us: The Coalition of the Eager had nothing to do with Sir Antoine Ruggeri's shooting in Sarajevo earlier today. To put it another way, we understand that Sir Antoine Ruggeri headed an evil, murderous organization (the IMF) but we do not take credit for his shooting. Somebody else did it, which comes as no surprise. Scores of people around the world are sick and tired of the ongoing abuse of the bloodless globalists. And a growing number of those dissidents are not only becoming organized, but have started to take action. Perhaps we have inspired them, but that remains in the realm of conjecture. One thing's for certain: the liberal establishment better get accustomed to radical actions unless radical change is brought about, effective immediately. This is the new world.

Together in harmony, strength, and eternal good will,

Blood and Soil America – Earth Rescue Brigade, USA – Nonaligned Federation for Neoliberal Termination – Fourth Group Classified.

Pluribus est Unum: The Coalition of the Eager

Somewhere in the contiguous core of the sacred United States of America

"I need a drink, *compadre*."

"Good idea, bro."

Though she held it back in her voice, tension could be perceived on Jen Cornell's brow as she introduced a foreign correspondent.

"And now, Tim Collins, live from Sarajevo."

"As most of our viewers know by now," said Collins, *"security camera images of the shooting of the International Monetary Fund's president, Sir Antoine Ruggeri, near the Bosnia Convention Center, were made viral today, shocking the world, particularly due to the emergency developing in the Gulf of Mexico where a cruise ship was seized by a multi-cell North American organization. There were subsequent unconfirmed reports that Sir Antoine Ruggeri had been pronounced death on arrival at the Sarajevo National Hospital in the center of the city. Due to security measures around the hospital, it has not been possible to confirm the reports. However, a succinct memo from the Belgium Embassy, which has been sanctioned by officials in Brussels, confirms that indeed Sir Antoine Ruggeri, president of*

the IMF, or late president of the IMF, excuse me, was declared deceased upon arrival at the Sarajevo National Hospital, as the early unconfirmed reports had stated. It has been officially confirmed now, Jen, and Fox News viewers back in the United States. And well, first of all, we want to send our condolences to Mr. Ruggeri's family. That's all I have for now, Jen, unless you have any questions."

"Yes, Tim, as you said, first of all, our condolences go out to Mr. Ruggeri's family. I understand Mr. Ruggeri, who was born in Belgium, was a father of three children, two of whom go to college in the United States."

"Yes, that's correct Jen."

"My question for you is, what will happen to the International Monetary Fund's convention, which had controversial market integration negotiations taking place, in particular between Russia and the West. Will the convention go on?"

"No Jen, the convention between economic and political leaders of North America, Europe and Russia has been called off."

"Is that official?"

"Yes, the IMF issued a press release minutes ago. Also, I had a chance to personally speak to Petros Demetriou, the agency's press secretary, who confirmed the cancelation."

"Will the economic and political leaders be heading back home right away?"

"Yes, some have already left, I'm aware."

"What about the alleged shooter? Has he been apprehended?"

"Well, as you know, the alleged shooter appears in the security video that has now been watched over a thousand million times, making it the most viral video of all time. And it's a rather clear image. Security cameras have come a long way. As you know they can now be combined with facial recognition technology devised in England."

"It has been reported here that the alleged shooter has been apprehended by Bosnian authorities."

"What I can tell you is that there are credible reports that the alleged shooter has been detained, not by Bosnian authorities but by CIA operatives, who are now negotiating jurisdiction with the Bosnian and European Union authorities. However, all of that remains, as of yet, unconfirmed."

"We will certainly keep following this story closely, Tim. Thank you Tim Collins from Sarajevo. Please take care of yourself. It's a tremendously volatile situation."

"Thank you, Jen. Regards to all back home."

"Thank you, Tim. That was Tim Collins, reporting live from outside of the Sarajevo National Hospital, in Sarajevo, Bosnia. And now, after the pause, we're going to talk to our panel of experts here in Chicago who will try to make sense of an incredibly complex set of events."

Alvo Garzón turned the television off.

"Let's go fucking grab a drink, bro," he said. "This shit's too over the top."

Mamadú got up and stretched his arms over his head.

"You're right," repeated the Liberian, taking one last glance at the improbable Cézanne painting. "Let's go."

"We're heading to the hotel bar," said Alvo out loud, as they walked out to the main room, but neither Yusuke nor Fumihiro were there anymore.

There was a well-dressed older lady with short hair in the room instead. She bowed. The Ecuadorian and the Liberian bowed back. With the aid of Google Translate she let them know that Yusuke had gone to do a press conference with Fumihiro and the Japanese Ambassador to the United States.

"I wish we'd met you under different circumstances," said Mamadú.

"So do I," said Mrs. Furukawa through Google translate and a sad expression in her face.

Alvo, who wished he'd been better dressed to meet her, awkwardly asked if she wanted to come to the lounge with them. She said her husband was soon arriving at Miami International. They offered to take her. She said Fumihiro was already at the porte-cochère. Alvo and Mamadú bowed. Just then somebody knocked at the door. It was a Miami Police Department detective, one Ramírez. The cop had lots of acne on his face. For some reason, the Trump Hotel suddenly felt like the set of a bad detective flick or the center of an old, neglected nightmare.

"You cannot talk to anybody about what I'm about to tell you," were the first words out of the detective's unusually large trap.

No G.P.S. in the Ancient Sea

Back at the Reggaetón Cruise, the terrorists were tense. Night had fallen and Delfín Quishpe was nowhere to be found. They proceeded with their agenda even as they looked for the viral star.

"You will be asked some questions," said the beardo professor from the bullhorn. "Do stick to the truth. If you want to get home safely, do stick to the truth."

Lots of green-clad youths walked around the clusters, tablets in hand, asking a series of questions. The questions ranged from the numerical (age, weight, height), to the biographical (nationality, marital status, level of education), to the bizarre (number of sexual partners, least favorite cuisine), to the philosophical (belief in God, the meaning of life, favorite book), to the imminently political (takes on abortion, political party), to the anodyne (favorite clothing brand, preferred mode of transportation, number of lifetime visits to Disney World). Then each passenger was asked to describe a recurring or recent nightmare that they might have had. The interviews took hours. And shifted the mood of the Reggaetón Cruise even more than the earlier slaying of a man. The nature of the fear changed. The outward fear became internal fear after the interviews. A projection was set up then (the hijackers had brought in their own devices). A woman took over the microphone. She was well spoken and stern. Her eyes were piercing and blue. There wasn't any make up on her face. She must have been in her mid-30's. She explained that hundreds of thousands people all over the world would be watching the same images online. "What you're about to see took an enormous effort to produce. And we advise you to pay attention. Perhaps some of you will be forever changed. We see you folks as potential allies." Even though her words were conciliatory, there was an implicit threat in her tone. Then came the material. It wasn't so much in the professionally-produced videos, which were earnest in their desire to show the various evils of the globalized world (and the need for radical action). It wasn't there. Yes, the videos showed cows being slaughtered in bloody conditions, cruises dumping trash into the oceans, conclusive statistics of illegal hiring practices, tax evasion schemes, reverse racism, outright racism, misogyny, ageism, and theft. Yes, it was all there. And well-produced too. The videos contained threats to both the general citizenry and to those in power. They contained exhortations to radicalism, and examples of radical activities — organizing secret guerrilla cells that focus on pointed activities such as blowing up mail boxes, for instance— which were the opposite of the current self-deceiving, merely conscience-appeasing actions of most, like throwing plastic bottles into recycling bins or voting in democratic elections (democracy being not a sham, or something that needs improvement, but a real evil, something that needs obliteration, the videos said). This hijacking *moment* was *actual action, a good deed*, the video stressed over and over.

People reacted differently. Some in awe, others in disgust. Little Eime was one of the people who reacted in awe. Unfortunately for The Coalition, most of the Reggaetón Cruise passengers weren't inclined to follow along, much less be moved by the information, except perhaps a widespread sense of horror at the bloody cows in the first part. The video ended. Eventually the beardo with the bullhorn ran out of things to yap about, and all the lights were turned off. It was exactly then that the true darkness began to expand. The mysteries of sky and sea seemed to turn up. The ship's Geographic Placement System had been turned off. All cell phones had been taken away and nobody knew where they were or what time it was. The alcohol, or whatever stimulants passengers had been on, began to wear off. The previous music and entertainment felt like a mirage lost in the inscrutable immensity of the sea. Many got seasick at this point. But no one dared complain. The deep silent blackness that followed, so steady, so beyond radicalism, and meaning, like the soil, and the sky, was the real impact. Minutes upon minutes transpired. Both mad anti-globalization terrorists and decadent global tourists floated on, rocked slowly in the minutes, increasingly feeling not so much the pulsations, which did beat, but the gravity of that complex self-contained beast as it allowed itself to be felt (to be seen through, as if transparent in the core) in its unimaginable depth of time and power—the ancient sea. And there, it carried the Reggaetón Cruise, with its rosy mirth and the young idealists, with their verdant terrorism, it carried them all lightly, the sea, like the wind carrying a feather, which it could, if it wanted to, swallow down, that tininess. The sea, a pre-Biblical monster; that was the feeling under the ship after the minutes and hours of absolute darkness accumulated. The sea, the thing that rocked it; the sea, the thing that carried it above. Captives and captors were simply waiting as yet another world emergency (political, economic) unfolded, as the paradigm imploded, whatever that meant. Silliness. That's what the paradigm was like on the darkly rocking ship. And they all felt it. And that was the actual moment. Because, as much as the ancient sea, the mother sea, was below: the sky was above. With its avenues and undying shards of glass and hints of breath and a movement and violence so remote and so geometric it inspired ontological unsteadiness. And some had fallen asleep, headed on into dreamland, looking up above, as if it were below, an inscrutable abyss of inscrutable depth—the night sky. Not radical or political, but material, elemental: full-on nighttime in the middle of god-knows-where, all the hearts, green and red, floating on, like ancient mariners.

The Spitting Trucker

Jimmy's worry was justified. The next day after finding out who, indeed, that *cipote* was, Sandrita Iriarte did not wake up in time to go to work for the first time in six years. The last time she'd been absent had been because she'd just given birth to the twins. Jimmy didn't wake her up. He turned on the computer and looked at her browsing history. Nothing stood out, except the dismal Ecuadorian viral star about whom, of course, Jimmy had heard because of the *No puede seeerrr!!!* thingy. So it hadn't been a dream: Sandrita had really awoken him at the crack of dawn to ask him what the meaning of *irony* was. And she'd been extremely sweet to him. There was definitely something wrong with Sandrita. Jimmy turned off the computer and headed to Anahí's room, but the old woman was already up, making breakfast for Petra and Gladys. He told Anahí that Sandrita wouldn't be coming into the *pupusería*. She must be sick, Anahí thought.

"Don't worry, I'll take care of her," she said.

Anahí's words made Jimmy feel better. After Petra and Gladys were done with breakfast, Jimmy took them to school, and headed over to the *pupusería*. It felt strange being there without Sandrita. As the day unfolded, Jimmy felt tempted to turn off the televisions, or to at least change the channels, but didn't dare. Sandrita wouldn't have approved. He kept the same channels on. Though there wasn't much time to watch television before lunch, he paid attention to the *Crónica Roja* shows out of Miami in the afternoon.

"Nothing but bad news about fucking terrorists and international killings, and shit that has nothing to do with El Salvador," he told the dishwasher, a young guy nicknamed *Pollo*. "I don't know why Sandrita is so into this crap. Must be because she really wanted live in Gringo-land when she was young. It's like a failed dream of hers."

And then a close-up of the very face of the indigenous viral star Sandrita had been looking up all night popped up on the screen above. Apparently the little dude was at the center —nay, the epicenter— of an international terrorist attack in the Caribbean.

Ecuadorian Singer in Hijacked Reggaetón Cruise Has Contacted Authorities—read the vermilion caption at the bottom of the screen.

"These fucking terrorists are insane in the brain," Jimmy told *Pollo*.

"The whole situation's so wacky," said *Pollo*.

"The little dude hiding somewhere in the ship!"

And that's how the rest of the evening transpired: *pupusa* orders taken (in a nicer way), followed by Miami-generated news, followed by commentary between Jimmy and *Pollo*. At some point, Jimmy brought his cellphone into the bathroom and looked up the full meaning of *irony* from the toilet. He wanted to tell Sandrita all about it when he got home that night. Perhaps that'd make her feel better. But lots of dishwashing and mopping came first.

Back at the lavender house Sandrita had talked to her mom for the entirety of the day.

"After we crossed the river," she had said in a kind of trance, as her mom made lunch for the girls, "I got *El Gallo* to kick the little *indio* from our group because he was pretending to be Guatemalan. *Did you know he wasn't Guatemalan?*"

"Of course I knew, *bebé*. But he reminded me of your father because he was a native, and so I went along with the idea that he was Guatemalan. It wasn't such a big deal, was it?"

"I got him kicked out of the group."

"He was a good boy, if I remember correctly," Anahí said. "He worked with me for a few days. It's been so long, *mija*."

Sandrita sharpened her eyes.

"*El Gallo* pulled a gun on him. We left him right by the riverbank, on the Honduran side of the Lempa. We took his cash and split it between all of us, like damned hyenas. I thought the little *indio* was a spy or a creep, that's what I was thinking, I swear to God."

"What is past is past, *bebé*. Don't beat yourself over it. He was a resourceful guy. Most *indios* are. So was your father. I'm sure he made it okay, don't worry so much sweetie."

"I know exactly what happened to him, momma. He made it okay, that for sure, but *we* didn't. We didn't make it okay, as you well know."

"Don't, sweetie. No need to go through that again."

"I need to tell you momma. I've never told you the whole story."

"Let me make you some coffee, *bebé*," said Anahí and quickly rode her wheelchair to the stove.

"I've been a bad daughter, momma. I didn't even tell you how Big Toño died, and it's been seven years," said Sandrita, eyes wide open. "Look at all you do for us. *I* should be the one making *you* coffee."

"Ah, don't be silly, *bebé*," said Anahí. "I might be on a wheelchair, but I'm not an invalid. I'll throw a little *ron criollo* in there, so you can relax, okay?"

"Thank you, momma," said Sandrita standing up. "So after we took that guy's money and left him to his luck in the Honduran bush, by that turbulent Río Lempa, full of fucking river creatures and devils and ghosts, without a penny, nor food, we got into an old red truck *El Gallo* had arranged to take us through Honduras all the way to Guatemala. We were concerned for our safety because at that time there was news of Salvie migrants being jacked or kidnapped in Honduras, but actually the trip through The Country of Great Depths was blah, except for heavy rains that pushed landslides and flooded roads, to the point where we had to wait a long time for one of the roads to get cleared, and were scared because there were some jungle thugs (the kind we used to call *cusucos*) they might have been good people but they looked like *cusucos* to us, and we were keeping an eye on them as we waited for the waters to clear off the road, and I told *El Gallo* to make sure the *cusucos* saw we were armed, and *El Gallo*, who was such a sweet guy underneath, actually did as I said, and started playing with his little *cuete* and then the *cusucos* actually came up to us, and asked us where we were from, and said we were from The Country of Great Depths, and they said, no way, you're fucking *Guanacos*, heading up North, that's what you look like, you fucking *crispetas*, and you better stop hyping your *pewpewpew* like you own these hills, because we got real *cuernos* ⌐╥╥ , and you don't want us wildin' on your ass, do you? So we stopped making eye contact with them. They were keeping an eye on us, and ugly mocking us, but we played dumb. In time, the water came down, and everyone got through, including the *cusucos*. But that shit soured things between our men, who hated being clowned, and particularly not being able to talk back. The geezer who was driving us, a former commercial truck driver named, I forgot what his name was, but he was a former trailer dude, and he was pretty up there, one of those mens you can tell have been through a lot, thievery, jail, murder, alcohol, all kinds of shit, you could see it in him, anyway, he told *El Gallo* in a pretty bad way that he was out of his mind to take his *cuete* out like that, as if he were a fucking cowboy or something, and *El Gallo*, who was pretty sour after the *cusucos* had clowned, told the former truck driver not to talk to him like that, that he was no fucking kid, and that he was trying to protect his old ass too, but the former truck driver kept at it as he drove, and I don't know what the hell was wrong with his teeth but he kept spitting out the window as he drove, he'd been doing it all through the Honduran roads actually, but as he argued with *El Gallo*, he started spitting more often, and it was gross, because I was sitting by the window right behind him, and more than a few times, fucking spit hit me in the face, not to mention wet ash from his cigarette, that I thought could stand, and I got tired and tried to close the window though it was still rainy, the heat was unbearable, so I told the driver *quit fucking spitting baby, you're giving me a facial*, like that, and as he was already pretty dizzy from his argument with *El Gallo* (that's how heat is, a fucking monster that feeds off itself) I should know, well, this crazy old timer driver, who wasn't that bad otherwise, he had a lot of crazy jokes, all ass and titties stuff but super funny, except when he was dizzy and his jokes became insults, well, he said *shut the fuck up*, like that, that he spit as much as he liked because this was his truck, and that we weren't paying him as much as the trip was worth, anyhow, *so if you want*, he said, *jump right out baby, I ain't even slowing down for your ass*. You're probably asking yourself where Big Toño was in all of this, because, though he could be an asshole to me, and he was, a lot, he never ever allowed any other fucking *hombres* to be assholes to me, that is the honest to God truth, and it's one of the reasons why I loved him, growing up without a dad, you know, so many fucking assholes try to get wise. Anyway, it's not like Big Toño, my sweet José Antonio Torres Cepeda Jr., q. e. p. d., was just quiet up to that point: he was stunned. And I'll tell you why. I'm tired of holding this shit in momma. Like I told you, we kicked off that fucking lying *indio*, who turned out to be smarter than all of us put together, and he might even be in the news right now, but I'll tell you about him later. Well, for some reason Big Toño was against us kicking the Ecuadorian *indio* out of the group, and tried his best to get him to stay, but we outvoted him. I'd always been better at convincing people than he. And that got him cunty, but the worst for Big Toño was that we took the *indio*'s dough, and even his rainbow bag, which Big Toño flung out the window daring anyone to talk back. José Antonio was a tough man, you know. And in some ways he was the most straight-up *hombre* I ever met. Though in other ways he was a complete crook. Anyway, he was mad about that whole situation and so later in the trip, when we were splitting the little *indio's* bread, Big Toño said, he didn't want any of it, and I told him he was crazy, that we needed the dough, and so we started throwing down, by then it was already late, and the former trucker stopped in a cave he knew from his trucking days, and shared stories of how he used to bring prostitutes there, and how one busty one turned out to have a hanging nozzle between the legs and he'd already paid and didn't want his money to go to waste, it sounds bad now, but they were really funny stories actually, anyhow, we were supposed to sleep there, but Big Toño and I kept throwing down, so we walked off from the group to let them rest, and at some point Big Toño pushed me pretty hard, and I slapped him on the ear, and he was going to whack me, and so I told him what I'd been waiting to tell him in the US, go ahead whack me, you fucking *hijodeputa* fag, you're going to hit a pregnant woman, and that's how he found out I was with baby, not in Uncle Sam's, like I'd planned, but that's the thing about plans… they seldom come true, I should know, so Big Toño found out in the darkness, like that, though he didn't know it was twins of course, nor girls (*I* didn't even know that, though I had a feeling), he thought it would be a boy, he was certain, he didn't say, but I could see it in his face the next day. He didn't hit me of course. He sat down on a big rock and asked me if I was sure. I said *for sure baby* and the argument ended right there, as if someone had thrown water on it, and I tried to see his beautiful manly face in the dark, I think I managed, my feeling is he was crying. We stayed a while like that until we heard some animals or monsters or devils or ghosts in the bush and headed back to the cave, actually

laughing, that's how we were, swinging moods all the time, and then we laid
down and slept, or tried to sleep, and in the middle of the night I felt that he
hugged me with his thick hairy arms, momma, I've never felt such thick
manly arms around me before I swear. The next day he didn't say a word.
That's what I'm saying. He was stunned. He was pretty nice, sometimes,
you know that momma, but always without words. He was sweet and frail
with body language and looks. It was funny how finicky he got. So when the
thing between the former truck driver and *El Gallo* happened, Big Toño
didn't get into it, he didn't even tell me off for asking *El Gallo* to show his
cuete to the jungle thugs, though I knew he didn't approve, I knew it all from
his body language, I knew that man like the palm of my hand, momma. But
when the former truck driver told me to shut up, after I told him to stop
fucking spitting, Big Toño snapped, and you know how he was when he
snapped, sorry I don't mean to laugh, but all hell broke loose, the red truck
was a nightmare, and it was raining and thundering outside, and this old
timer kept spitting, and I don't know if it was the rain or the spit that was
hitting me on the face, or my warm pregnant blood, but I wasn't going to put
my window down so he could spit away, and I couldn't help myself,
somehow got to a place where I could aim at the dude's face and, sweet
momma, I spit right in his left eye. Self-control has never been my strength,
well, you should have seen that poor *señor*, we almost crashed, and that
should have been an omen, life is full of God's omens, momma, but we're
so dumb we pay no attention to them, it's our damned faults. He slammed
on the brakes and the red truck almost fell off a cliff before coming to stop."

"Now all of you *cerotes* are going to get the hell out of my fucking
truck," he said.

Everyone tried pleading with him but he wasn't having it. He was an old
timer. He'd seen a lot. And so I looked at *El Gallo*, my dear cousin, we used
to call him *Pepito* when he was young remember how mad he used to get,
fucking *colorado* like crazy, and I have always communicated like that with
him, and so *El Gallo* knew exactly what I was asking him to do. He put the
little *cuete* right on the former trucker's temple. And so the dude had no
choice. *El Gallo* tried to be pretty nice about it though. He was such a sweet,
gentle guy inside. Most rough men are. I knew him like a brother. He told
the former trucker, it really sucks it has to come down to this *caballero*, or

some high-sounding word like that. *Just get us to the Guatemalan border and we're cool. We can split after that. The one thing we're not going to allow is for you to leave us in the middle of a fucking mountain in the rain. We hope you understand that caballero.* I swear he sounded just like Pablo Escobar. It was the gun, obviously, but the former trucker pretended to be convinced by *El Gallo's* deference, men are like that, they need to be talked to like that, sideways, so their pride don't get hurt, and *El Gallo* knew all about that, he grew up with us women, he was sensitive like that. Big Toño on the other hand, didn't have a way with words, he was a man's man, all action, no explanations. And I knew him so well, I knew he was about to obliterate the former truck driver with his fists, part of me wanted him to (I mean, what do I got a man for?) but I knew this wasn't the right time, so I held Big Toño's hand sweetly, like a little boy, hoping he wouldn't snap, and I pulled it off. We got back in the red truck…but you're not going to believe this ma, ten minutes later, as we were coming down a steep hill, the fucking asshole driver geezer put the window down and started spitting again! *Do not fucking spit—please, please, please,* I said. We were really close to Guatemala. The former trucker tried to talk back to me, you could tell he hated me, but as he opened his trap some white and pink shit flew out of it and he slammed on the breaks again. *Mis dientes! Mis dientes!* he yelled out. And believe it or not we all got out and tried to find the mother fuckin' trucker's fake ass *dientes* in the rain. That's why he'd been spitting so much! It'd been some fake *dientes* that didn't fit well, or whatever the heck. I'm such a bitch for laughing. The whole shit was so outlandishly tragic. The thing is we couldn't find his fucking fake *dientes*. We tried begging, all of us soaked, but the old trucker said something like *you can kill me right now cipotes, but I'm not going to go anywhere without my grill, seriously. It was my wife's Christmas present, you have no idea how much she saved for them, she's a seamstress, I can't let her down like that.* And that's when Big Toño snapped. *Your choice,* he said drily, and then he swung at him, and he hit him so hard that it was good the old trucker didn't have any fangs in the gummers because if he did he would have lost them again. *I hope you find your fucking pearls,* Big Toño said, *I can't have a pregnant wife getting wet and spat on like that. We won't steal your ride, we know you use it for work, you'll get it back, I promise, but we got to go.* The old trucker didn't try to stop us all at. He just looked at us with hatred and that hatred might have washed all over us, like an acid, bitter rain, because those things exist momma, good omens, bad omens, *mal de ojo,* hexes, all of that, when somebody looks at you like that, with real actual fucking hate, *mierda*, evil gets rubbed off on you, and in this case we got soaked in geezer hate."

"And then you crashed," stated Anahí, matter of fact.

"Yes, and then we crashed. It was a steep hill, and it kept raining, and there must have been something wrong with the breaks, or maybe the former trucker did something to the breaks before getting off, I don't know, the thing is we crashed, there was another car involved, and then we fell into this deep hole, I guess that's why they call it Honduras."

"I'm sure it was a trick with the brakes. These old trucks are full of *mañas,* sweetie. That's what I think life is sometimes, one big fucking incomprehensible *maña* we all have to contend with."

"Yes, I'm sure it was the breaks, momma. It wasn't the tires because the thing had good traction, you could feel it on the pavement. It was the brakes. The geezer knew how to handle them, and he wasn't there anymore and, well, that was that. We crashed and now Petra and Gladys are growing up without *papá* to take care of them."

"Who was driving, sweetie?"

"It doesn't matter who the heck was driving, momma. We were in it together. What matters is that the twins have no dad, and that *El Gallo* is gone too, and he never got to see his dreams to join the American army come true. In a way, the whole thing was my fucking fault. And the whole story is so indecent, so precarious, it would be funny if it weren't so horrific," Sandrita said, now crying. "That's why I never told you, momma: besides a tragedy, it's a deep fucking embarrassment."

"No *bebé*, come here, sweetie," said Anahí hugging her daughter from the wheelchair. "There's no need to feel embarrassed. You got nothing to be embarrassed about."

"I'm not embarrassed, momma," Sandrita said, sharply. "That's what I thought, but now as I tell you, I can see I was wrong. This situation is not *my* embarrassment to deal with."

"Whose embarrassment is it?"

"It's God's embarrassment."

REGGAETÓN CRUISE | 135

"Don't say that, *bebé*."

"No, seriously, obviously."

"Why are you thinking about all these things now?"

"Momma," said Sandrita, exhaling. "I have something to ask you that has nothing to do with this. Well, in a way, it has everything to do with it, *mamita*."

"*Sí, mi amor.*"

"My father didn't just leave like you always said he did, did he?"

Anahí got suddenly fidgety as she always did. Then she physically tried to roll out of the kitchen, but Sandrita cornered her. It wasn't hard. Her mother was an old woman in a wheelchair. She'd been an old woman in a wheelchair for years. And yet, it was the first time Sandrita, the big muscular woman, who cursed at big muscular men, had used her power with her crumbly, sugar cookie of a mother. Sandrita would simply stand there in the kitchen for as long as it took. All the niceties in the world wouldn't melt Sandrita's resolve now because she'd come to feel that living life ducking behind a heap of sugar wasn't any better than charging forth all the time, choking on your own bile. It was the same thing. Sandrita needed some of Anahí's sugar as much as Anahí needed some of Sandrita's powerful ire.

.

A Presidential Message, Muffled

Alvo Garzón and Mamadú Anderson ordered a couple of Sapporos at the Trump Hotel's bar. There was so much to talk about —Yusuke, the presidential suite, Mrs. Furukawa, detective Ramírez, The Coalition, and now the killing of the IMF president— that they let themselves be on the stools in silence, simply sipping cold ones in honor of the Furukawa sisters instead. What good would talking do? They just wanted it all over with. Not only the Reggaetón Cruise thing, but the great American nightmare that had emerged around them. They did not want any of it. Alvo Garzón had come from a country that couldn't hold a president for any reasonable length of time before the citizenry flooded the streets like a new bride who's realized she's chosen the wrong groom and wants out. Seven presidents in ten years…What a beauty! Mamadú had fled a civil war that had killed maybe 200,000 thousand people in about the same amount of amount of time. And now King George, former FIFA World Player of the year, who'd helped in the peace efforts, was in charge. But not only that. Two hundred goals in about 15 years was indeed terrific! It wasn't lack of faith, but Mamadú wasn't waiting around in L-I-B. Neither was Alvo in *la mitad del mundo*. They simply wanted to keep making it in The Core. They wanted to keep earning money because it was easy here, and paying taxes, and saving, and spending, and eating, and traveling. They were in the game. But now they'd been dragged into the center of some global nightmare, which was of a political nature in appearance but of a neurotic thrust in reality.

And so they drank one, two, three icy Sapporos, looking at the Dolphins charging against the Patriots and then at the Patriots charging against the Dolphins and then at the Dolphins charging back against the Patriots and then at the Patriots charging against the Dolphins, and not getting it, until the thing was cut off by the Commander in Chief himself, though the bleached-haired bartender muted the volume as soon as the president began to yap. The Liberian and the Ecuadorian looked at each other in disbelief. And yet, they made no attempt at getting the bleached-haired bartender to unmute the address. They let the hip-hop beats take up the air and stared at the gesticulating leader instead. The captions were too small to be deciphered.

"Must have got in touch with the terrorists," said Alvo at last.

"How do you know?" asked Mamadú.

"Body language, bro."

"Aha," said Mamadú. And after a long sip: "Fuckers already killed a tourist."

"How do you know?" asked Alvo, annoyed.

"Reports," said Mamadú, looking at his phone on the stool and feeling deep hatred for it.

"Has to be bull, brother, nobody knows. Don't believe the media."

"You're something else, *amigo*," said Mamadú, letting out his long acidic giggles.

"You know what I really want to do next?" said Alvo.

"Go crash some balls?"

"Go in the nearest church and pray for like two hours straight. Either that or, like…"

"Drink some more, *amigo*," said Mamadú, picking up the giggle. "The net effect is the same."

As soon as the Message to the Nation ended, the bleached-haired bartender shut off the music and turned the football game back on. Alvo and Mamadú watched the green and blue men in helmets for a while until they couldn't watch anymore and walked out into the parking lot. It was extremely bright outside. A gang of Japanese bloggers, podcasters, and new media types rushed in towards them. *How, when, why* and a bunch of other stuff that was hard to make out. As Yusuke had requested, Alvo and Mamadú tried not to answer, but the swarm of questioners was adamant, so much so that one of them jabbed Mamadú on the side with a microphone.

"Shit-menh!" yelled out the Liberian, and instinctually shoved the reporter away like a small rag doll.

Mamadú was polite, but the minute his anger was tapped, it came in whooshing over considerations. Blood came rushing too, on the pavement, where the Japanese reporter's head had bounced. All the cameras turned towards the hurled body. Taking advantage of the confusion, Alvo yanked the Liberian and pointed to the yellow Camaro. Both men bolted, not necessarily soberly, nor in a straight line, but quick enough to get away.

After some yelling and —it must be said— some snickering, they made it to the Motel 6 in Hialeah. Unfortunately for Mamadú, it wasn't only the blood, but the bombastic nature of the clip that did it. Because: of course the whole thing had been turned into a clip. Multiple angles! Crisp sound! Stills of the gaping media. The oscillating Ecuadorian in the background. The shove. The fall. The blood. Video game sound effects. The Miami sun. The sloppy run. The yellow Camaro's screeching tires. How American was that? Viral gold! Mamadú Anderson, a formerly anonymous Liberian, had now entered the arena. For the tabloids, the clip was the beginning. First post: *who'd been in the right?* Second post: *would charges be pressed?* Third post: *Was that really, as rumors had it, Yusuke Furukawa's sister's kareshi/boo?*

Surge of the Andean

The green-clad youths had looked in corridors, cabins, storage rooms, saunas, steam rooms, movie theaters, casinos, and all sorts of game rooms, so that the night had worn off and daybreak was upon them from every side, but the god-forsaken viral star was nowhere to be found. Frustrated and tired, some of the searchers joked that "the dolphin" might have jumped off into the ocean. But that was First World disdain talking. The *guagua* who'd left the Chimborazo province on foot, and who'd survived the perilous trek to the United States, and exploitation, and the deprivation, and the English-learning process, and the trappings of viral celebrity, plus all the ridicule followed by mainstream acceptance, wasn't one to simply jump off into the ocean and die. Ha! Those green Uncle Sam's radicals had no idea who the Andean was. Like all the poor of the deepest South, the obdurate *guagua* was used to swimming against the tide. The worse the odds, the greater the pay off.

After the blast, the son of the deepest south had caught on to the looming clusterfuck and quickly scurried back to his cabin, where he'd instinctively grabbed the nearly ripped wiphala bag (the same one he'd crossed over with) he kept for sentimental reasons. The wiphala bag contained a small book of inspirational quotes, a Rambo knife, a compass, a magnifying glass, a flute, and a red poncho. Yes, for a second, he'd considered getting into one of the little lifeboats, like he'd seen it done in the Titanic, but his fear of sharks, and the fact that he didn't know how to swim, had deterred him. Then he'd heard the second blast. Self-preservation had him bouncing around like a headless chicken, until he'd stumbled into a metal kitchen that looked like the inside of a robot's belly. Upon hearing shouts, he'd holed himself up in a dark cavity that turned out to be a huge walk-in refrigerator.

The poncho came in handy then. To think, Veronica, his Dominican girlfriend, had always made fun of him for carrying all that mountain stuff around. *A poncho in the Caribbean, coño!* he could almost hear her. *Well, there you go*, he whispered from the belly of the ship, half-smiling, as he put on the red poncho. It was frozen! Thank God Veronica had stayed in New York. She'd probably be on the platform with the rest of the passengers and that would've been a death sentence to Delfín because he would've tried rescuing her. Ironically, being undocumented had saved Veronica Rodriguez from the Reggaetón Cruise. He didn't have to rescue anybody. All he had to do was pray that the green-clad terrorists wouldn't blow up the ship, in which case...

But that was unlikely. There was no *kamikaze* mindset in those kids. It was also unlikely they'd find him, crouching in his poncho, like in a Diego Rivera painting, between two gigantic bags, one of Thai shrimp, the other of Canadian lobsters. The only danger was freezing to death, but if anyone had a shot at surviving in a refrigerator, it was Quishpe, who'd been born right in the paramo. As a child, he'd spent days in the cold, with llamas and cows, or hunting tree doves with Byron, Antay and his kid brother Güily. Suddenly, as in a whisper, the old Honduran Garifuna's words came to him: *All dreadful things have a break built into them, comrade. Seek the break within and use it as a source of power.* Delfín took out his phone, which was charged. But there was no internet and no reception in the big fridge. He'd have to come out to the kitchen. He wrote three messages at once: one in Quichua for his family in Guamote, one in Spanish for Veronica in New York, and one in English for the president in Washington. There wouldn't be enough time to contact each one individually, so he'd post the messages on Photogram. His millions of followers could help him. He approached the freezer's door, which had a small window, and saw that the kitchen was still empty. He stepped out. Then, quickly, as much as the shivering allowed, snagged a wisp of the world wide web. The postings went up.

To his family in Guamote, Chimborazo province, written in Quichua:

I'm doing fine my loved family and would love soon to see you. ¡Hasta la victoria siempre! – Delfín hasta el fin.

To Veronica Rodriguez in Harlem, New York, written in Spanish:

Amor I love you 100 percent. These hdps will not defeat us. ¡Cásate conmigo, bebé! – Delfín hasta el fin.

To the president of the United States of America in Washington D.C., written in English:

Mr. President, I'm hiding somewhere in the Reggaetón Cruise. Here's a photo of our exact G.P.S. location according to Google Maps. I'm safe and awaiting further instructions from you good sir. God bless America. – Delfín hasta el fin.

Delfín Quishpe's viral instincts said he should upload a selfie. He took a picture of himself, but realized the terrorists could locate him that way. He took another photo with his fist up, eyes flooded with adrenaline. He knew he'd use the photo for his autobiography's cover someday. He lit up a makeshift torch with wrapping paper in the stove, brought the little torch into the walk-in fridge (closing the door with his foot) and made a small fire with ripped pages from the inspirational quotes book. He wrapped himself in his poncho and placed his head over the lobster bag. Two or three hours later he awakened with a melody in his head. With stiff little fingers, he took out his flute. *This is going to be bigger than Twin Towers song,* he told himself.

His arms and legs were going stiff. He needed more fire. He stepped out again. All three Photogram messages had gone viral. It seemed that half of the world had reacted to his messages. He must have broken some type of record. But most importantly, Puramama, Güily and Karina had sent him a video in which they'd said a prayer for his return to safety. In the background you could see the mud hut and a baby llama. It was just like a postcard. Delfín, who knew what stuck, shared the video at once. Veronica had also sent him a message, saying she'd love to be his wife. The message was already public. It had millions of likes, including many by celebrities.

Lastly, Delfín opened a confidential message sent by the president of the United States in conjunction with the Head of Homeland Security, one General K. Gary Gordon. They were asking him to do three things: 1. To send a second screen shot of the ship's location. 2. To, at some point, preferably in the middle of the night (for his safety) take a photo of the cruise ship's massive superstructure, and forward it. 3. To stop sharing anything on social media, as it could compromise the success of the rescue operation, which was underway. The president's message ended with the attachment of a detailed map of the ship, for reference. Also, the president labeled Quishpe an American hero, which sent shivers down his spine. The first request, Delfín took care of right away. The cruise was about a hundred and seventy miles off the south-eastern coast of Jamaica. As to the second request, it wasn't the middle of the night yet. He would cross that bridge when he got there. Delfín loved that English phrase. As to the third request, it was too late. He'd just shared more stuff on Photogram. He wouldn't share anything else thereafter.

He lit up another cone of paper and brought it back into the walk-in refrigerator, hoping for the best, or rather, praying his heart out to the *La Virgen del Quinche* and to the other Apus of the mountains. At some point, the lights went out. The Coalition's decision to unplug the ship's generators was done to avoid being located by the authorities. They were unaware that Delfín had already shared that information. With the power off, the big refrigerator stopped working, which was a gift for the freezing Andean. He took it as a sign from above. At around midnight, Cellphone map in hand, he marched through the dining hall, up the ship's side stairs, through the boutique zone, and into the commodore suites, which were near the top. The power outage had caused the locked doors to unlock. The green-wearing terrorists had so focused on developing the conceptual grounds for their attack, that they had ignored the nuts and bolts of the operation. Also, it must be said, Delfín was lucky. A dark petite man in a red poncho could surreptitiously maneuver in obscurity better than all others onboard.

So he made it to the main deck, near the Watersports Marina™, and from there, an odd but effective angle, he captured a flurry of images. *This shit's too dark*, he thought to himself, *but I'm dead meat if I use the flash.* His hope was that the authorities could clear up the images. After capturing what the authorities had asked him to capture, he bolted himself down the side stairs (from where you could see the waters, and the waters were wild) and through the dining hall again (where he grabbed some butter buns from a basket). When he got back to the walk-in-refrigerator, it wasn't so cold anymore. Getting rid of the power had backfired on the hijackers, but it had also presented an obstacle for Quishpe. How could he send the requested superstructure pictures without an internet connection? He thought hard and fast. *The trick is finding the right angle,* he recalled Uncle Abe saying in relation to a guerilla escape in the Congo. Staying out in the kitchen was too dangerous. He put his phone on silent and left it outside, under three lettuce leaves, in the process of sending the image. His hope was that at some point there would be intermittent reception, the same way it happens on airplanes. He couldn't wait to see it through. He could hear the terrorists nearby. It pained him to leave his cellphone behind, as his cellphone was his link to millions of worldwide fans, to his family in the Andes, to Veronica in New York, and even to the leader of the free world in the White House. But he had to. Goodbye cellphone! Goodbye world!

He snugged back between the Thai shrimp and Canadian lobster bags. This time he'd locked the door behind him. The minutes went by. The fire died out. Delfín was worn out and hungry. He took out a lobster tail from one of the bags, smelled it, and flung it across the room. His head was bruised from the blast. He brought out his flute and took a long look at it. His heart was racing, he wanted to do something, but there was no action to take. Racing thoughts took off and he started to nod off as the floor swayed from side to side. Like the rest of the passengers outside, Delfín Quishpe felt the pulsating beat of the monster below in the unplugged night —the timeless sea— as it opened up its depths. He had no idea as to what the authorities would do or when. The sway of that monstrous being below was all that was real. It might have been the rocking, but Delfín felt a stirring inside. His mind went back to that drunken night by the San Pedro River in his hometown, when Antay and Byron, the Guamán brothers, his old buddies, had tried to convince him not to make the trek to Uncle Sam's McDonald's Republic. *That damned place might not even exist for all you know*, Byron had said, while Antay had tried to dissuade the migrant-to-be by rashly offering him *Fantasma*, his baby horse! But Delfín Quishpe had made up his mind. Though quiet by temperament, he was deeply obstinate. They had drunk and fallen asleep on the grass. And though Delfín was floating in the middle of the sea now —a viral star inside a cold tin box— he felt as if the equatorial night sky was above him, and the wet grass under him, and that the Thai shrimp bag to his left was Byron Guamán, forever taking apart discarded engines and machines by the shed, and that the Canadian lobster bag to his right was Antay Guamán, the eternal lover, already back then planning that first trip to a steamy *chongo* that never did materialize, and that the metal ceiling was wildly alive with stars and comets, and fleeting clouds fat with water and gas above (or under) the blackest equatorial sky, and that it was real, indeed, because he felt utterly and thoroughly intoxicated. The U.S. of A. had attracted him like a magnet, he had no idea why, it was just a force that had driven him, and he had left Guamote and pushed upwards through the continent, meeting people, skipping deathtraps as best he could, and that ring of fire that is the border between The Core and The Periphery—and it would be a mistake to say the ring's fire hadn't burned, oh, it had burned alright, like a pig's fur gets singed before you slice it to get the innards out, except he hadn't been sliced into two, he had been singed, but he had survived, there he had been (there he was!) in a floating arena, disoriented and hungry as a motherfucker, seeking some type of further center because as he arrived in the U.S. of A. (which did exist!) with Pedro and Simón, the little Honduran boys, beat up, spat on, and shaken, he couldn't just walk up to a government office, or a given business, stand at the gate, and say, well, here I am, I made it to the U.S. of A., give me power, give me *chusqui* motherflower, he couldn't do that. *Legal or not, here I am,* was all he'd said, standing there inside the gates of The Core, singed like so many migrants, but so many others had gotten raped, or kidnapped, or mutilated, and they were all, thousands, standing there, in The Core, with no G.P.S, no compass, no map, except the heart, which is good, and better off, because so many others had drowned in rivers, or roasted in deserts, or fallen into rocky chasms, or been eaten by snakes in jungles because this may sound like wild fantasies to some naïve fuckers, but it does happen, alongside the killing hands of fellow man, fellow *latinoamericanos*, that is, because here's the thing, the perils of the trip up to the gates of The Core are The Periphery's price of the ticket, so when Delfín Quishpe, like so many others, meandered around that zigzagging snake of a line between sunny *Playas de Tijuana* and the not-so-sunny *Nido de las Águilas,* that was simply the end of the Latin American part of the ordeal, followed by the deepest sigh, the deepest relief, but also the absolutely overwhelming knowledge (a kind of horror colored by hope) that the trip in its central phase, with its own, shall we say, complications, was just beginning—*the land of the free*, all that.

That first shower... Jesus fucking Christ! That first shower! A kind of baptism into capitalism, freedom, and democracy (at the very least, the hopes of it); an elongation of the first sight, and then you get out of the shower, and look at yourself in the mirror, your face and body nearly broken, and you dry your limbs and your torso, and your face, carefully, nobody knows as much as you do, how near utter collapse you have been, so you eat and you sleep, and even though you're nearly broken, the thrust of unadulterated hope is such that you draw fuel from your wounds, and that carries you forward through the first few months, perhaps the first few years, and in some exceptional cases, the first decade. Only then do you turn around and attempt to take a sweeping look at the entirety of the thing (the landscape) that your life has become, and the vertigo that follows the realization of how far you've come is such, that you could collapse as if no time has passed since your arrival.

But that comes much later. First comes the view. Delfín Quishpe. His name.

Upon entering The Core, he'd followed Pedro and Simón east to New Orleans. In New Orleans, the boys had found out their father was in Sacramento, California, working in construction. They had stayed with an uncle near Tulane-Gravier, a somewhat tough neighborhood. The kids' uncle had allowed the Ecuadorian to stay for a few days. Those few days had turned into three months as the uncle got Delfín a job first chopping off, then packaging chicken legs at a plant way south in Lafourche Parish. Those first trips up and down the Bayou, the raw chicken blood smell that seeped into his clothes, the fluorescent light as he fought off sleep in the night school, were Delfín Quishpe's first impressions of the dream. Then he'd moved to Pennsylvania, where he'd worked in construction all over the place as the Honduran boys moved west to their father. Delfín had hurt his shoulder. The boss had fired him, but he couldn't sue because he was illegal. Then he'd worked cleaning buildings all through the night (which in a way was tougher than construction) in Pittsburgh as he improved his English in the day. At the English school he'd met Juan José, a party guy from

Nicaragua. He'd hang out with Juan José on weekends, and they'd go to a cumbia bar called *La Bailanta*, where they got to hanging out with some *bichas* from all over Central America, and one of those nights Delfín Quishpe had been deflowered by a pasty and thirsty plumpette in Juan José's Nissan, while back at *La Bailanta* Juan José kept trying to charm the bounciest Panamanian like all the others. Delfín hung out with that crowd for a while but then Juan José had had a drunken car accident, and had become suddenly religious, and had dragged Delfín into a parking lot called *Agua Viva* Pentecostal Church. Delfín had gone to the parking lot church a few times, but the pastor had wanted more and more of his time. Quishpe had agreed with Juan José that drinking and partying wasn't going to take them far, but he didn't want to become a church mouse either. He'd never liked church mouses. Not even in Guamote. Like all Andeans he believed in doubt. So he stopped going to the *Agua Viva* Pentecostal Church, and that was the end of his friendship with Juan José, who was a cool guy and had a way with words, to the point that he'd manage to drag half of *La Bailanta* into the parking-lot church with its screaming pastor and its veiled ladies. Hanging out at *la Bailanta* without Juan José wasn't fun anymore, so Delfín stopped partying. Then the owner of the office cleaning building, Yuri, a guy from Georgia (the country) who was a doctor in his country and spoke like five languages, had fired him because somebody had said that immigration authorities were going to raid local business. It was time to move again. A couple of years had gone by. Delfín had some savings and nobody could say he didn't speak English. He even wrote it a little. So he took a bus and some trains to Harlem, New York. His second cousin, Marina Quishpe, lived there. She worked in the garment industry and had a job for him. Working in the garment industry did not pay better than cleaning office buildings in Pittsburgh, but it seemed better for his unhealing shoulder. Plus Marina's husband, a funny guy from the Manabí province whom they called Colorado because of his skin color, worked as a superintendent in the same building where they lived. Colorado needed an assistant. If Delfín wanted to, Colorado could teach him how to fix things. Delfín was already pretty good at fixing things so he jumped on the opportunity. He'd arrived in Harlem in the summer and it had been crazy humid and dirty with trash on the streets and gigantic rats in the subway. He'd hated the Big Apple at first. He'd thought Marina would cook Ecuadorian food, but all she and Colorado ever ate were hamburgers, pizza, and hot dogs, which Delfín considered "an awful shame." *How could Marina, a woman from the highlands, where they had the most delicious cow stomach lining and peanut sauce stew — guatita— and Colorado, a man from the Pacific coast where the black fishermen handed you the fresh seafood to make ceviche which you ate with fried green plantains, how could they?* Delfín thought but didn't complain because he wasn't an idiot. In Harlem Delfín had felt blue all the time and on top of that he'd developed stomach issues from diarrhea to constipation, sometimes both at the same time, which defies logic but, as the Andean found out then, it is indeed possible. One thing he'd had access to in New Orleans and in Pittsburgh that he did not have access to in New York was nature. There was Central Park but Central Park was a joke. It was a park! It wasn't nature. *Fucking newyorkinos…* he would say and laugh. That Marina and Colorado had recommended he should go to Central Park when Delfín said he needed some nature, had made him laugh, because it had been laughable. And the garment factory was bad for his shoulder due to the repetitive movements. On top of that, one of the managers, an old man that stunk of piss, who thought he could speak Spanish though he couldn't, had got it into his head that headphones hurt productivity and forbid that garment employees listen to music in their headphones. Instead he'd started playing English oldies on a dusty radio which absolutely none of the workers, who were all Latino, liked. Looking back, the one good thing Delfín had gotten out of the *Agua Viva* Pentecostal Church experience with Juan José over in Pittsburgh had been music. He'd gotten back in touch with it. In an effort to keep him in the church, the pastor had allowed Delfín to play in the church. He'd gotten to play the flute over drums and an old synthesizer. A couple of times he'd gotten to fool around with a synth, but he'd done it quickly for the pastor only allowed Jesus songs to be played, not the Andean songs about *karishinas* and *machashcas* (bitches and drunks) Delfín wanted to play. Anyhow, the seeds of mixing electronic beats with the Andean flute had seeped into his head then. So when the piss-smelling manager in New York had stated they couldn't listen to their headphones anymore, the obdurate Andean had quit the job and had started fixing stuff around the building with Colorado. That's when music had begun a-brewing in his heart again. *One of the best things about living in America is that you can actually afford stuff even with a crappy wage, unlike in Ecuador where only the rich can afford stuff*, Delfín thought to himself.

That's how one day, he'd simply walked over to the neighborhood pawn shop, and bought himself a secondhand synthesizer. A few weeks later he'd bought some microphones, then a drum machine, and so on. All second hand. Though he only knew how to play the Andean flute, he'd started playing with the new equipment. Things had started looking up. Fixing stuff around the building was more suited to his abilities for one. Colorado had been surprised at how much Delfín already knew. There had been no need to teach him how to use a snake to unplug hairy bathtubs, for instance. Within a couple of weeks Delfín had been allowed to do minor jobs around the apartment complex on his own. Within a couple of months he had been offered a permanent position. Less than a year later, he'd gotten a job as head handyman at another apartment building, all with Marina and Colorado's help. That's when Delfín had learned what it meant to be a co-national. Before he mostly thought of himself (if he ever thought about that at all) as a Quichua-speaking *campesino* from the Chimborazo province in a country that was in denial and at war with people like him. Slowly in New Orleans and Pittsburgh he'd realized that he was what they call a U.S. Latino. The more he learned English, the more this notion settled in, particularly by seeing how non-Latin Americans saw him. His piss-smelling boss at the garment factory, for instance thought Delfín was Puerto Rican, which was laughable as there was nothing further from a Puerto Rican than himself (at least in his mind). And yet, he understood where the piss smelling old man was coming from. Something else had happened when Delfín arrived in New York. He'd thought of Marina as related by family ties, however distant, but then, as she'd introduced him to more people from Ecuador, he realized that there were chains of self-established camaraderie and even obligation among people who called themselves Ecuadorian, some of whom hadn't even been born there, but were the children of the natives. It was one or the other. Immigrants from Ecuador either helped each other like family or they hurt each other like enemies, for no other reason than their common nationality. Some fools tried to re-establish the old country's rigid social class structure in the United States to comedic effects. Everyone —Latinos, Asians, Blacks, and Whites alike— knew that *cushqui* (money baby!) established relationships of command in The Core. That was the beautiful thing about America! Another good thing about America, or maybe just about Delfín's job, was that he got to meet all kinds of tenants in various buildings. Many of these folks, particularly the Dominican grandmas took a liking of the guy. A tiny dolphin who could unplug their bathrooms with a smile, what's not to love about that? The Dominican women gave him food and coffee. Sometimes, when he'd already eaten at another unit, they gave him stuff like *mondongo* to go. He never ate American food again. It was the only thing he hated about the country. Everything else he adored. Eventually, his stomach issues had improved. His English, however, was not improving. Because there was so much Spanish spoken in the units, whenever he encountered black or white (rarely) households, he made sure to practice English as much as he could. In fact, because that's who he practiced the most with, a sparkly black English patina glittered over his heavy Quichua accent. Delfín Quishpe did not have a Spanish accent in the least. He had learned Spanish at the age of ten from Mr. Ibañez, the old rural teacher.

"What are you, Indian or Mexican?" had asked Simone, as Delfín was changing her door locks one day.

The question had taken Delfín aback. He did not know whether she'd meant Indian from India, or Indian as in *indio*, which is what he was, but since so many people throughout Latin America said it as an insult, he didn't know how to take it. The black woman before him didn't seem to have said it in a bad way. He looked at her.

"I'm not Mexican," he said.

That much he knew.

"You got a strange accent, that's why," she said.

"Where you from?"

"Ecuador."

"Where's that?"

He didn't know how to explain so he'd shown her a map. They'd got talking and it turned out Simone, whose father was American and whose mother was Trinitarian, had just divorced her Brazilian husband and was afraid he'd return to take her stuff. Hence the new locks. She had two kids but had been laid off from work. It would be a lie to say Delfín was good to her out of pure good will. A light bulb had gone on in his head from the minute he'd meet her. It was her single mother situation, but also her modus operandi. Simone had been so straightforward with him, he felt he could be straightforward with her. Or, as straightforward as somebody from the Andes could be, which wasn't that straightforward to begin with. Anyhow, every time Delfín was around her unit, he brought Simone and her daughter, Shaun (or Shaunee) something to eat, usually the stuff the Dominican housewives gave him. Sometimes he brought colored pencils or notebooks. One time he'd even bought Simone a bottle of perfume.

"What is it you want, 'phin?" Simone had asked.

"I wants to marry you, Simone," he'd said.

"You crazy? We're not like that, man."

"I mean, I need help."

She'd got it right away.

"You didn't have to bring me all this stuff."

"I wanted you to see I'm not a bad guy."

"I know you're not a bad *hombre*, 'phin."

"I know you needs money, Simone."

"So how much am I gonna get if I marry you for your American papers, bro?"

"I don't have no money."

Simone had cracked up so hysterically, the Ecuadorian had walked away. Still, they'd be married within a week. She couldn't turn down his offer. He'd arranged it with the building's manager to switch Simone's apartment to his name, and to give him a sizeable employee discount. He'd pay for Simone's food and rent for a year and a half. He'd also talk to people around the apartment complex to try to get her a job. And so just like that, less than a year after the arrangement, Quishpe had his American papers. And a new ally in Simone, whose ex-husband couldn't open Delfín's double lock on the door.

To celebrate the new legal resident, Marina and Colorado had ordered pizza, of course. Folks from around the apartment complex came to get a slice, including some of Delfín's Dominican benefactors. One of them, *Doña* Rosario, brought her niece, Veronica. The Andean had been smitten right away. Veronica Rodriguez had curly hair, big brown eyes, and a broad smile.

And she danced bachata, swaying her wide hips better than anyone he'd ever seen. To think he used to hate bachata! Before leaving that night, he'd begged *Doña* Rosario to let him take Veronica out. "I'm going to try my best," the old woman had said. But Veronica hadn't been interested in Delfín. He was too short for her. Plus she'd left her boyfriend in San Pedro de Macorís. She apparently talked to him every day over Skype. Plus Delfín was a married man; everyone knew. So it'd befallen Simone, the supposed wife, to explain things. The time would arrive. Simone had gotten a job at a pharmacy chain and needed someone to babysit Shaunee. Delfín had recommended Veronica as babysitter. As the weeks and months had gone by and Veronica's relationship with her boyfriend back in San Pedro de Macorís had fallen apart (obviously, *amor de lejos...*) the two women had become friends. Simone had explained to Veronica that the marriage hadn't been real and that Delfín, despite his short stature and overly mild manners, was extremely ambitious. "He's a beast in the good sense of the word," Simone had said. Veronica hadn't been convinced. At around this time, Delfín had uploaded a video of his music on YouTube. At the end of the music video he'd put his phone number in case anybody was interested in hiring him for any parties. He'd been trying to branch out as they say. Veronica had watched the video, and like most everyone else, she'd thought it was either funny or horrible, or both. And yet, it was also intriguing. A migrant love story loomed at the heart of the song. Delfín had interwoven it with the most horrific, most awfully global terrorist attack ever. In a way, the little guy had brought all of the peripherals into the heart of global darkness: the very crossroads of the world. Such had been the naïve force behind his ambition. Who would dare create such a viral monster but a child-like maverick? Veronica saw that Simone had been right. The dolphin was a shark! Veronica and Simone had talked about it over drinks at Simone's place. More accurately, they both had laughed about it. As the night had progressed, a sort of impromptu building party had formed.

Everyone had been interested.

"How did you upload the video? Who helped you with the camera? Who recorded the song? How did you get the electronic beats in? How did you insert the Twin Tower attacks into the video? Where did you get the matching hat and boots? What about that oversized leopard-print jacket?

How much was it? Can you get arrested for something like that?"

"You mean my dance moves?" Delfín had answered back.

"Those too," someone had said opening another beer.

"Can you show us the dance?" Marina had asked.

Simone had seconded her. Colorado had dragged the coffee table to the side.

Delfín's dance was ridiculous… and yet… they couldn't get enough. The artist was skirting the oncoming waves of ridicule with raw sincerity. That smile! It was the opposite of the extraordinary secrecy with which he'd skirted most questions about the production. Even years later, as he was interviewed on TV show after TV show, he wouldn't say much about the making of the phenomenon. It'd been instinctual. There'd been something magical and secret in how he'd put his finger in the belly of some sort of monster: the zeitgeist. He didn't want to mess with that.

But Veronica Rodriguez had been something else from the get-go. Hey eyes, her hips, her bachata-dancing. He was in love and couldn answer her with neither secrecy nor jokes. During the impromptu party she'd looked him in the eye.

"So did you have a girlfriend who actually died in the Twin Tower attacks?"

Her Dominican accent was like a song to the dolphin's ears. And yet he was taken aback. Veronica almost never talked to him directly.

"I'll tell you all about it later tonight," he'd said, maybe too loudly.

He'd been serious and un-ironic. His plan had been to walk Veronica home. But the crew at Simone's apartment had taken it as an outright attempt to "ring her bells." Innuendo-filled remarks were made. Veronica had gotten embarrassed at first, but as she'd already had a couple of drinks, and the whole thing was so preposterous, she'd loosened up.

"At least take me out on a date first, *tigere*. I'm not that easy!"

Banter and jests pregnant with innuendo had ensued. Though she'd blushed, it was the first time Veronica had felt at home since she'd left the Dominican Republic. She didn't know one could laugh like that in New York. You could see it in the way her eyes shifted. And everyone knew what that meant. She'd finally give the daring young Andean a chance in love. Delfín couldn't wait for the party to be over so he could walk her home—or whatever.

After seeing the change in Veronica's attitude towards the dolphin, the guests at the party had experienced what hundreds of thousands would within next 24 hours. Laughter and mockery first; then, surprise and even secret fear at the fool's unintentional magic. Actual admiration or fandom at last. Nobody at the party (nor the majority of millions of followers afterward) had been able to put it into words, but deep within felt what philosophers have always understood: that the fool is the precursor to the sage. Delfín Quishpe had accidentally —or through a haphazard combination of naiveté, ambition, daring, and a positively reckless belief in his own destiny— come upon a different take on reality. Some call it tapping into the zeitgeist; some, fingering the hot wet cunt of culture. The peripheral Ecuadorian dolphin had done the impossible.

During the last of the innocent days, what Delfín Quishpe, the man, hadn't known back then in Simone's apartment with his love-crazed eyes for the hip-swaying *bachatera* was that the tiny minority of prodigies who get to tap the zeitgeist with their images (or philosophy, or acting, or singing, or rapping) get all eventually ripped apart by the pulling forces generated by that same culture. It's the using up of the magic; the magician's inevitable malignment, or worse, abandonment, or worse, deletion.

The Reggaetón Cruise was swaying from side to side. The walk-in-fridge wasn't cold anymore and the huge Thai shrimp and Canadian lobster bags were beginning to thaw and smell. Delfín closed his eyes. He wanted to bring the memory to a conclusion. He needed to. There it was! When Simone's party had ended, he'd walked Veronica across the complex over to her apartment. Before kissing her, he'd told her the truth. The love story in the song hadn't happened to him. It had happened to Colorado, who'd told him about it as they fixed a water heater in the South Bronx one day.

"If you think about it, I'm too young for it to have happened to me," Delfín had told Veronica. The 9/11 attacks happened in 2001. I didn't even know what love was back then. Colorado did. He'd been in love with this beautiful brown-eyed girl. An Ecuadorian immigrant in New York, like him. This is all before Colorado met Marina, my cousin. Way before. The girl he was in love with worked cleaning offices in the Twin Towers. And she was in the second tower when the planes hit. He was destroyed. Even considered blowing his brains out. Please don't tell anybody about this, particularly Simone, because she has a big mouth. She's super nice but she has a big mouth. I'm not afraid to say it because she's a real friend. Colorado doesn't want Marina to find out about it because he doesn't want to make her feel like a consolation prize. He has an old Ecuadorian way of thinking. I respect it. So please don't tell anybody. Anyway, what I sing about in the video is what happened to Colorado. He saw the planes hit the towers from his living room and he knew his girl was there. "*No puede seeerrr...*" are Colorado's very words as he told them to me. I just added the emotion when I decided to make a song about it with Andean flutes and electronic beats. People laugh about it, but I didn't mean it as a joke at all. It's a dance song with a dark theme. Sad music can be danced to. We do it all the time back home. I hope it does well."

Veronica was touched by Delfín's insistence in keeping his friend's secret. It showed he had a good heart, but she knew that already. He'd helped her out with babysitting jobs in the apartment complex and he was always there to run all kinds of errands for her. And he'd told the truth about his situation with Simone. He wasn't necessarily her type, but he was good.

"It's cool that you show that there were Latinos in the twin towers too," Veronica said. "I hope your song does well. But don't worry if it doesn't. And pay no mind to those who make fun of you, *corazón*. You're different. That's what makes you especial, Delfín."

There was nobody in the hallway. For a minute there, he savored the way Veronica had said his name. From the windows you could see some Little Leaf Lindens and their flowers, yellower still under the streetlamps. It was the place: Delfín stood on tiptoe (he had to) and kissed Veronica. She let him kiss her. Perhaps she kissed him back too.

They walked in silence to *Doña* Rosario's apartment.

"You know," Delfín said before she closed the door, "I don't care if people like me or if they make fun of me, as long as you do me the honor of becoming my girlfriend."

"Let me think about it," she said, smiling at his extreme Andean politeness.

He was like an alien to her. A mysterious man of destiny. A native Napoleon.

An abrupt noise was heard then.

"It's my *tía*," Veronica said. "She's trying to eavesdrop on us."

"Say hello to *Doña* Rosario for me," he said, loudly.

Scampering noises were heard. They both laughed.

Delfín tried to kiss her again but Veronica smiled and quickly walked into the apartment. The next day she had a viral star for a boyfriend. Fans have debated ad nauseum whether the Dominican said yes to him before or after the Andean became an international phenomenon. The viral star himself has indignantly stated that that's none of anyone's business.

It was the infectious song, of course. The *no puede seeerrr!!!* The beat. The video. The clothes. And the dance moves... But it was also Quishpe himself. He was the most unselfconscious performer anybody had ever seen.

People's covert desires to see a buffoon triumph was behind their adoration. That covert desire, and the ruthless mockery that masked it, had taken Delfín Quishpe not only all through Latin America as an ongoing gag, but also into the heart of The Core, as an actual star. And now, he was all over the news. He, out of all people on the Reggaetón Cruise, had contacted the authorities. It seemed preordained. His cellphone was hidden under three lettuce leaves outside the fridge. But he didn't need his phone, nor an internet connection to know that everybody in the media, and in the Oval Office itself, was talking about him. He was at the core of The Core. The conflict, the culture, the power. In a way, he'd become the core itself—and it burned. Movies and books would be written about him. The part of him that sought fame was joyful, and yet, a wave of self-hatred overtook him as the stench of thawed shrimp and lobster became ever more noxious. It was the other side of him. The serious, quiet part he related to *taita* Yuyay, his father. Delfín, the man, imagined everybody laughing at him. The fans, the media, the terrorists, the generals, and even president himself. Deafening laughter all around. Veronica, Simone, Marina, Colorado, Juan José, the Honduran boys. The Mexican mountains. The young Salvadorian volcano. The cities. Even the United States, as an entity laughing, laughing, laughing at him, the little ignorant countryside *indio* gone American celebrity. Anger surged. He would show them Delfín Quishpe was no joke. He had a bully pulpit now and he would use it alright. He had seen more than they could ever imagine.

Dead serious matters. He'd experienced poverty and hunger. He'd seen murder and backstabbing. He'd killed and stolen alright. He'd gotten his ribs broken on the way to The Core. If they wanted to talk about serious shit, he could talk serious shit. He rushed to the door in utter panic. But he couldn't get out. He'd locked himself in. Or had he locked himself out?

"Am I locked in or am I locked out?" he asked himself in Quichua. I don't even know, I'm such a fool. "Am I locked in or am I locked out?" he yelled out as he trashed the walk-in fridge completely. He started banging on the door besides himself. "Let me out! Let me in! Let me out! Let me in!" he repeated making a little dance. "I can make a fucking song about it," he yelled out in anger. "Let me out! Let me in!" he repeated, childishly, dancing. "See, I carry my little flute everywhere I go." And then, in an angry voice: "I'm the king of YouTube. And you know what, as the king of fucking YouTube, I say, to you all dear and loved audiences all over the word: I'm not your *shunsho* no more! I came to this country to work because mine is broke and you can't make real money even if you work hard. I made a song because I love music. I dress like this and dance like this because that's how I dress and that's how I dance." He started playing the flute. He stopped and looked at his flute in disgust. Screw you! *Runtuyta ch'unqay!* You turned me into a *shunsho*! A herd-less lost goat! And I went along with it. No more! All I have in this world is my balls and my word and I don't break 'em for no one. Do you understand?" he yelled out as he broke his Andean flute with his knee. "You wanna fuck with me? Okay. You wanna play rough? Okay." He went over to the lobster bag and started flinging lobsters at the door violently, one by one, yelling obscenities in Quichua. The entire room was full of thawed lobsters. Delfín was sweating. "But see, I'm so god damned lucky not even when I want to do bad I get caught," he whispered, exhausted, "and not even the terrorists take me seriously because, even as I fight, I'm a joke, even to myself."

He laughed out loud before collapsing over the big shrimp bag.

When he woke up again, he reached for his phone, but his phone wasn't there. It was then he felt farther from the Chimborazo province than he'd ever been. Like he could never come back home. He hadn't simply migrated elsewhere. He'd entered a different dimension. No GPS. He had no clue as to the ship's latitude or longitude, or whether the passengers above were alive or not. He felt suddenly exposed to the topography of his own life. He turned around, as it were, and saw his own trajectory, the real man's trajectory, not the viral star's trajectory, which had surged over the horizon, beyond itself. A vital singleness of vision had driven him forward (and taken him pretty far) but he knew that from then on he'd have to be aware of himself on multiple levels. A weight like an anchor settled inside as he saw himself promising to the Apus, the protector spirits in the mountains, who surely inhabited the ocean as well, that if he pulled through this, he'd move back to the real center of the world, *como runa que soy.*

A Delicate Man, as Delicate as a Spring Flower in May

Back in Santa Ana, El Salvador, the twins had been put to bed. Sandrita, Jimmy, and Anahí, were glued to the news in the living room. There were protests against the apparent savagery with which the US government had solved the Reggaetón Cruise crisis in the Caribbean. Some experts on channel 4 were arguing that the protests were being orchestrated by anti-democratic actors. Others adhered to the idea that orchestration didn't coincide with the magnitude of the marches, particularly in Western Europe. The marches, and levels of anger displayed, were too substantial not to be at least partially spontaneous. Both sides said it was the first time in history that huge protests in defense of terrorists were taking place. And that this had put the American government and its allies at a crossroads. And that political alliances had begun to crack. Some of the experts were talking World War III, others scoffed at the prospect. It was a deep moment of global confusion, both sides concurred, right before the commercial break.

"Why are they burning so many cars?" asked Anahí from her wheelchair. "They could just send us one of those Audis if they don't want them!"

"Germans and Swedes are not happy with what the American government did," said Jimmy.

"It was pretty macabre, you got to give them that," said Sandrita.

"Macabre…" said Anahí, "I like that word, baby, whatever that means."

"*Horrifying because of involvement with death and injury*, momma," said Sandrita with pride, as the online classes had started paying off. "I've added a new word to my vocab."

Jimmy was immersed in the situation.

"Those hippies complain about everything, *maje*," he said. "Imagine if we had what they have. We would be thankful, not angry. In my mind, the *gringos* did the right thing. They're fed up with terrorists. The Europeans are just jealous. They don't have the guts nor the capabilities to pull of something like that."

"But to have it all shown live… that wasn't good," said Anahí.

"I think the recording was probably an error, Anahí," said Jimmy.

"That was no error, *amor*," interjected Sandrita.

Jimmy wasn't surprised that Sandrita disagreed with him. That was normal. He was surprised by how sweetly she was talking to him. Something had changed. The worst of the bitterness seemed to have been squeezed out of her heart.

"What do you mean?" he asked.

"They did it to show the world, I think. A show of force."

"I guess," said Jimmy, "to keep other terrorists scared."

"But showing all that killing," said Anahí, crossing herself, "that was not good."

"Sometimes you got to show the awful part, Momma," said Sandrita, staring.

"I don't buy the World War III predictions," said Jimmy. "Pure scare tactics."

"What's that?" asked Sandrita.

"Supposed experts warning people that a great war is approaching," said Jimmy.

"*Dios no quiera*," exclaimed Anahí. "We can't afford another civil war in El Salvador. I lost so many loved ones."

"Don't worry, Momma," said Sandrita. "El Salvador is not part of the world."

"What are we then?" asked Anahí, smiling, "*marcianos*?"

"Yes, to the rich world we may as well be *marcianos*," said Sandrita.

"I guess it pays off to live in a different planet," said Jimmy.

"Not a different planet, *amor*. More like another galaxy," said Sandrita.

"What about that guy?" asked Jimmy.

"What guy?" replied Sandrita.

"Your hero," said Jimmy with a hint of irony. "The little *indio*."

Sandrita pursed her lips like a little girl.

Anahí looked at her daughter.

"Sandrita used to hate that boy's guts," she said, rocking back and forth in her wheelchair.

Both Anahí and Jimmy looked at Sandrita, expecting a big blow up.

"Delfín Quishpe is not a boy anymore," Sandrita said, calmly. "People do grow up, you know?"

"But he was... I met him, a nice guy, a very nice guy," said Anahí.

"Yes, momma" said Sandrita, "you're right, he was."

"Talk about irony..." added Jimmy.

"What's irony?" asked Anahí.

Jimmy looked at Sandrita. They both smiled.

"Shhh!" Sandrita let out before Jimmy spoke. "Irony is," she went on, confidently, "the full significance of one's actions. That's irony!"

"Poor thing," said Anahí.

"Who do you mean poor thing, momma," said Sandrita, sharply.

"The guy," said Jimmy. "She means the guy."

"Right, look at the signs," Anahí said. "The protesters hate his guts."

"Oh, those protesters don't know shit," said Jimmy. "You both met him in the flesh."

"Yes we did. And he was nice," said Anahí.

"Yes he was, but that's it—*se acabó*," stated Sandrita like the commander in chief she still was.

The sharpness of her sentence cut the damp Santa Ana night air at once. Jimmy looked at her with unrestricted admiration.

Anahí, looked within: "Yes, exactly—*that's it*, baby," she echoed from the rocking wheelchair. "Change the damned channel. I'm sick of all this globalized American bullshit!"

Jimmy had never heard a single bad word come out of the old woman's mouth in all of his life. And he'd known her since he was a little *cipote* in

Tamarindo Beach. He let out a clean, nay, a pristine, an immaculate chuckle. Sandrita looked at Jimmy's tiny white teeth like little nascent moons under his slightly blushing cheeks and then heard a sweet apology come of his mouth. Sandrita, the big bad woman, was going to say something sarcastic to her pale, brittle man, but she stopped herself with a new force she'd found within. It was a force that came right from the belly. She held on to it until the moment passed. And it did pass; it was a feat. Her eyes lit up. Well, then, this delicate man, as delicate as a Spring flower in May, was the man Jesus had selected for her. There was no doubt about that. She would marry him as soon as he asked.

THREE

The Hog Farm - Lebanon, Kansas

Artjom closed the door to the suburban house he shared with Cheryl, formerly known as theNeverwhöre and looked up at the sky. The thunderstorm had ripped up tree branches and the winds had knocked down power lines which —*thank dog*, as he liked to say— hadn't affected the power supply. Except for a diffuse orange spot, which looked like an apocalyptic blast far in the horizon, a kind of milkiness permeated the heavens. He looked down. There was still hail on the ground. He thought of riding his bike there, but it was hot and humid. Artjom Pärn liked humidity, but he didn't like riding his bike in it. When he rode his bike in muggy weather, he began sweating at once. His bike seat was getting too small for him anyway. He had to either get a bigger seat or to get smaller himself. He was planning on taking up Muay Thai soon. That would complement biking around deserted neighborhoods, preferably those with train tracks, which was his favorite activity. But it was muggy today, so walking it was. If he walked slowly he could keep from getting the sweats and so enjoy what he actually liked about this kind of weather: the chilly airstreams that unexpectedly hit him in the arms or in the neck or in the face. It seemed so unlikely that a cold stream could hit you in this humid heat. And yet it did. It was real. The proof was in the quickly melting hail which had somehow made it to the ground. Then it was gone and you were back in the heat, feeling the aftereffects or the meteoric debris left behind by the thunderstorm forces. Artjom put on his headphones and made his way on the sidewalk by the decrepit houses. The music —now mathcore metal— awakened his inner vigor. He walked on down James Street. When he felt the beginnings of a sweat, he put his hair in a ponytail and slowed down, feeling the cold gusts he so loved. Even through headphones he could hear the sky roaring. At first thunder would scare him, but he'd come to enjoy this also. There it was. Boom, boom, the colossal roaring of the heart of America! He was in a mood alright. He was about to turn 21 years of age in an Oklahoma City suburb. That might've had something to do with his feelings. Walking was the right thing to do.

After about four blocks Artjom could see the 7-Eleven sign looming large above the only bus station around. He walked four more blocks to get there. It was quite a ways; sixteen blocks, to and from. But it always got him in a better mood. The food helped too. He got four hot dogs, two for Cheryl, formerly theNeverwhöre, and two for himself, $doomMetalBo, war game wunderkind. To drink, he got two Slushies, a lime-flavored one for himself, and a Coke-flavored one for Cheryl. He also bought e-vaper cartridges, menthol for himself, cherry for Cheryl, and lavender-scented toilet paper for both (they had run out). "Hello," he said to Rodney, the clerk, upon entering. Rodney knew Artjom was $doomMetalBo and wanted gaming advice, but Artjom he wasn't in the mood. He thanked him for the discount, paid in cash and left. He couldn't wait to get back to Cheryl. Things were going well. Which was alright because it hadn't always been the case...

Right before they had graduated from Raleigh High School, Cheryl had gotten pregnant by Tookie10, the young Mexican skater who'd appear in $doomMetalBo's video tutorials from time to time. Though she wasn't religious (quite the contrary) theNeverwhöre couldn't bring herself to abort the baby. As it often happens, her religious upbringing kicked in at the most critical moment. She got insecure about her own thoughts and went with what she felt—*aborting was killing*. Nevermind that the father hadn't even officially started the 11th grade. Tookie10 didn't want her to abort either. In his limited English he told her he would marry her. theNeverwhöre said no; she didn't believe in marriage. If Tookie10 wanted to, they could raise the child together, as a couple, but there would be no marriage. Tookie10 accepted theNeverwhöre's conditions. He dropped out of high school and began working with his father, first in a car wash, then as a janitor at Raleigh Community College. As this transpired, teenage Artjom felt pushed to the side. He was making money developing outreach projects for the U.S. Army, but what good was that? He had lost Tookie10, his best friend, and theNeverwhöre, who was his other best friend (and his crush) in one fell swoop. The Youtube channel he'd started suffered the consequences. Without Tookie10's skating tricks and theNeverwhöre's bosomy rants, Artjom lost interest in his own channel. He started posting less and less until at one point he stopped. In addition, he'd begun to detest his work with the Army. Unlike what Kirill, his big brother, had anticipated, the U.S. Army's Summer Program for Teenage Developers wasn't action filled. It was a veiled way to get young brains as consultants without hiring them as such. He still got more adrenaline out of playing war videogames. There seemed to be more at stake there. Moreover, Artjom had seen a video by one Freedom89now who claimed the Military Arcade Center (M. A. C. ™) was targeting working class teenagers to send them to war. *The idea behind it,* said Freedom89now, *is to make the teens believe that it's all fun and games, but in truth, once they enlist, they get sent out there to do real killing, and most importantly, as far as the teens are concerned, real dying.* Those words got to Artjom Pärn. He was even considering moving back to Estonia. But then events took an unexpected turn. Tookie10, his father, his uncle, his cousin, and many others who worked for the same janitorial subcontractor at Raleigh Community College, got deported back to Guanajuato, Mexico, in a fierce National Security Administration raid one day. theNeverwhöre was considering moving to Guanajuato to be with Tookie10, but the truth was that theNeverwhöre wasn't in love with Tookie10. She merely loved him as a person. The Estonian tried to be there for her, but she shut herself off from all. Well, she took off somewhere. Nobody knew where she was. Not even her family. Artjom Pärn didn't see her for five months. He knew she was alive. She sometimes said hello on messenger, but she never divulged her location. He was losing hope —and smoking more weed than ever, to the point that he seemed to be developing an allergy— until he ran into theNeverwhöre's cousin at a metal show on a rainy Sunday night. The cousin, one Kallan, confirmed that theNeverwhöre was no longer in Raleigh. She had moved to OKC where she was working at an AT&T call center.

"*What about the baby?*" Artjom asked, in a sweat.

"You can ask her about that."

"Can I have her phone number?"

Kallan said she wouldn't have given it to him, but that "her cuz" was doing pretty terrible and could use a trustworthy friend.

"I'm trustworthy," said Artjom.

"I know, that's why I'm giving it to you," said Kallan. "You got to go see her in Oklahoma City. I can't go now 'cause I'm dealing with some shenanigans myself, but as soon as I'm able to, I'll go see her too, man."

The Estonian felt something surging inside.

"Come with me, Kallan…" he insisted, "I'll front the plane tickets, food, everything."

"Call her first," Kallan said. "She's going to kill me, but call her first. If she says it's okay, I'll do my best to go with you, bro."

Artjom called Cheryl as soon as he got home. Surprisingly, she was receptive. Artjom and Kallan went to see her a few days later. Artjom saw the change right away. Cheryl was clearly not the theNeverwhöre anymore. She had dyed her hair brown and taken out her nose rings. She was also thinking about erasing theNeverwhöre tattoo she had on her back, but that would cost her a lot of pain and money, so she was putting it off. Losing her baby had traumatized her. Well, she hadn't precisely lost the baby. She'd had a late term abortion. And she couldn't face her family so she'd moved to OKC.

"Why this small town? Artjom asked.

Both he and Kallan thought the place looked awful.

"I don't know," Cheryl said.

But that was a lie. The truth was she'd met an older biker online and the biker had seemed pretty stable but it had all been, well, another lie. She'd left him right away, but since she'd already gotten a job at the AT&T call center, there she was.

"There's a military base not too far from here," Artjom said, unafraid to seem desperate. "I can ask if they'd let me work from there."

When the U.S. Army's summer program ended, the Army had hired Artjom as a legitimate military consultant. Most of his work was done remotely.

"Go back where you came from," Cheryl said. "I don't want to ruin your life too."

Artjom tried explaining to her that she hadn't ruined anybody's life. Kallan, who saw Artjom's good intentions, tried to convince Cheryl to give the Estonian a chance. After a while Cheryl got quiet and then said in a dry voice: "I'm addicted to painkillers." Then she cried. Within a month, Artjom Pärn had moved to Oklahoma City. Slowly, he'd helped Cheryl, formerly theNeverwhöre, to kick off her addiction. Exactly a year later, Artjom and Cheryl had gotten secretly married in the city of Broken Arrow. Not even Kallan knew about it. Two years after the marriage and four years since Artjom (who now spoke perfect American English, and went by Art) had first come to the United States, he'd become an American citizen. Everything had changed, including his career. After his U.S. Army contract had ended, he'd joined the CIA's prestigious *remote war drone operator* program (REWADRO). He was shy of 20 years old. His war video game experience, his successful completion of the Army's Summer Program, his stint as a consultant, and the fact that he'd become a U.S. citizen had laid it all out for him. Also, Artjom was making more money than his older brother, Kirill, now. His capabilities as a REWADRO were unquestionable. This former video game champ, with long greasy hair and gory black metal t-shirts known as $doomMetalBo had quickly become one of the top drone operators in the world. The other top REWADROs were in China, Russia and Japan. The CIA, which had done extensive psychological testing on Artjom Pärn, knew that he was creative and lazy and would not show up to work on a Monday through Fridays basis. He was hired as an independent operator who was legally bound to the organization for a period of five years with an option to renew. Additionally, $doomMetalBo was mandated to take part in an undisclosed number of remote operations per year, including training sessions in which he was the trainer, not the trainee. He had achieved such a high drone-operating proficiency that hardly anyone could teach him anything. Still, he hadn't changed either his look or his lifestyle. He still preferred videogames over actual war operations.

"That's him!" Talent Management Director Herman Moore told CIA Director, Captain George Armstrong, as soon as Artjom's figure could be seen on James Street.

"Let's go get him," said the Captain.

The small group of men in suits got ready.

"No. It's better if we wait here sir," said Moore, who had known Artjom for years now. "We don't want to make him nervous. He gets into these strange moods..."

Moore went on to explain to Capt. Armstrong, who was in contact with the Secretary of Defense, how if Pärn felt trapped or too hurried or, worse yet, pushed around, he could become difficult. In the past he had, for instance, faked an allergic episode to avoid working with a certain team he'd found obnoxious.

"Pärn's contractually mandated," stated Capt. Armstrong. "We could throw him in military prison if he defies our orders."

Herman Moore turned around and made eye contact with his assistant, whose eyebrows were already raised.

"Frankly, sir," said Moore. "The boy doesn't give a damn about anything. He's lax. Has always been what we used to call a slacker."

"Perhaps we got the wrong man for our mission then," said Capt. Armstrong as worry tensed his brow. "You well know that this is the most important military mission of our lifetimes."

"That's why we're here, sir," added Moore. "Agent Pärn might be a negligible idiot in his personal life —look at where and how he lives— and he might be hard to deal with, as indeed he is, but as REWADRO he's one of the most accomplished pilots ever. I'm sure you're aware of that. Agent Pärn is, if I may say so, sir, an unparalleled genius in performing surgical drone operations under extreme duress *because of that odious laxity of his*. It grants him an easy flow, a strange focus (some kind of Zen really) in situations where most would and do crumble. We have come to think of him an artist, not as a soldier, and treat him accordingly. As you know, he came through the U.S. Army's Summer Military Program for Teenage Developers. He was a video game champion from a very early age."

"We're familiar with the Artjom Pärn's dossier, sir," said Armstrong. "There's no need for you to try to sell the boy to us. He's the one, alright. I will not walk on eggshells around a barely legal *slacker*, as you have stated yourself."

"He's the top Remote War Drone Operator in the world, Captain," asserted Moore, who took pride in having brought Pärn up the ranks.

"Be that as it may ..."

"With all due respect sir," interjected Moore, before Capt. Armstrong completed his sentence, "I can bring Artjom from his front door to your helicopter in an unproblematic way. My rapport with the agent tells me that I'm the only one who can make that happen. Once you have him in your helicopter, you can do what you need to do. But I must warn you: if the agent begins to get problematic, as he's bound to, remember, he's an artist, not a soldier. And you're right, Captain. This is perhaps the most important mission of our lifetimes. I want to make this happen as much as you do. Hence my unusual candor with you, sir."

"Alright then," said Capt. Armstrong, crossing his arms across his mile-long chest. "You get doughboy to our helicopter, Mr. Moore. I'll take over then."

"Alright fellas," said Moore to the dark suited men behind him. "Back in your vehicles."

Capt. Armstrong assented with his head.

The men went back into their dark SUVs.

"You too, sir," added Moore with a smile.

Capt. Armstrong walked away huffing and puffing. Mr. Moore waited by himself as Artjom Pärn arrived. Artjom moved slowly, but not only that, he had headphones on and was in his own mathcore world. He seemed to nearly come to a stop every few feet to better enjoy the music. Moore suspected that Artjom was perhaps playing with the authorities.

"Hey, Herman," said the Estonian loudly, taking off his headphones at last. "You alright?"

There was sweat on Moore's brow.

"There's a bit of emergency going on in the Caribbean," said Moore.

"Hold on," Artjom said, handing his hot dogs and Slushies to Moore.

The Talent Management Director held on to the food, getting some ketchup on his suit. Artjom kneeled down to tie his shoelaces, making part of his ass visible at once. Some of the dark suited agents couldn't keep from laughing.

"Shut the hell up, you morons!" exclaimed Capt. Armstrong, banging on the dashboard.

The agents got quiet at once. Still, they couldn't believe that this greasy haired grunger was the top REWADRO in the world.

"We have to be guided by facts," said Capt. Armstrong, as if guessing what his men were thinking. "It's too risky an operation not to."

It was true. Artjom Pärn, aka $doomMetalBo, had been in charge of flying the drone that had hit and killed the head of ISIS in Syria. He'd also performed operations in Afghanistan, Pakistan, Yemen, Venezuela, and Somalia—*always successfully*. The Estonian was gifted not only at hitting moving targets, but also at minimizing collateral victims. He'd flown all kinds of war drones, including The Reaper and The Global Hack, which had its pluses and minuses, but his top drone was The Predator-RPA. That particular drone was loaded with AGM-114 Hellfire missiles, which were unrivaled in targeted deletions.

"Let's go in for a minute," said Artjom.

The living room wasn't tidy, but Moore was used to it. He laid out the complexity of the situation before the agent. Artjom seemed surprised not so much at the seriousness of the mission, but at the gall of the hijacking itself.

"You haven't heard of it?" asked Moore in disbelief.

"I try to stay away from the news," said Pärn. "It's not good for the soul, *vennas*."

"You're something else, Pärn," said Moore, drinking from the cherry-flavored Slushy.

"Wait!" said Artjom. "That's Cheryl's. Have some of this one."

Artjom gave Moore the Coke-flavored Slushy. Then he got up and brought the hot dogs upstairs to his wife.

She noticed something in his face.

"Moore's downstairs. The CIA is outside," Artjom said.

"I know," she cut in sharply.

Artjom heard disappointment in Cheryl's voice. She'd come to disapprove of his REWADRO work on political grounds. *I'd rather have a gamer for a husband than a remote drone assassin*, she'd said before. That had gotten to the Estonian. He was now full of doubts.

"This will be the last mission I do," he said, taking a quick bite at the dog.

"You have a contract with them."

"I do."

"I'm heading out to work soon," she said, turning her head away.

Cheryl had matured. She'd become a certified X-ray technician. There was no trace of theNeverwhöre nor of the painkiller addiction left in her.

Artjom gave her the food and kissed her.

"You taste like Dijon," she said. "I hate that pretentious shit. Tastes like pigeon barf."

"Cheryl," Artjom said. "This time I'm saving innocent people."

Cheryl got serious too. And she did not flinch.

They both knew about the Reggaetón Cruise. They had talked about it extensively, and had even expressed some sympathy for The Coalition. He knew they'd call him and had done preliminary studies on the ship, the weather, and the green-clad radicals. Cheryl had helped him. His ignorance was a put-on. It had always been.

"Radicals are people too, you know," she said.

"They're not radicals, they're terrorists," he said.

She looked him in the eye without saying a word.

"This will be my last mission, babe,' he repeated.

"Be careful Arty," she said, letting her worry out, "*Ma armastan sind.*"

"*Ma armastan sind,*" he repeated, smiling at her accent.

Cheryl got near him and wiped the Dijon off his lips. Then she kissed him again.

"But if you don't quit ruining good dogs with pigeon shit, I'm dumping your ass."

Once $doomMetalBo and Talent Management Director Moore came out of the house, CIA Director, Capt. Armstrong, exited the vehicle.

"George Armstrong. It is time we met."

"Hi there. Art here."

"The President sends his warmest regards."

"Neat."

"Please let me know if there's anything I can do to facilitate your mission."

"Sure."

The top men got into different vehicles as per protocol. It was a short drive across the city. Artjom thought how much he'd come to love OKC. As plain as it could be, OKC had allowed him to set up a life. He couldn't have done it anywhere else. Perhaps he'd need the thunder.

The heliport was on top of Mount Sinai Hospital.

"You're not coming with us?" Artjom asked Moore, after they parked in the back.

"This falls under higher jurisdiction, *vennas*," said Moore, eyeing Capt. Armstrong, who frowned. "They'll take care of you."

The elevator brought the Estonian and a small group of men to the top floor of Mount Sinai. Artjom started getting anxious. Performing high risk operations from a remote computer was nothing to him, but riding in a helicopter with a bunch of strangers felt different. He saw a bathroom sign and went in before stepping out onto the terrace where the MH-65 Dolphin hummed. An agent stood by the door. Capt. Armstrong eyed his watch until Pärn came out. The pungency of cannabis swirled all around as they boarded the helicopter. Capt. Armstrong was dying to tell off the Estonian as he would his kids, but he couldn't. Pärn's dossier stated the agent performed better under the influence of the leaf.

And so, the nimble MH-65 Dolphin went up into the air, tilted its blades, and dove straight across the turbulent heartland sky.

"Where we headin'?" asked Artjom, stepping into $doomMetalBo mode.

"The Hog Farm, agent," replied Capt. Armstrong cryptically.

"Neat," replied $doomMetalBo, putting on his headphones, though he knew not what The Hog Farm was.

"Wait," said Capt. Armstrong. "I need to fill you in…"

"Herman Moore already did."

"Some details haven't been disclosed outside the Oval Office. Moore's not in that circle."

"Be quick as a bunny, *vennas*. I get nauseous up in here."

Soon after Capt. Armstrong's update, or perhaps even before it ended, $doomMetalBo figured out the MH-65 Dolphin was heading north. It wasn't too long a ride. From above, the scattered trees looked like green broccoli bunches and the little lakes like gravy over mashed potatoes. It was odd. Perhaps the Estonian was just getting the munchies. As the helicopter descended, he saw a vast ranch with something of a golf-course on the left and a horseless equestrian field on the right (there was no sight of a hog farm). Artjom deduced they were in Lebanon, Kansas, the center of the contiguous United States, a nothing place he'd been to as a tourist before. The nothingness of place —his life's bouncy journey there— seemed to reach further into the heart of his dreams than any videogame vision ever could.

They landed. $doomMetalBo followed Capt. Armstrong. They headed in the opposite direction of the silly stone pyramid with a flagpole (the place of his old tourist memento), down a stone path for about 10 minutes, or half a mile, opened an unlocked private gate, and stepped into an unremarkable wooden ranch house with the words "The Hog Farm" engraved on an old bronze sign at the door. The room was wide. There were six backgammon tables scattered around. An elk head hanging on the suede walls caught Artjom Pärn's eye, but there was no time to wonder. A side door that led to a set of deep reaching escalators, such as the ones found in subway stations, was cast open. Before the darkness subsided, $doomMetalBo had the feeling that he was entering the belly of the beast, except the belly took the form of a bright and surprisingly airy computer room. $doomMetalBo was used to working from odd locations (pretend nail salons, massage parlors, bowling alleys, nursing homes) but this was different. The Defense Secretary and the Head of Homeland security were standing by a digitally blown-up photo of the Reggaetón Cruise captured by one Delfin Quishpe. The cruise was a vortex of joy and extravagance, the culmination of all that is wonderful about Uncle Sam's star-spangled nation. Something about it dizzied up the Estonian, who had chosen to live on the flip side of that. But he ignored the vertigo. Capt. Armstrong quickly stood next to the other two men. Looking at those three men before him, $doomMetalBo was invaded by a sense that they were three heads of a single body—the body of the State.

After shaking their moist hands, he heard them go on about procedures and goals. He did not nod. Not even out of politeness.

"That's nonsense," he finally let out as soon as they stopped.

The three heads glanced at each other as $doomMetalBo snatched the laser stick from one of their hands. This wasn't the same puffy guy. He was suddenly slick.

"There's no need to fly diagonally over the funnel," $doomMetalBo added. "We'd be giving the bad guys time to flee or even to shoot us down. It's best to come in... right on the waterline."

"That's dangerous," said General Gordon, Head of Homeland Security, reaching for the laser stick with one of his hands, at which point $doomMetalBo shifted his own hand almost playfully, holding on to the thing.

"Let me ask you something, sir," he said, playing with the stick. "Has the drone been camouflaged?"

"Yes, it has," said Gen. Gordon.

"What color?"

"The color of the sea," intercepted Gen. Lewis, Defense Secretary, "obviously."

"That's terrible, *vennas*. It should be the color of the sky. Change it. There's still time. The best way, as I say, is to come in low. The terrorists might have satellite access for all we know. Foreign intervention or simply hacking. So we come in low and at forty feet from the ship, we fly up vertically, here, by the anchor, and then over the deck in a flipped L fashion. Yes, I agree. It's tougher in terms of target location. We'll find ourselves face to face with the targets, but we must do it like that. I can do it."

"The terrorists are wearing green," added Gen. Gordon.

"Their clothing color has nothing to do with it," said $doomMetalBo.

The authority with which $doomMetalBo spoke was different now. It wasn't the voice of a gamer anymore. It was the voice of an international agent at the top of his game.

"I think what the head of Homeland Security is alluding to, if I may," said Gen. Lewis, "is the fact that the Predator-RPA is equipped with movement-sensitive cameras that can effectively zero in on certain shapes and colors—in this case, green."

$doomMetalBo pretended to write something down. He was trying to cool off.

"That's for amateurs, man, general, sir, with all due respect. Let me ask you something: How many civilians are wearing that same shade of green on the Reggaetón Cruise?"

"We don't know," said the Gen. Lewis.

"Right. That's why we should not, under any circumstances, rely on the bird's color recognition program. Mission Freedom Remote is too critical for duty deferment."

"I see you point…" stated Gen. Gordon.

"Thank you, *vennas*," said $doomMetalBo tapping him on the shoulder. "We don't want to spend half of the time cancelling bad shots generated by the movement-sensitive cameras. If we let ourselves be pressed for time, we could end up shooting civilians. It's the same thing with war videogames. Never depend on the machines if you can do it yourself. It's a principle I've communicated to my online followers repeatedly."

"We *are* expecting civilian casualties," said Gen. Lewis. And then, reacting to $doomMetalBo's intense look. "The Commander in Chief recognizes this as well."

"We should minimize casualties, not maximize them, general."

"We're well aware of that, agent."

"You're proposing is that we let you use your naked eye," cut in Gen. Gordon, annoyed. "That's playing with fire."

Gen. Lewis and Capt. Armstrong made eye contact.

"Are you daft! Jesus on a stick…" exclaimed $doomMetalBo. "Forgive me for being so blunt here, dear sirs, but explaining REWADRO operations to people who've never videogamed in their lives is like explaining calculus to five-year-olds. You simply do not have the background to grasp the intricacies of the situation."

"I advise you to hold your horses, Agent Pärn," said the Secretary of State.

"We're on the same team, young man," added Gen. Gordon, somewhat at a loss.

"Have any of you guys ever flown a Predator-RPA before?"

The three-headed Hydra turned into a headless chicken all of a sudden.

"General Lewis is a Purple Heart veteran of the War on Terror," said Cap. Armstrong.

It was the first thing the CIA Director had said so far.

"I don't give a hoot about the War on Terror, Armstrong. It wasn't too much of a success, was it?" said $doomMetalBo. And then, catching himself a bit: "In all fairness, those are pre-historic times in terms of drone operations. Wait, wait, wait. Let me talk now, *vennas*. Answer my question. Have any of you in your grand, purple-hearted lives ever flown a Predator-RPA before? How about shot an AGM-114 Hellfire missile? Have any of you ever shot warheads from a remote post in real time? Have you even played a war videogame before?"

"Not in real combat, we have not, agent. You know that," stated Gen. Lewis.

"Look. I get it. I might not look like Ethan Matthew Hunt here, but you know and I know and your enemies know that I'm one of the world's top experts in this kinda thing, so let's cut the hierarchical crap, please If you want to call China or Russia to request help from one of *their* agents, go for it, shit pumpers, but if I'm going to be the one to take on the burden, Imma do it my way."

"You may be detained if you refuse to follow directions," said Gen. Lewis.

"Having to shoot at people blindly is the worst kind of detention, General. My guess is you know a thing or two about that."

A blond woman in a grey uniform stepped in.

"It's the President."

The three heads fidgeted about nervously. The woman walked away. Capt. Armstrong remembered what Herman Moore had said about Artjom Pärn back in OKC. He tried a different approach, though what he really wanted to do was to slap the arrogant tinkerbitch.

"Alright Pärn... alright dude, *vennas*, if I may," he said, loosening his red tie, while he looked at the other two heads, as if telling them to roll with it. "Please share what you have in mind. What's your plan? We're all ears."

The Estonian smiled. He saw Moore's hand in this.

"Hold on," he said, and sucked hard on his e-vaper, twice.

"What in the...!" exclaimed the Secretary of State.

"It's in his contract..." said Gen. Gordon.

"Yerp," added Capt. Armstrong, covering his nose. "Helps him focus."

A few tears came out of his $doomMetalBo eyes as he coughed out a cloud of light purple vapor. "All I ask for, um, chiefs, is that the movement-sensitive lenses and all other motion-activated detectors be off. That's it. It's a moral choice. I'll take care of the rest. I promise."

"A moral choice?" asked Gen. Lewis.

"If civilians die —and I'm not naïve enough to think otherwise— it will be *my moral responsibility*, general. Not yours. I'm not a child anymore. I don't want to hide behind a computer program. I'm not a coward. I've never been one. I've been blind or ignorant, which is another thing. You get me? Life's not a videogame. Life might be just as strange as a videogame, and it might be set up like a videogame, but it is not a videogame. I'm trying to confirm that to myself. If you'd spent most of your life your life glued to a dynamic screen you'd develop a sense of unreality too."

"Are you really capable of doing this, Agent Pärn?" asked Gen. Lewis.

$doomMetalBo adjusted his ponytail.

"Not me, the eye. Is it capable? Yes," he declared. "Consider the incredible human eye. Furnished with automatic aiming, automatic focusing, and automatic aperture adjustment, the human eye can function from almost complete darkness to bright sunlight, see an object the diameter of a fine hair, and make about 100,000 separate motions in an average day, faithfully affording us a continuous series of color stereoscopic pictures. All of this is performed without complaint, and then astonishingly, while we sleep, it carries out its own maintenance work – Dr Scott Huse, *The Collapse of Evolution*, a dreadful book, but one inspired description of the human eye. I might be a slob, my man, but I got the best hand-eye coordination since Wang Nan!"

"Wang Nan?"

"Google it."

"This is preposterous…"

"Say what you will. But if in, so's my naked eye."

Smithereens of an Overheated World

Something broke in the global village then. The strongest protests spread from local citizens to global governments. Formerly docile heads of state began speaking up against the United States for what came to be known as *The Reggaetón Cruise Butchery*. The German, Canadian, and Italian governments, among others, recalled their ambassadors from New York. For the first time since World War II, the West seemed truly anemic. Perhaps the event created a wound on people's consciences. It became a kind of litmus test. Individuals had to be either for or against the drone attacks. The media talked about it for days, watching and re-watching the footage from different angles and in slow motion, as if it were a sports match. Spirited demands for justice, which meant not only different but opposing things to different people, were countered with widespread curfews. Some called Artjom Pärn a hero, others a cold blooded murderer. Nobody knew what would happen next.

One thing's certain: for Artjom Pärn, the videogame wiz; Delfín Quishpe, the viral migrant; Alvo Garzón, the estranged champ; Mamadú Anderson, the investor refugee; and for Yukiko, Kaori and Eimi Furukawa, the roaming sisters of Japan (alongside family members and others involved) the present age became a sort of multidirectional ejection. A transnational array of futures and destinations greeted their shifting dreams.

The Young Survivors of Claretown FC

Kaori was released from the University of Miami Hospital, after which the Furukawas reconvened at the Trump Hotel's presidential suite. Mamadú Anderson and Álvaro Garzón were not invited to the family reunion and resented the fact. For 72 hours they had to make do with inaccurately captioned media reports out of Japan. All kinds of things were reported. That the Furukawas were taking a charter plane back to Tokyo; that they were suing both the Reggaetón Cruise and the US Department of Defense; that the Japanese government was behind the impending lawsuit; that friction was growing in the family due to Little Eimi's support for The Coalition; and that Yusuke was gathering funds for a film version of the events. Media conjecture, and circular talks about *il calcio Italiano*, were all the Liberian and the Ecuadorian had, until at the end of the third day, they were finally asked to come up.

Little Eimi had either borrowed or rented a separate room in the same hotel just so that she could meet with Mamadú. She did not want her parents to hear what she had to say. It was true! She was displaying Stockholm-y support for The Coalition, though her support wasn't, as the reports had stated, unequivocal. She agreed with the reasons for the hijacking, though she disagreed with The Coalition's methods. Which was bizarre to the Liberian. Not only her words but her face: it was changed. Something had cracked inside. Or rather, a step had been taken, which can be the same thing.

Mamadú grabbed her hand. She let go at once.

"I'm not going back to Japan with my family," she said.

Mamadú's eyes lit up. That's what he cared about. He hugged her.

"But," she added stepping back, "I'm going to make some changes. Sit down."

He sat down, his long legs stuck out of the couch, as Little Eimi walked around the room in a flowing dress or whatever that floral thing was, talking about the research she'd done. She began with the evils of the cruise industry, which Mamadú had already heard *ad nauseum*. He looked at the artwork on the wall as she talked. It was the same painting as the one in the presidential room. Well, it was a chopped-up or zoomed-in version, but it was the same. The same impossibly forlorn (to him) Cézanne landscape. How foolish could he have been to think it was an original? If you wanted an original, you had to go to a museum or you had to go buy your own. You could go to Walmart or you could try to paint one, yes, yes, you could try to paint your own Cézanne. His mind was moored to the painting as she went on about capitalism, which was apparently destroying the world. And then materialism, which was destroying the soul.

"And you're going to fight all of this by staying in America?" Mamadú probed, regretting his brusque tone at once.

"Let me talk man, for too long men have been silencing women around the world," she said. And then, as if assimilating his words: "So what, *you want me to go back?*"

"Sorry: You've been through a lot, babe. Of course I don't want you to go back-ya."

"I have a plan, Dú," she said, holding his fingers in her small right hand, which he noticed with horror, had the words *rebel fleur* freshly tattooed on top. "I mean, it's not set on stone. We have options."

Mamadú leaned forward. She hadn't even told him about the tattoo. It was written in the crude, cursive writing formerly associated with jail ink. What was next? A kiss on her neck? A tear under the eye? He placed his gold watch on his knee which sparkled in the light. She began pacing around the room again and spoke of a vegan-yoga collective near Eureka, California, where members lived in equality and balance with nature. It was clear Little Eime had a gift for words, both big and small, but Mamadú was already aware of that. He wasn't uplifted by her words. Not this time.

"I just want to try it out," she added, reading his face. She wasn't deranged, she'd merely been radicalized, which is different. "I think it'd be good for you too. A faraway ranch is the perfect place to face our fears together, Dú-Dú."

"And how are we supposed to work there?"

"And why is it that one needs *to work* anywhere?"

"Why is it that one needs to work..." he repeated drily, holding the weight of the question inside. The weight was Biblical, that is, impossible to sustain. "Bah!" he chuckled.

She said the vegan-yoga-collective folks worked for each other, not just for themselves, and that the nature of the work was limited because it wasn't about amassing wealth, but about keeping well, because that's what humans needed in this life, to keep well.

"In *this* life? I see, as opposed to all our other lives. And what's the name of this wonderful home where we're to relocate-ya?"

"Not if you ask like that!" she snapped back. "What's so wonderful about amassing wealth anyway, Mr. money man?"

Mamadú loved her bite. It was so compressed in her. He stayed silent, not because he was considering the question, whose answer to him —a war refugee turned investor who could conjure up America, Japan, and Liberia's *per capita* GDP at will— was insultingly obvious, but because Little Eimi looked so beautiful then. He held her in the eye for as long as he could instead.

"Well?" she queried, as perky as a cat.

"I don't know," he slurred, feeling a wave of sorrow.

It was that or a burst of anger, but he wasn't about to get angry at her, not anymore, not ever again. He understood, he really did. In many ways she was right, which was the whole tragedy of the junction.

"The only thing," she added, looking slightly deflated and deranged for the first time, considering the sideral distance between them, which she either misjudged or willfully ignored, "is that to come to Eureka you got to become vegan, Dú-Dú. And it's not only because of the people at the ranch, but because I got to draw the line for myself. I cannot be with someone who eats animals. Not with the meat industry being what it is. I got take these steps for myself."

"What if I don't go vegan?"

"You should've seen the butchery at the cruise, Dú-Dú. And the videos they showed us. It was some crazy, eye-opening stuff."

"Answer me. What if I don't go vegan?"

"Then we can't be together anymore."

A bitter smile emerged between the Liberian's heart and himself. There had been a tension in their relationship before. Everyone saw. And that tension, which had made things so tight and sexual had now snapped. Hence the bitter smile: completion of a death foretold. He placed the gold watch on his forehead and thought, as he often did, of how he'd killed his little friend as a child. There was a darkness in him Little Eimi would never, ever understand. It was that same darkness which generated his superpower: the way he could just walk through the eye of terror with the certitude that the other side would be fine. They'd emerged from different planets. It had always been the case.

"I love you Little Eimi, *my big jue*," he said, standing up.

My big jue, that's what he always called her. Her eyes filled with tears.

"Wait. You could start by becoming vegetarian and then work your way up to veganism. I'm already at raw, it's doable. You don't even like red meat anymore. I know you don't. You never did. Come on, Dú-Dú."

"Eureka, Afree-ca, paprika," he uttered, ruthlessly playful and utterly sappy all at once.

The power was in his smile, in his acidic giggle, and in his ability to hold on to it, though the situation burned.

That was that. He hugged Little Eimi and then he left.

As he went down the Trump Hotel's gilded elevator, he felt something like relief. He'd travelled across country to ask Little Eimi to marry him, and had ended up breaking up with her instead. But he'd also travelled across the United States, it turns out, to give back to her, as best he could, a little bit of the understanding he'd previously withheld from her. He knew she knew, or would eventually know, that he approved of her crazy move. Not because he respected Mc-yoga, raw diets, or cult-y retreats with quack-y gurus in the hills —screw all that shit— but because he knew Little Eimi craved the rupture. It was right. She needed to find her darkness, and in it, her own superpower. If anyone could in that family, it was she. She wouldn't last in the Eureka collective, he knew. And the crash or hangover or would be terrible. But that would be her trip. It would have been nice to be thanked for driving across country just to see her, no doubt, but oh well. It's not like he'd apologized for all of his angry outbursts. He'd seen what he needed to see. And they'd also hugged.

Back at the bleach-smelling Motel 6, he answered a call from a Japanese agent.

"I'll think about it-ya," was all he'd replied.

Money. A guest appearance. Fuji Television. A chat with the injured reporter. Questions about the Furukawas. His own side of the story. It would be too much to say the Liberian played with the idea. He considered it in its full ridiculousness instead. Even pictured a spotlight on his face. *Bah!* He thought of King George as he showered, and just how the old bossman had made his way up the ranks. From the Young Survivors of Claretown (a team without a coach), to Paris Saint-Germain, and finally to A.C. Milan, where he'd been the first African to win —to earn— a *Ballon d'Or*. A high school diploma at 40. Then the Liberian presidency. Focus. Discipline. The empirical compass of work for its own sake. Those were the things Mamadú Anderson wanted the most in life, actually, not turning into an exotic media plaything for overworked Tokyoites, nor spending hours meditating in the Eureka bush with a bunch of blue-eyed yogis. He took a nap, during which he had a dream: he was sitting in a Trump Hotel room again, not a guest-room, but a sort of storage room, where the staff kept towels, bed sheets, pillowcases, Clorox, brushes and lots of basil-scented soap. He was sitting in a chair, looking at the Cézanne landscape, as the cleaning ladies went to and fro chatting and singing in a sort of jubilation of work, but the landscape wasn't a painting because the hills were afire with animal vibrations. So he stood up and stepped in, and behold, it wasn't Europe but a pristine corner of the Bong Range in LIB. He was right. He had been right. There were songs coming from the river.

After he woke up, he texted his annoying puffy-chested *amigo* and within an hour he was at Miami International. As he lingered at the crowded gate, he thought of all the ways one could go across the U.S.A. By car, by train, by airplane. Some fuckers even walked! And the reason for that was that they all wanted different things from the same land. The Liberian was no different. He had a personal relationship with America to honor. There were ritzy apartments to be placed in L.A. and a long road home to be laid down across the fields.

Torrid Guayaquil

"Come with me to Guayaquil," Alvo said.

The ring seemed to pulsate between Kaori's elegant fingers, but it wasn't magic. Perhaps it was the bright Atlantic in the expansive windows. Perhaps it was the Florida waves crashing on the rocks below. Perhaps it was the doctor's pills. Whatever it was, the presidential suite's media lounge seemed to gyrate all around.

"I love you like the 10th grade!" is all Kaori replied.

Back in the main room, Yukiko and her parents could hear the giggling next door as they packed. The flight to Tokyo would take off that same night. Still, the attack (all the crazy fee fees in it) had cemented the former ballerina's attraction to Sergio Tortelli, who'd landed in Rome the day prior. They'd agreed to meeting in neutral territory next summer; Santorini, Pattaya, and Punta del Este were options. The question was whether their attraction —and the world's stability for that matter— would last a year. The shared trauma certainly would. As for the lawsuit, the rumor was true. The Prime minister of Japan himself had asked Mr. Furukawa to sue. "A matter of national pride," he'd called it. Mr. Fumihiro, Yusuke's assistant, would handle the paperwork in Florida. The young star was now back in Tokyo, securing funding for The Reggaetón Cruise movie. Yusuke's plan was not, as it'd been widely reported, to star in it. He wanted to direct it.

The days went by.

Once in torrid Guayaquil, Alvo had taken care of stuff, just as his Liberian friend had suggested. Despite his aspirations, and Mamadú's pro-tips, smoking a washed-up former coach was not in his character, but a few shoves and a whole lot of *carevergas* were. Which had made him feel infinitely better, particularly that first burst... which had symbolized a child's ability to stand up for himself. The old lack, the source of his malaise, had been addressed then. A racing of the voice and a dilation of the nostrils before an old fart had materialized like a revelation to the former champ, who was still, indeed, in his 30's. After that, he felt like a man. A young man! A weight had been lifted. But in truth it was also seeing what that Córsica, the child slapper, had turned into. Not because Álvaro Garzón was happy to see the suffering of a man, but because it spoke about the law of unintended consequences or retribution or whatever. And it could have been naïve, or excessively Catholic of him, but then again, he was who he was and proud of it. Life had given the old fucker what he'd deserved. God and none other had put things in their place. In this case, ill health and unsanitary conditions. So once the grievances were expelled, there was nothing to do there. Alvo left that dingy suburb, and particularly Córsica's messy house, which was already abstracted in his memory, like a symbol, not before dropping some dollars on the floor, for food or drugs or whatever. Not out of selflessness: the old fart would have to pick up the dough with the same hand he'd slapped a child with. "*Buenas tardes*" Alvo said at last, courteously, like his well-off parents had taught him, and closed the door, making a point not to slam it, not because he couldn't slam it, but because he didn't want to slam it, the same way he didn't want to wait to see the other's afront, but to let the wounds heal inside, where they actually were.

Kaori, soon to be Kaori Garzón-Furukawa, was waiting for Alvo at the ritzy beach town of Salinas, drinking a Piña Colada by yet another pool. The view from the hotel's terrace was even better that the view at Miami Beach. It was amazing how far his little country had come, though in truth, to Álvaro Garzón, the Republic of Ecuador had never ever been deprived. The marriage would take place at the Guayaquil Tennis Club, where Pancho Segura, Andrés Gómez and Nico Lapentti had played. Not that Kaori nor her family cared about those foreign national luminaries. Neither did the former champ, actually, not that much, but holding the wedding at the club would be like extending an olive branch to his family, who at the end of the day were just a bunch of people who had tried their best, and at times, but only at times, failed, because (he was coming to accept it, particularly as he took pride in his own actions) at times they had succeeded as well. He was living proof of it.

But the matter of staying, like his folks had suggested, was something else.

"If you don't like Guayaquil, we don't have to stay, you know," Alvo said.

Kaori knew him well. That's how Latin men got requests across. By pretending they were asking for you.

She looked on.

"How about Okinawa?" she finally asked.

"Or wherever you like..." he replied.

"Aha," she said, and softly waited.

Her softness was caramelized further by the equatorial sun on her shoulders.

"What's Okinawa like?" he asked.

"Okinawa's like Hawaii."

He smiled.

"Like Cancún."

"Right."

"Like Bali, but with less nature."

"I see, I see," he said, noting that he'd been stuck in the middle of a bridge for too long.

And that it was time to cross. And that the crossing was the main reason he'd fallen for her. And her golden tan. And the eternal summer in her ways. And that wonderful naiveté deeper than his own. They were similar people. There wouldn't be disagreements as to how to raise children, for one.

"Okinawa is so humid, with a beautiful ocean, and slow time," she said, rolling a strand of highlighted hair in her manicured finger. "If they say we're meeting at 3, it usually means 4!"

"So, it's the same as Guayaquil..."

"You guys drink rum. In Okinawa they drink soju made the old fashioned way."

"And the food?"

"Lots of seafood. I love Okinawa noodles."

"And...?"

"And...Okinawa people really, really love Okinawa."

"I could teach tennis anywhere, *mi amor*."

"I'll go wherever you want, Alvo-san," she said, "so long as it's not back to America. It's just too primitive over there."

He spread open his right hand. She handed him her Piña Colada. It was frosty still.

"What about Shibuya?" he asked, brain-frozen and giddy. "What's Shibuya like?"

Like Champagne

Delfín Quishpe was more sought after than ever, though his permanence in America had become problematic. Like the Estonian REWADRO, the viral star, had become controversial despite himself. American conservatives hailed him as a hero. Signatures were being collected to get him the National Medal of Honor. American leftists, on the other hand, considered him a foolish instrument of State murder. There was talk that the remnant members of The Coalition, now further radicalized, had put a price on his head. It was unclear how Quishpe saw things himself. As soon as The Reggaetón Cruise had docked in back in Miami, he'd deleted his social media accounts and vanished from the public eye. Not until his autobiography, *Pequeño Gigante*, came out had the public learned of the man's whereabouts and, it must be said, of his new zazzle. He'd pierced his nose, attempted to grow a beard, changed hat colors, and gotten a large condor tattooed on his chest—all featured on the book cover.

The book detailed how he'd married Veronica Rodriguez in Harlem, securing her American papers before taking a cruise around the Mediterranean, where he'd powered through his fear of ships with curses, prayers, and jokes. The rest had been the typically profligate Mediterranean honeymoon of *nouveau riche* émigrés with new American passports. The fact that Delfín didn't care to hide his wealth, nor where it came from, earned him further online adoration. He was the dream's proof. And said so in his autobiography: "For someone who came up in a mud hut, money in America does indeed grow on trees. You just got to grab it!" (Quishpe 178). After the trip, however, the newlyweds did not head back to the United States, but secretly south instead.

The plane landed with difficulty, as it often does in Quito, Ecuador, which is perched upon an orgasm of volcanos and chasms. Delfín put on Ray-bans and a mask. So did Veronica and her aunt, *Doña* Rosario, who would help out with the coming baby. Once in the Escalade, he put his head on the window and slept through the ride along the Avenue of the Volcanos. He woke up in Guamote. Nothing seemed to have changed, except the old bus station, which had been turned into fruit stand. When the vehicle couldn't go on due to the rough terrain, the three Americans as they later, and perhaps bitingly, came to be known in the town, shook their tingly legs and began the trek up the Santa Rosa trail. Veronica and *Doña* Rosario talked to each other in the overwhelming Dominican fashion all the way through, so that they didn't even notice the extreme altitude. Delfín was hauling the luggage several feet behind. He'd neglected to hire help. Eventually the three Americans arrived at the ancient plateau. There were lots of people there. Veronica and *Doña* Rosario waved back.

Delfín looked around: same trees, same blue hills, the same sun plunging at exactly the same angle. Only the faces had changed. Or rather, the faces were the same, but they now belonged to different personalities. As he noted in *Pequeño Gigante*: "Those who'd been *guaguas* had adult masks on now; those who'd been adults, had old masks on now; and those who'd been old, had shrunken masks on, like fallen fruit on the earth, for time is like a dance in which the same masks are passed on from generation to generation. My plan is getting this thought tattooed on my ribs someday" (Quishpe 294).

Many weren't there anymore. But Puramama was there. And the old teacher, Mr. Ibañez, was there. And further along the ancient plateau, near the cliff, Antay, and *Fantasma*, his old horse, and Karina, and a bunch of babies, who weren't so much babies anymore, but grown kids who'd sprouted like yellow corn on a field, which was the same field, were there. Suddenly, as if prompted by the mountains, the Andean thought of the day he'd crossed into the United States years and years ago. He recalled the funny drunk's directions in Tijuana. *Seven kilometers to the east, turn left, avoid the hills, do not enter the red valley, hide behind the cone-shaped rocks, wait for the right moment, hours if you must, then cross.* He'd learned the whole thing by heart, pauses and all. And not for aught. He'd made it into The Core with the two little Hondurans! And then there was all that had come to pass. Their lives, his own, events, circumstances, outcomes, years. And now he was standing on another verge. The verge of homecoming.

He stood still before the ancient plateau. *Then cross* —he repeated to himself feeling the pulsation of mountains and rocks as if they were breathing— *then cross.*

All of his Guamote *paisanos* were watching him like he was some kind of hero or something. It was then he understood that he too was wearing a different mask. An older, weathered one. Something settled inside then, like a click, a click he was silent enough, Andean enough, to hear. And so he realized that you can't just bring yourself home like a corpse that a transnational jet transports in a coffin. You can't leave your spent years behind. "If you do, you run the danger of turning into a goat, or into the ghost of a goat, which is worse" (Quishpe 300). Delfín Quishpe had lived under the sun and stars of the United States, under the gravity of its gold. That was not fake. It was real. He patted his own chest (though what he really wanted to do was beat it like a silverback king). It was alright. One could not step back in like the one who had stepped out. Too many years had passed. Something had to be done. The body shifted, but the heart stayed put.

He kept looking.

Embarrassed at her husband's frozenness, Veronica, who was quite taller, elbowed him in the tummy. His arms were heavy but of course he waved back at his people. He waved back! Then, hurling his smile forward, he allowed it to brand his face, his unequivocal Inca face. As if on cue, Chuco's descendants dashed down the hill, frantically waving their tails. Delfín kneeled down in joy. He pet each little pooch. Same eyes, same lick, same smell. Old Chuco incarnate. "*Hi beautiful babies,*" he said in English (Quishpe 322). The words had come from the inside and, for some reason, in Uncle Sam's beautiful tongue. Somehow the path was cleared then; the threshold, crossed. The *arrivé* flung off his shades into the chasm and the *indio* began to cry.

Three days of well-earned celebrations ensued. Pigs, chickens, and guinea pigs were slaughtered galore. Kegs of *puntas* and *chicha* were drunk. Guamote's marching band played *San Juanitos* for two days. Ecua-volley tourneys took place that weekend. Then, just like that, the masks settled. Things went back to normal again. Except for the Quishpes, whose lives were in flux. Within a month, famed Swiss architect Pierre Herzog arrived in the country and began the construction of a modern house next to Puramama's hut. Herzog's idea was to build the new house around the hut, incorporating ancient Quichua motifs into the building. The result, as documented by *Modern Design,* was a breakthrough in Latin American architecture. Not that Delfín cared about such things. He devoted himself to raising his baby girl, whom he and Veronica had named Anahí. Now and then he'd hear of book sales, page clicks, and such. He'd been willfully overlooking that stuff for years, but the numbers proved it: he was still the most famous Ecuadorian in the world. He let it be. Two more years passed that way. Only after his second child, Comrade, was grown a little, did Delfín step back into the public eye. The next step was bold —he'd gained confidence by living where the Apus live— and from the heart. He signed on as presidential candidate for the newly formed *Unidad Nacional Party.*

One campaign image stayed in people's eyes: on a crowded wooden platform full of dancers and confetti, a nerdy Telemundo journalist asked him, the wildcard candidate, whether he was left wing or right-wing. Delfín Quishpe looked at Felix Matamba, former Vasco Da Gama striker, whom he'd artfully picked as running mate for the battle. Matamba, who as former Captain of the national Ecuadorian soccer team commanded respect, hollered at the rowdy crowd of poncho-wearing Andeans below to quiet down. The cameras zoomed in. It was a tense moment. One could've heard a pin drop, but Delfín did not rush. He'd seen a lot in life and knew better than to rush. He grabbed the mic and stepped forward at his own pace.

The arresting length of the hush kept echoing throughout the joint.

"Neither left nor right, comrade," he finally declared, raising his index, "I'm a *runa* candidate for the *runa* people of the center of the world. A little bit Che, a little bit Uncle Sam, and very much Taita Rumiñahui hahahaha!"

The public knew Delfín, but that laughter was new. It was crazier, bubblier, and soaked in guts because it had come from the belly, which carried the depths of all he had seen. And it was with that laughter that the *Unidad Nacional Party* crushed the national polls, like champagne rushing from below.

Supreme Warrior Tier II

As requested by $doomMetalBo, the Predator-RPA drone was stationed on a unit camouflaged as a fishing boat off of Guantánamo Bay. $doomMetalBo flew low at first, then straight up about forty feet from the Reggaetón Cruise. The first group of Coalition rebels to be annihilated mistook the drone for a big pelican. By the time terrorists and tourists (who in their horror were the same) saw what the big pelican was, the AGM-114 Hellfire missiles were upon them. Exactly four minutes and thirty-two seconds later, $doomMetalBo turned off the computer, leaned back in his ergonomic chair, and withdrew a thick cloud of cannabis from his e-vaper. When his eyes opened, he saw, as if in slow motion, a bunch of Special Forces gorillas charging.

Within 48 hours, the Estonian's mother and brother were on planes from Tallinn and London, respectively. It was baffling. Military experts agreed that Artjom Pärn's performance constituted the most remarkable tour de force in the history of military drone operations. The gaming wunderkind had blasted every single terrorist on the Reggaetón Cruise deck by —in rogue policy transgression— flinging the Predator-RPA through the ship's superstructure, and doing so with the panache of one who's playing a videogame in a suburban PC Room, and not one who's performing a high-stakes anti-terrorism operation from an undisclosed bunker near the heart of an empire. The flamboyance had paid off. Just three members of The Coalition had survived for the subsequent SWAT operation. But most outstandingly, not a single crew member or tourist had been neutralized. Yes: $doomMetalBo's hand-eye dexterity would land him in the books. And yet, if charged in a military trial, he could get the death penalty. The grounds were clear. In an act of rebellion, whistle-blowing, or youthful idealism, he'd surreptitiously activated the Predator-RPA's eagle-eye cameras and had also, *somehow* —that was still under investigation— linked the resulting video to a live feed on his YouTube channel, thus allowing web surfers all over the world to witness aghast as scores of young green-clad terrorists (radicals? ideologues?) were shredded to pieces. The *Reggaetón Cruise Butchery Feed,* as it was called, spread like wildfire through an overheated field; a field that was, indeed, the entirety of the planet earth's internet connection.

Artjom Pärn felt the sharp karate-chop on his fleshy neck. The Special Forces gorillas dragged him to the bathroom, stripped him naked, and took away his possessions, e-vaper, phone, and all. Then he found himself back in the same MH-65 Dolphin, above the unremarkable wooden ranch house known as The Hog farm, the little broccoli clusters in Lebanon, Kansas. This time the helicopter flew far. When Artjom finally inquired about the destination, a s*hut up, you traitor*, was the reply. And so he stayed quiet until sleep came encased in the drowning hum of the engine. The Estonian gamer, for that's what he still was, began dreaming of the Ghost of Tsushima, of the sacred skies of Halo, and of the wondrous strips of fire in Infinite Warfare. Abstractions. All of these landscapes, the landscape, and the hero, himself. He half opened his eyes. Mountains vary, but clouds are the same everywhere. From above, again the trees looked like little pieces of broccoli, or like the medieval forests of Nagasaki, which he'd traversed, or like the entrance to the Dilapidated Field of his years, so many rooms, so many screens, controllers, keyboards, and chairs ago, but most of all, the Hollywood PC Room in Tallin, the bright lime BMX he'd ride back home by the medieval towers or along the train tracks, Motörhead blasting in the ears. But as the purr of the blades subsided and the bodies descended in the flying machine, which could have been an Annihilator-X75, it became apparent to $doomMetalBo, Artjom Pärn, the Estonian, who was also an international agent, that they weren't touching ground in a videogame world, nor in The Land of Memories Old, but oddly, vexingly, in actuality, the place of his entrapment: a vulgar American prison somewhere.

In a world already on the verge, the *Reggaetón Cruise Butchery Feed* (now, of course, the most viral of all time) had exacerbated matters. Thus his incarceration. The best Artjom Pärn could hope for was a civil trial. His mother, brother and wife moved heaven and earth, but to no avail. The very apparatus that had propped him up for years had now swallowed him up with the same inexorable dexterity. National Security: box, keeper, and lid. A mute darkness settled in.

Then, a year and a half later, the following image took traction:

As requested by $doomMetalBo, the Predator-RPA drone was stationed on a unit camouflaged as a fishing boat off of Guantánamo Bay. $doomMetalBo flew low at first, then straight up about forty feet from the Reggaetón Cruise. The first group of Coalition rebels to be annihilated mistook the drone for a big pelican. By the time terrorists and tourists (who in their horror were the same) saw what the big pelican was, the AGM-114 Hellfire missiles were upon them. Exactly four minutes and thirty-two seconds later, $doomMetalBo turned off the computer, leaned back in his ergonomic chair, and withdrew a thick cloud of cannabis from his e-vaper. When his eyes opened, he saw, as if in slow motion, a bunch of Special Forces gorillas charging.

Within 48 hours, the Estonian's mother and brother were on planes from Tallinn and London, respectively. It was baffling. Military experts agreed that Artjom Pärn's performance constituted the most remarkable tour de force in the history of military drone operations. The gaming wunderkind had blasted every single terrorist on the Reggaetón Cruise deck by —in rogue policy transgression— flinging the Predator-RPA through the ship's superstructure, and doing so with the panache of one who's playing a videogame in a suburban PC Room, and not one who's performing a high-stakes anti-terrorism operation from an undisclosed bunker near the heart of an empire. The flamboyance had paid off. Just three members of The Coalition had survived for the subsequent SWAT operation. But most outstandingly, not a single crew member or tourist had been neutralized. Yes: $doomMetalBo's hand-eye dexterity would land him in the books. And yet, if charged in a military trial, he could get the death penalty. The grounds were clear. In an act of rebellion, whistle-blowing, or youthful idealism, he'd surreptitiously activated the Predator-RPA's eagle-eye cameras and had also, *somehow* —that was still under investigation— linked the resulting video to a live feed on his YouTube channel, thus allowing web surfers all over the world to witness aghast as scores of young green-clad terrorists (radicals? ideologues?) were shredded to pieces. The *Reggaetón Cruise Butchery Feed,* as it was called, spread like wildfire through an overheated field; a field that was, indeed, the entirety of the planet earth's internet connection.

Artjom Pärn felt the sharp karate-chop on his fleshy neck. The Special Forces gorillas dragged him to the bathroom, stripped him naked, and took away his possessions, e-vaper, phone, and all. Then he found himself back in the same MH-65 Dolphin, above the unremarkable wooden ranch house known as The Hog farm, the little broccoli clusters in Lebanon, Kansas. This time the helicopter flew far. When Artjom finally inquired about the destination, a s*hut up, you traitor*, was the reply. And so he stayed quiet until sleep came encased in the drowning hum of the engine. The Estonian gamer, for that's what he still was, began dreaming of the Ghost of Tsushima, of the sacred skies of Halo, and of the wondrous strips of fire in Infinite Warfare. Abstractions. All of these landscapes, the landscape, and the hero, himself. He half-opened his eyes. Mountains vary, but clouds are the same everywhere. From above, again the trees looked like little pieces of broccoli, or like the medieval forests of Nagasaki, which he'd traversed, or like the entrance to the Dilapidated Field of his years, so many rooms, so many screens, controllers, keyboards, and chairs ago, but most of all, the Hollywood PC Room in Tallin, the bright lime BMX he'd ride back home by the medieval towers or along the train tracks, Motörhead blasting in the ears. But as the purr of the blades subsided and the bodies descended in the flying machine, which could have been an Annihilator-X75, it became apparent to $doomMetalBo, Artjom Pärn, the Estonian, who was also an international agent, that they weren't touching ground in a videogame world, nor in The Land of Memories Old, but oddly, vexingly, in actuality, the place of his entrapment: a vulgar American prison somewhere.

In a world already on the verge, the *Reggaetón Cruise Butchery Feed* (now, of course, the most viral of all time) had exacerbated matters. Thus his incarceration. The best Artjom Pärn could hope for was a civil trial. His mother, brother and wife moved heaven and earth, but to no avail. The very apparatus that had propped him up for years had now swallowed him up with the same inexorable dexterity. National Security: box, keeper, and lid. A mute darkness settled in.

Then, a year and a half later, the following image took traction:

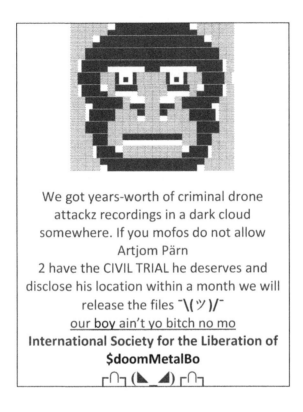

We got years-worth of criminal drone attackz recordings in a dark cloud somewhere. If you mofos do not allow Artjom Pärn
2 have the CIVIL TRIAL he deserves and disclose his location within a month we will release the files ¯\(ツ)/¯
our boy ain't yo bitch no mo
International Society for the Liberation of $doomMetalBo
┌∩┐(◣_◢)┌∩┐

Experts dismissed the image as a teenage hoax, or a stupid meme, but the bomb was actually real, and it did drop. A mammoth file teeming with hours of Predator-RPA videos landed at Human Rights Watch International. Artjom Pärn and his family claimed no relation to it. The State Department thought otherwise. They went after Cheryl Pärn, his wife, who sought asylum in Estonia. The EU steeped in, so did Anonymous, and even the remnants of The Coalition—and thus, the real mess began... in The Core, that is, for most of The Peripheral world remained uninvolved, beautifully uninvolved.

FINITO.

Afterword

Sometime around 1999, when I wondered into a sort of boutique west of La Brea looking for art supplies, I discovered globalization. Having lived in L.A.'s Chinatown and Koreatown, the global world had been my reality for about four years. I had already gotten my first American kiss from a black girl named Tina while spinning the bottle in the apartment complex where we lived. I played soccer with Hondurans and Salvadorans in the afternoons by the Lafayette Park courthouse. My best friend spoke Russian and Armenian, and understood the true weight of the term war refugee. I'd gotten into a first fight with a boy from Mexico during class break and been to Disneyland during summer break. My Algebra teacher, Ms. Agatep, was from the Philippines. My English teacher, Ms. Laughlin, from Canada. My favorite food would soon be *sushi,* and then *phở*, and then *pad thai*

We were L.A. immigrants alright. We no longer lived in my grandparents' estate on the outskirts of Quito. Though our beautiful *quinta* had a pool, a tennis court, and a grass soccer field, it did not have a phone connection, nor the internet. In L.A. we had a phone and the internet, and cable, but we lived in a small apartment. My stepfather who was an architect back home now worked as a security guard in a smoky Mexican joint. It was different. Not only had our tourist visa expired a while back, but also, there was a sort of tension we had stepped in. It's the same colorful tension one feels at an airport waiting room. I'd call it the preamble of hope. The whole city had that tension because the whole city was an airport. We were the passengers! I was extremely taken by it, but also, well, disoriented. The city rhythms were becoming my own. Though part of me still had trouble accepting (not mentally but, like, physiologically) that in our North

American reality, as rich and as dynamic as it was, there was no pool, no court, and no soccer field at home. Grandma wasn't waiting for me with *sopa de bolas de verde* or some other coastal Ecuadorian concoction after I got home in my white shirt, blue tie, and a cotton cardigan with the golden pin on the left, right over the heart. We wore no school uniform in Hollywood High. Our attire was individually haphazard, urban baggy, or goth. As for food, Taco Bell wasn't the norm, but I had come to know the difference between combo number one and combo number two; same thing with Carl's Junior.

Well, that afternoon in 1999, when I wondered into a sort of boutique west of La Brea looking for art supplies, I came across Manu Chao's album *Clandestino*, and discovered globalization condensed. The songs were about migrants; the rhythms French, Arabic, Latin, and Punk. The output was multilingual; the aesthetic, pastiche. It was a global quilt of sorts. I couldn't buy it then because I was in the 11th grade and did not have the money. But I had wandered into a global chamber, in art form, in this case music, which is liquid architecture, as Goethe said. The point is, I was already immersed in the city-airport, that colorful tension, had been for years, but it wasn't until I encountered a musical object that boiled it down to 45 minutes or 16 songs that I felt it *as a thing*. It was like holding a mirror to your own face for the first time after a four year expedition. *Oh wow, that's me now!* I can't convey the exhilaration, but the cognitive grasp. Nirvana, Guns and Roses, and all of the other angry rock bands I had worshiped thus far could not do what Manu Chao's *Clandestino* did for me conceptually. Here was indeed the work of art that opens up a whole field for the young artist. Baudelaire was supposed to have done the same for T.S. Elliott. Now, Manu Chao is not Baudelaire and I am certainly no T.S. Elliott, thank God, but I understand how art opens up worlds, especially ones that had already been your own.

I wrote this novel, *Reggaetón Cruise*, for my students. Or I wrote it for myself to better understand the contemporary world, in order to help them grasp it, so that they could consider it for themselves. By contemporary world, I mean the distinct atmosphere that starts emerging after the fall of the Berlin Wall in 1989, when most of the glove becomes a superhighway of open commercial, cultural, and racial exchange between faraway lands.

Of course the world had been heading in that direction for a while. Take the Immigration and Nationality Act of 1965, through which the USA opens up to the Global South, which readily steps in. Incredibly, the global acceptance of Malcolm Mclean's standardized shipping container, which has huge implications for world trade, happens at essentially the same time. Yet it was the post-Berlin-Wall opening of the global economic superhighway that fires up the contemporary atmosphere. Everything gets quickly intense after 1989. Part of that is technology: the chip in your MasterCard, the cloning of Dolly, the booming supernova called internet, the GPS in your car, AI, Viagra, lab-grown meat, facial recognition, and SpaceX's reusable rockets. There are also key events that seem far apart in time (from up close) but which with a little distance will seem to have taken place almost simultaneously: 9/11, the rise of Amazon, the cultural embrace of smart phones, Chinas 14.23% GDP growth in 2007, war drone attacks, Facebook, Uber, the Covid, and suddenly you're right there in the thickness of the thing.

The thing is so thick, its atmosphere so hazy, like floodlights on a misty field, that none of us really knows when it coagulated or how to go about navigating it. Many try to push against it or pretend it is not here. But we know it's here. We're all plugged in. All we need to do is open up a window and breathe in the pixels. There's also the question of when and how it will end. It might not be possible to shut down the window, which is scary. That movie *The Matrix* comes to mind. All we know is that the floodgates broke around the time the USSR fell and McDonalds set up shop everywhere. This is almost a joke, but many youngsters are so deep in the thing, the pea soup fog of the current world, that they feel history began like 40 years ago. And that a trip or a wedding don't count unless posted on Instagram. In a way they're right. I'm no spiritual purist. The folks of The Coalition are. I pay for my Disneyland tickets with plastic and post the pictures online, and at the right angle too. My late friend, artist Aldo Tambellini, rightly called us "primitives of a new era."

Of course there's a chance I'm making too much of the present. Today's is just another era as there have been so many eras before. The world is not new. The world is old. The whole idea of the advancement of humanity is iffy to say the least. It's all tradeoffs, as Thomas Sowell would put it. Still, we live in a time and that time has an atmosphere, a style, a compression, and a speed. Now and then it feels like it's all about to burst into flames. But it might just be a feeling. Contemporary neurosis. The Communists thought they were creating a new man ☺.Whatever it is, the distinct atmosphere of the times is worth looking into. We're all traveling on its superhighway anyhow. Think of how you got this book or where the chair you're sitting on came from and how. It's all quite dynamic, not to say dizzying, not to say nauseating in the Six Flags kind of way. One of the books I consulted to get a grip on the ordeal was Thomas Hylland Eriksen's *Globalization*. A few years back I tried teaching it to my students. It was a bit too dry for them. They needed the sweet juice of art to go with it. Turns out I needed the sweet juice of art too. In Delfín Quishpe's ordeal I see one of the possible trajectories of our uprooted times. In Mamadú Anderson I see a plausible ethics. In Alvo Garzón I see hope. In Artjom Pärn, I see a warning and an attempt at redemption. It's hardly an exaggeration. My characters are my gurus. Now I understand the present a little bit better —my fears are better formed— and I hope this is true for my pupils as well.

I should say that *Reggaetón Cruise* owes its spirit, and some of its lexical exuberance to *Heart of Darkness*, except the journey here is to a different epicenter. In fact, I almost titled it *Heart of Lights* and still believe that would've been a more lasting name. But I wasn't going for timelessness. I was going for the seductive vulgarity of the present. One should not go about easily changing names anyway. Another journey I drew from was Doyle's *The Lost World,* particularly in its lightness. Doyle the novelist is something like the flip side of Conrad. There was also the film *Babel* by González Iñárritu, which alongside García Márquez' first novella, *La Hojarasca*, showed me multi-perspective structure. And of course: Delfín Quishpe's daring song. The real one. And the viral video. The comedic punch I felt upon encountering it online wasn't unlike the conceptual punch I felt upon encountering *Clandestino* years prior. There were also the sketches of Utah in the book *America* by Baudrillard, who must have been on philosophical acid. And the life summaries in Graydon Miller's stories "The Hit" and "American Paranoia" from his *Havana Brotherhood*. Miller, like Borges, knows that a well-done life summary is an artform in itself. I must also mention the photo book *The Americans* by Robert Frank. In particular, the picture of the young brown guy looking at a shiny jukebox in an empty saloon as if that shiny jukebox were The Burning Bush itself. God, can I relate to that. From all those symbols, and from my experience as a Global South migrant, who grew up invariably falling in love with women from the furthest corners of the world, writing yet another book in English, the world language, comes what I hope is a compressed mirror of the times, or at least the feeling of the thing. I hope I have captured some of the rewards of that beautiful vertigo, which if seen at the right angle might be nothing but momentum. I hope that's how the future sees us. The Age of Momentum.

Lastly, a deep contradiction. This novel is made of people, not just of ideas, feelings, or atmospheres. Quishpe, Pärn, the Furukawas, Alvo, Mamadú, Sandrita, the stories they tell, the people they meet, the things they go through, *that's the tale*. At the end of the day, a novel's success rests on its characters, on that which is eternal in their struggles. Even beyond that: the value of a novel rests on the tangential anecdotes of peripheral characters. In this case, Puramama, the Honduran boys, the TheNeverwhöre, Abraham, Big Toño, the spitting trucker, the eco-terrorists, the CIA agents, Chuco, and all the others. Sometimes I think I cooked this whole thing up so that I could access the tangential anecdotes of my beloved peripheral characters. See, eras and atmospheres change, but people are people. Gossip is all we are. And gossip is all that shall ever be known of us.

Patricio X. Maya Solís
April 17, 2021
West Hollywood, California

Patricio X. Maya Solís (1982) was born in Quito, Ecuador. After attending various school—Catholic, military, Waldorf, and college prep academies—he was brought to Los Angeles, California, where he attended Hollywood High. The clash with North America upended his perception of the world. In boastful moods he claims to have swallowed down and digested the entire continent. Published books: **Walking Around with Fante and Bukowski** (essays), **80 MPH** (poetry), from Grady Miller Books. He holds an M.A. in Arts Journalism from Syracuse University. Maya is currently at work on his second novel, **Too Much Sweetie**, which has been called an unlikely lyrical novel of ideas.

Also by Patricio X. Maya:

80 MPH (poetry in Spanish; antologia poética)
ISBN 978-0-9862734-5-2

"Maya puts his foot on the pedal and hurtles through the fragile American dreamscape, from California –a "stolen star" to Castro, from Escher to Echo Park, from Nikes to nothingness. . . The view through Maya's windshield is crystal clear: a tacky jumble of cultures; a frenetic nostalgia for nostalgia's sake; a Puritan wasteland of trash, chaos, hate, violence and urban blight, punctuated by rest stops and temporary *"I'm home, Honey!"*'s where, hopefully, we find a hearth, or *por lo menos* a willing heart, to keep us warm." **Paul Dell'Amico**

WALKING AROUND WITH FANTE AND BUKOWSKI (essays)
ISBN 978-0986273407

Part poetic autobiography, part harbinger of a new critical sensibility to emerge from colliding world cultures, Walking Around with Fante and Bukowski fuses a poets' fire and a journalist's unblinking eye. The title piece is a gripping quest to find a remnant of a lost-and-found L.A. literary masterpiece. "Staring into Vaginas," looks at the photographic legacy of a seedy Hollywood strip club. The haunting "It's Always Quiet in the End" celebrates poetry and friendship, and brings us face to face with one of life's deepest secrets. "The Brightest, Bluest Swimming Pool Water," is an evocative mosaic memoir of the writer's one way jet flight from Ecuador to California at an early age.

"Maya's riveting debut collection of essays takes the reader by the heart and throat, and never lets go." **Pio Tapia**

80 MPH (Bilingual Anthology #1)
ISBN 978-0986273476

Bilingual literary anthology presenting daring new voices from the US, Latin America, and Europe (GMB- Pato Cuervo Productions). Antología literaria bilingüe presentado excelsos nuevos valores de Europa, Estados Unidos, y América Latina.

Poetry and new Spanish fiction

Aldo Tambellini **LISTEN: SELECTED POEMS (1946 – 2016)**
ISBN 978—0-9862734-4-5

If you think you're alone and crazy in the struggle against complacency and the current world order, Aldo Tambellini is there. Youthful, righteous, and bitterly funny, he has been with us, painter of the written word, a caster of shadows and lights in the Lanterna Magica tradition, a one man gran guinol for 70 years. He has lived under Mussolini, contemporary American fascism --which he predicted-- and everything in between. There are over 70 years of great poetry in this anthology.

"This is an important book." **Ishmael Reed**

Graydon Miller **MUJERES CON NAVAJAS** (in Spanish)
ISBN 978-0-578-63639-6

Graydon Miller, el gran Mago de la ficción, vuelve con una novela poderosa, de alcance universal. En 'Mujeres con navajas' el lector encontrará que tras los efectos de la llamada novela social también se puede hallar una sutil trama de intriga familiar; una antigua historia de amor. El logro de Miller es conmovedor, máxime si se toma en cuenta que el escritor Estadounidense elaboró 'Mujeres con navajas' en la lengua de Cervantes durante unos veinticinco años de trabajo (había perfeccionado su dominio del español durante una prolongada residencia en Guadalajara). Para la casa editorial 80mph es un placer presentar los resultados de dicha labor. Aparte del drama, el humor, y el comentario social, esta novela logra revivir la tradición narrativa hispana en California.

(Spanish Audiobook and Paperback)

Made in the USA
Monee, IL
16 July 2022

99792088R00132